Thirsty Thursdays

Palm Springs Poolside Book 4

J. L. Brannick

To Marie-Pierre, the fabulous French Canadian beta reader who assisted with the French phrases and Titus's pet names, and who also has a fascination with "tentacle fetishes and tentacle porn as a thriving sub-culture." And, again, to all my fellow voracious readers who'd rather be home in their pajamas, with a spicy book and their favorite adult toy. The Cherry Box episodes are for you. Enjoy!

Chapter 1

We sat in the driveway, staring blearily at Titus Tremblay's sprawling white mid-century modern house through the bug-splattered windshield of my ancient sedan.

After our three-day drive from Seattle to Palm Springs, the car smelled like stale food and dirty socks. My heart thudded painfully in my chest as I gripped the steering wheel with sweaty palms, worst-case scenarios chasing through my exhausted mind.

My best friend Isabella patted my shoulder encouragingly. "You can do this, Abby, one step at a time. Just let go of the steering wheel and open the car door." We'd been out here for at least five minutes.

"What if this doesn't work? What if he decides we're too much trouble? Or he thinks Stella is too loud, and he gets angry and hurts–"

Isabella interrupted my budding panic attack. "He's not your father, and Titus would never do that. He's calm and levelheaded–except with other hockey players. I've needed to use the bathroom for the past two hours, and I'm about to burst. I'll get Stella out of her car seat while you pull yourself together, okay?"

As Isabella got Stella out of her car seat, I turned back to the expensive-looking house and focused on the pretty mint green front door. Exhaling, I carefully peeled my hands from the steering wheel and got out. Then I gathered my little girl into my shaky arms and followed Isabella to the front door to meet my new roommate and fake boyfriend.

Adrenaline raced through me as we approached the house, but I tried to calm myself. I mean, how bad could he be? He didn't hate kids if he wanted custody of his little boy, and he was one of Isabella's best friends. And she swore he was even-tempered.

The front door opened and my eyes slowly traveled up the body of a massive, tattooed man who stood glaring down at me with his hands on his hips. When he growled low in his throat, my stomach cramped, and I came close to peeing myself. Stella buried her face in my neck and pulled her worn yellow blanket around her head.

My new roommate had a hard muscular body, messy dark blond hair, and a striking, craggy face. He also terrified me. I instinctively flinched when Isabella reached out and smacked his shoulder. "This is Titus. Titus, Abigail and Stella. Now quit staring at her like a serial killer, and let us in so we can use the bathroom."

When he wordlessly shifted to the side, Isabella disappeared into the house, but he continued to glare at my face.

Isabella had brought us together. She'd just completed an internship with his hockey team and was seeing one of Titus's best friends and former teammates, Connor McCoy.

She explained to me that Titus needed a live-in girlfriend to help with his custody case. Apparently, even a fake one would work. I needed a safe place to live, far away from my parents. Her plan still sounded crazy, but I was desperate, and Isa thought we could help each other out. So less than a week later, here I stood on his front doorstep.

My stomach pitched, and the ugly bruises on my face seemed to throb under his gaze. My ribcage ached every time I breathed, but luckily, he couldn't see those injuries. The black eye was bad enough. I looked down, trying to hide behind my long, unruly, ash-blond hair.

I might have turned around and run if Stella hadn't needed a break so badly, but three days in her car seat was more than enough. I hoisted her higher on my hip, my ribcage howling in protest.

"Who in *the fuck* did that to your face?" Titus asked in a low, gravelly voice. "Because I'm going to kill them."

"I'd rather not lie to you." I shifted again, trying to ease the pain. "And I've been told countless times liars go to hell." I tended to joke when I got scared or nervous.

His hands fell to his sides. "Are you hungry or thirsty?"

Over the past year, I'd been hungry many times, but I was too terrified to think about food right then. "We'd really like to use your bathroom if we can. Please."

He immediately stepped back. "Isa's probably in the guest one. Come on, I'll show you yours."

Letting go of Stella, she slid down my side and started crying a little, her hand clutching mine. I reminded myself Titus might *seem* scary, but he had a mint green front door, and an asshole probably wouldn't paint their door that lovely color. Tall palm trees and flowering desert bushes also dotted his lush front yard, but I was too anxious to fully appreciate it right then. His house gave me a spark of hope, though.

As we walked to the bathroom, I glimpsed a large, comfortable family room with a sprawling sofa next to a bright, modern kitchen.

He stopped at a door. "Here's your bathroom. I'll show you the rest when you're done."

"Thank you." We stepped inside and shut the door. When we came out, he stood by the first bedroom.

"This is yours," he said, glancing at my black eye. His mouth tightened, and he looked away. There was a queen-sized bed, a nightstand, and a desk. The room was a typical guest bedroom, except everything was white. It seemed like heaven since we'd been living in my parents' damp, dark basement.

"It's very nice. And very white."

His eyebrow went up. I hadn't meant to be flippant, and I turned away and gazed at the room without seeing it. Worry, shame, and a blurry determination swam through me. I would make this work.

Titus turned and continued down the hall, stopping at the last door. The smaller bedroom had a twin bed and a dresser in it, but not much else. A couple of stuffed animals sat perched on the pillow, one a little moose and the other looked like a raccoon.

"This is your little girl's room."

"Her name is Stella, and I'm Abby." I turned to Stella. "This is Titus. We're staying with him for a while, and you get your own room."

She gazed up at him with enormous eyes, her neck kinked way back, their size difference almost laughable.

He squatted down but didn't crowd her. "Hey, Stella. I got a couple of stuffed animals to keep you company and protect you. They're sitting on your bed."

She looked over, then continued staring at him.

Isabella came down the hall and stood behind me, checking out the bedroom. "Nice. I always thought this room was your dungeon."

He stood and shook his head. "My bedroom and office are on the other end of the house, past the family room."

I nodded. "This is more than we could've hoped for. Thank you."

Soon Isabella would leave, and we'd be alone here with Titus. My neck and shoulders tightened, but I trusted Isabella, and she'd vouched for him. I also had seventy-three dollars to my name, no steady income, and a few hundred dollars in credit card debt looming over me. It wasn't like I had other options.

He pointed to the kitchen. "Groceries are delivered on Thursdays, and a housecleaner comes a couple of days a week. I'm gone most of the time to practices or games, but let me know if you need anything or have questions."

"I can clean and grocery shop. I'm also a decent cook. It'll save you a little money and help us pay our way."

"The agreement is you'll help me get joint custody of Max, and then help me take care of him while he's here. You worry about yourself and Stella right now."

His rebuff stung, but I nodded. "I'll go grab our things."

Isabella threw him an exasperated glance. "We'll help."

They followed me out to my car, and we brought in our belongings. As they helped carry everything inside, I looked at my meager possessions through their eyes. Most of what I owned was secondhand and worn. While I lived with my parents, I'd barely been able to make rent payments, afford daycare, and have any money left over for medical costs or incidentals. They'd charged me just enough rent to keep me impoverished, but less than I could find anywhere else in Seattle.

Isabella looked around my room. "I'll help you put your things away later. Are you guys hungry?"

Stella nodded.

Titus straightened off the door frame and looked down at her. "I have chicken pasta or leftover pizza. What do you want?"

Stella just stared at him, and my anxiety ratcheted up.

"She doesn't talk much anymore," I admitted, my heart squeezing.

He didn't take his eyes off her, but waited patiently as the silence stretched.

"Pizza," she whispered.

I turned away and pretended to look through our things. He didn't understand what a major milestone that one word was.

He held out his big hand, giving her time to take it. "Good choice, and I have apple juice too. How does that sound?"

She nodded and slowly wrapped her little fingers around his pinky, and they walked to the kitchen together. Fear flooded me, and I turned to follow.

Isa put her hand on my shoulder and squeezed. "She's safe. He's only mean to other hockey players."

I sucked in air through my nose, then let out a big breath. "Okay. Alright."

She put her arms around me. "It'll be okay. Let's go get some pizza."

Two hours later, Isabella went home, and Stella and I continued putting our things away. We were alone with Titus, in his big, sunny house with its swaying palm trees and sparkling pool, but I just wanted to curl up with my little girl in the white bed, under the thick white comforter, and push away the nightmare that had become my life.

Stella slept with me that night. We were both out of sorts and a little scared, but she brought both the stuffed animals Titus had given her.

The next morning, I woke up early so I could check my freelance service accounts to see if I'd gotten any new clients. I could sometimes pick up odd jobs helping people design or maintain websites. I had to use my phone as a hotspot because I didn't have the internet password yet.

Then I showered and got cleaned up in case Titus came looking for me. I didn't know what he expected or how to act around him, and not knowing made me nervous and twitchy.

I heard Titus in the kitchen around seven, so I wiped my hands on my old, worn jeans and walked out to talk with him.

He stood at the fridge, filling a water jug, and a gym bag sat on the counter. He wore training pants and a hockey pullover with the Thunderbirds logo across the front—Isa told me that was the name of their hockey team. It looked like he was heading off to practice.

"Hello." My voice squeaked, and I cleared my throat.

He glanced at me. "Hey."

"Can I do anything to help around here today?"

He put the lid on his water jug. "No. Just take care of yourself and Stella."

"Okay. Can I make dinner, or do any laundry, or…" My voice trailed off when I saw his jaw tighten.

He reached over to grab his bag off the counter next to me, and I instinctively flinched and lurched back.

"Fuck!" He straightened and held his hands out. "I didn't mean to scare you."

My heart fluttered like a trapped bird in my chest. "I'm sorry. I'm so sorry." I backed up hard and hit the kitchen table behind me.

Carefully, he picked up his bag and stepped back. "You don't need to apologize. Don't worry about doing anything around the house, just get settled in. I'll be home late."

I nodded jerkily, and he walked out. When I heard his vehicle pull away, I slid to the floor, put my head in my hands, and cried.

Chapter 2

Titus didn't come home until late that night, and when I got up the next morning, he was already gone. I used a couple of his eggs and some bread to make Stella and me a late breakfast, and we split one of his frozen dinners for supper.

But I worried about eating his food, and fretted about the incident in his kitchen. Did he want us to leave? Was he already sorry he chose me to be his fake girlfriend? Anxiety and doubt ran through me as I thought about our tenuous situation.

We went to the store the next day to replace what I'd borrowed from him and pick up a few groceries of our own. Stella never begged for treats when we went shopping because I couldn't afford them, and she'd learned not to ask.

I pushed our mostly empty cart through the aisles, looking for any bargains. The older man stocking the produce gazed at me, and then his eyes traveled down to Stella. I put my hand on Stella's shoulder and pulled her into me.

"Would she like a piece of fruit?" he asked. "Kids can have one here if they want."

My worn, ancient runners had a split at the top, and Stella's pants were a little too short for her. I knew we looked exactly like what we were—a poor single mother and a small child barely getting by.

But thanks to Titus, I didn't have to worry about my father hitting me or grabbing Stella. Or having my mother call me a worthless bitch in front of her. They resented me, and when they'd started in on Stella I knew I needed to get out.

Shaking off the dark thoughts, I smiled at the man. "Yes. Thank you." I kept a careful distance and turned to Stella. "What do you want? An apple or a banana?"

She looked at me but said nothing. I took a page from Titus's book and simply waited for her to answer.

She finally whispered, "Nana."

The man handed me a banana, and I partially peeled it and gave it to her. "Say thank you." She brought her yellow blanket to her face and quietly thanked him. He smiled and went back to replenishing fruit. The man's kindness lifted my mood a little.

Isabella calling me last week had been a godsend. When she asked me if I'd pretend to be Titus's live-in girlfriend and help him with his custody case in Canada, I thought she was teasing me at first. But Titus lived in Palm Springs and my parents lived in Seattle, so I grabbed at the lifeline.

Stella finished her banana, and we checked out and went home to make vegetable soup and cornbread. Titus didn't come home until after we'd gone to bed.

Over the next week, Titus left a couple of post-it notes on the counter for us asking if we needed anything, but he didn't leave his phone number. He stayed away until late at night and left early in the mornings, and I worried we were driving the man right out of his house.

I got up the courage and left a reply, asking for the code to the front door so we didn't have to leave it unlocked every time we left the house. His home sat in one of the cul de sacs in the Indian Canyons neighborhood of Palm Springs.

The sunny feel of the neighborhood and the views of the mountains, with the tall, thin palm trees dotting the skyline, seemed to soothe my soul. The sweet smell of orange blossoms sometimes drifted through the open windows, and his bright, peaceful home, with the modern kitchen and light furniture, felt like a temporary refuge.

When I agreed to come live with Titus and be his "live-in girlfriend," Isabella said Titus would pay me a monthly salary to help watch his son, Max. But I didn't think that would happen until Titus gained custody, and I needed to find a way to make more money. Otherwise, I wouldn't be able to make a payment on my credit card or buy groceries.

Stella sat on the bed that evening while I folded laundry. She had one of Titus's stuffed animals tucked under her arm—it was the little moose with a black and red plaid shirt. I'd read somewhere that moose were one of Canada's deadliest animals. I also knew Titus was French Canadian, and he played hockey. But that was about it.

"Are you tired, or do you want to watch an episode of *Pawn Stars*?" I asked Stella.

She nodded.

"So you want to go to bed?" I prodded.

Stella shook her head. "No. Chumlee."

"Rick is way better."

She grinned and shook her head again. The first time Stella watched the reality show, *Pawn Stars*, she'd become attached to the Harrisons who owned the pawn shop in Las Vegas. But she loved their goofy employee, Chumlee. It seemed strange that a little girl would like a show about pawn shop owners, but I'd watched a few episodes, and we'd both gotten hooked.

Pulling her pajamas out, we got ready for bed. Then I realized I needed to get Titus's Wi-Fi password so we could watch it on my second-hand laptop.

I bit my lip. I hadn't seen him all week and didn't know how he'd react after what happened the first morning.

"I'll be right back." I headed to the kitchen, hoping Titus was there.

The overhead light under the microwave cast the room into shadowy light. I looked around, but I didn't see him anywhere.

"Titus?" No one answered. "Mr. Tremblay?"

I listened for a minute, then turned to go back to my room.

"Did you call me Mr. Tremblay?" Titus muttered from the darkened hallway on his side of the house.

My heart sped up, and I wiped my hands on my sweatpants. "Hello. We haven't really talked, so I didn't know what you wanted me to call you."

"Titus is fine."

"Okay. Can I get the internet password? Stella wants to watch something before she goes to sleep, and I need it for work." We'd been going to the public library nearby so I could use their free internet.

He folded his arms and studied me in the dark light. "What're you going to watch?"

"An episode of *Pawn Stars*."

He froze. "Porn stars?"

Despite myself, my lips twitched. "Yes. I'm going to show my three-year-old daughter an episode about porn stars." I shook my head. "*Pawn Stars*. About the pawn shop in Las Vegas? We watch a rerun or two a couple of times a week."

He smirked. "I need to get to know Stella better if she likes a show about a pawn shop in Vegas." Titus slowly walked into the kitchen and leaned against the table at least fifteen feet away from me.

I tried not to shift or flinch. "Can I get the garage code too? I'd like to leave Stella's stroller in there. It folds up and won't take too much room."

He sighed and rubbed his forehead. "I should have given you all this information already. Text me and I'll send it to you."

I pulled out my old, cracked phone from my back pocket. "I don't have your phone number. Can I ask you a few other questions while you're here?"

"Yeah." Titus crossed his arms. "You can ask me whatever you want."

He was never around, so that'd be hard to do. "What's your number?"

He rattled it off, and I plugged it into my phone. "Where do you want me to park my car? On the street, or is the left side of the driveway alright?"

"It's fine where it's at."

Whew. My car was a piece of crap, but I didn't want to park it out on the street.

"What's your address here?" I held up my hand. "In case we have an emergency or I need to mail something."

He pulled out his phone. "What's your number?" I rattled it off to him, and he put it in his phone. "Okay, *p'tite cocotte*. I'll send you the Wi-Fi password, the garage code, and the address. Now, what else do you need?"

I wondered what *p'tite cocotte* meant but was too chicken to ask. I slid my phone back into my pocket and fought to keep eye contact because the last item was critical.

"Can I install alarms on the back doors, or maybe an alarm in the pool? Stella is only three. She can't swim yet." I wrung my hands and gazed at him with pleading eyes.

Titus rubbed the back of his neck. "For fuck's sake. I didn't even think about that."

"I know it'll be expensive. I can pay you back over time. I'm sorry–"

"Stop apologizing. I need to make it safe for Max too. I'll get a company to install a wrought iron fence across the front of the pool, and a pool cover for good measure."

My shoulders sagged. "Thank you. Thank you so much."

"You don't need to thank me either. Now come out into the family room, and let's watch an episode of this *Porn Stars* together."

I rolled my eyes and smiled up at him. "Okay, I'll go get Stella." I felt so grateful, I forgot to be scared.

"I'll make some popcorn," he added.

Clasping my hands together, I grinned. "Ooh, she'll love that."

Titus cocked his head and studied me, and my smile faltered. I quickly turned to get Stella. She came out with her yellow blanket dragging and the little moose in her hand. Titus smiled when he saw it.

We sat on the large, comfortable couch in the family room, ate popcorn, and watched two episodes together. At first, I fidgeted and couldn't get comfortable. But Stella crawled into the space between us, and helped herself to a big handful of popcorn from Titus's bowl. He smirked, and she grinned back.

When Chumlee appeared she bounced up and down, pointed to the screen, and then patted Titus's leg.

"Why do you like that guy so much?" Titus asked.

"He funny." She stuffed more popcorn into her mouth.

My jaw dropped open, and I stared at them while Stella absently used Titus's shirt to wipe popcorn grease off her hands.

Titus glanced down and patted her head. "Yeah, he is pretty funny."

I ate a handful of popcorn to cover my emotions. After the episode ended, I moved to stand but Stella flopped herself against me. My bruised ribs screamed in protest, and I froze and sucked in a sharp breath.

Titus watched me as I sat perfectly still for a moment, trying to hide my injury.

"What's wrong?" he asked.

"She just hit a sore spot."

He sat on the couch, patiently waiting for me. I finally pushed myself up, holding my breath and not making a sound.

"I've had bruised ribs before. I know what it's like. What happened?" he asked again.

"It's better for Stella and me to let it go. Please, just let it go."

He ran his hand down his sharp cheekbones. "We're going to talk."

"We just did. We're good now."

He raised his eyebrow, then turned to Stella. "Do you want some chocolate milk?"

"Yes!" She ran into the kitchen.

I watched her go, and Titus turned to me. "What happened to your ribs? And don't lie to me."

My mind raced through the pros and cons of telling this man I barely knew my darkest secrets. I settled for the *Reader's Digest* version.

"My father didn't want us to leave. I disagreed, and he tried to stop me."

Titus studied me carefully. "He punched you in the face and stomach to stop you from leaving."

Turning my face away, I nodded once. "Yeah."

"How'd you get away?"

"I threatened to call the police. And this time, I had visible injuries to show them."

His hands clenched, and he took a deep breath and let it out. "If he tries to make contact, you'll let me know." He wasn't asking, but I took it as a question.

"I will."

We followed Stella into the kitchen, where she stood in front of the open fridge.

Reaching over her, he pulled out the milk and a container of chocolate maple syrup. "My recipe is a little different."

"You put maple syrup in your chocolate milk?" I asked in mild disgust.

"Yeah. And it's fucking fantastic." He deftly mixed up three glasses, then passed one over to me and handed a smaller one to Stella.

I tentatively took a sip. Then I took a bigger drink. "This isn't bad."

"You sound surprised."

"Maybe a little." I smiled and raised my glass. "I'd give you a toast, but I hear if it's not alcohol, it's seven years of bad luck."

He grinned. "Or seven years of bad sex."

Stella drained her glass and let out a long sigh, then wiped her mouth. And burped.

Titus peered down at her. "Good one, *ma puce*."

Stella held out her empty glass to him. "Is good."

I shook my head. "She hasn't said more than one or two words to anyone else but me in months. You're a miracle worker."

Chapter 3

Titus wasn't a miracle worker, he was the devil. When Isabella called him in a panic a few days later, he wouldn't let me talk to her.

I stood in the kitchen glaring up at him, but from a good ten feet away. We'd watched TV together a few times and were getting more comfortable, but I still got skittish.

"Why can *you* talk to her, but I can't?"

Titus hung up and his lip quirked as if my annoyance pleased him. Then he sobered. "Connor's ex assaulted her this morning. She and Elodie are safe at my condo, but she said Connor just got there, and they need to talk."

He probably had a point, but I wanted to know if Isabella was alright. During our drive to Palm Springs, she'd talked about Connor and his five-year-old daughter. And Connor's scary ex-wife.

"What happened? Is she okay?"

"It sounds like she got hit in the face, but she got Elodie out and they're okay."

My hand instinctively went to my own cheek, and my eyes strayed to Stella.

Titus watched me. "They're safe."

"Okay. Where's your condo?"

"In Vancouver. I used to play professional hockey there until I got injured. I'm playing on the feeder team right now so Vancouver can assess my injuries."

"You were injured?" My eyes swept his big, beautiful body. I also loved his tattoos.

"Yes, and I'm old for a hockey player. They also have to pay me a fuck-ton, so they want to ensure I'm healthy."

"Oh. How old are you?"

"Thirty-four."

"Wow, that's ancient," I deadpanned.

He grinned and reached over to tug a strand of my hair. "I'm going to take an ice bath in the spa, but do you and Stella want to go out to eat tonight? It's been a rough week."

I perked up but then remembered my bank account. "I can make homemade pizza here. My food budget is tight this month."

His lip quirked. "You and Isabella are the only two people I know who have food budgets."

"She's been a college student for six years, and I'm a single mother. We've had to learn to be frugal."

He glanced down at my clothes and bare feet. I knew what he saw—threadbare jeans, and an ancient Nirvana t-shirt. Long, streaky blond hair that hadn't been cut or styled in over a year. I also had central heterochromia, which was a mix of two eye colors, so my eyes were a strange combination of green and hazel. My shoulders tightened as he studied me.

"I invited you so it'll be my treat, and you two are doing me a favor. There's another place I want to take you to afterward. Do you have warm jackets?"

"We're from Seattle, remember?" I mentally reached for the backbone my father had tried to rip out of me. "Stella would love to get out. Thank you."

Titus nodded, grabbed three bags of ice from the freezer, and went outside to dump them in his spa. I'd wondered why his freezer was full of ice.

"What are you doing?" I asked as I followed him outside.

"My back tightens up sometimes and hurts like a son-of-a-bitch. This helps."

Kneeling, I stuck my hand in the spa and yelped. "That's already freezing! And you add ice and sit in there?"

He shrugged. "Yeah. It beats using painkillers or alcohol."

"Okay, that makes sense. Does your back hurt all the time?"

"Probably. But I don't notice it when I'm sleeping or playing hockey."

A few minutes later, I tried—and failed—not to watch him as he walked outside in his tight compression shorts.

His thick, ropy thighs strained his shorts, and his muscular shoulders and chest tapered into a tight waist with a delicious V leading down to his groin.

Stella patted my arm again. "Mommy. Mommy," she kept repeating.

Heat crawled up my chest and my cheeks burned. Titus grinned as he opened the patio door.

"Enjoy your polar plunge. Glad it's you and not me," I croaked out.

"I will. You should join me sometime."

I smiled sweetly. "That's never going to happen."

He smirked. "Never say never, *cocotte.*"

That evening, I pulled out my best pair of pants and a nice sweater I'd bought before Stella was born. Stella wore her best jeans and a cute red top, and I grabbed our jackets. Mine had a small patch on the sleeve, but we both looked respectable.

Titus had on well-worn jeans and a black Henley that molded to his muscular frame. He always looked good no matter what he wore.

When we walked into the kitchen, he scanned us and grinned "Let's get some dinner and then go to the zoo."

Stella gasped and jumped up and down. "With animals?"

"Yep. Lots of animals," Titus grinned.

I quirked my head. "Is the zoo open at night?"

"It is right now."

So Titus took us to a neat retro 1950s diner close to his house, and then we went to the zoo. It was hosting something called Zoo Lights, and I'd never seen such a beautiful display of luminaries. We gazed around, mesmerized.

"Look, Mommy!" Stella kept pointing and dragging us from one display to another. And between the displays, we glimpsed the animals.

We walked around a winding, illuminated Chinese New Year dragon, and passed by a jungle-themed luminary display. Then we stopped at a sea-themed one. A few of the displays had bubble machines, and Stella squealed in delight. I'd never heard that sweet, excited sound come from her, and my heart clenched.

We watched as she tried to pop some of the bubbles with a few other kids, and I turned to Titus. "How did you know about this?"

"Isabella dragged the whole hockey team here. She decided we needed to do some team building—at the zoo of all places."

I laughed and my eyes went misty. "That sounds just like her. Stella and I have never seen anything like this. And she likes you and talks to you, so thank you."

He smiled and patted my shoulder. "We haven't started preparing for the custody hearing. You probably won't be thanking me then."

Titus had a few days off before the playoffs began, so he flew to Vancouver to visit his son, Max.

"Where's Tie-Tie?" Stella asked me three times the day he left.

She had her little moose tucked under her arm. I'd made a batch of chicken and rice soup, and absently wondered if Titus would like some when he got home, then remembered he was in Vancouver.

We watched an episode of *Pawn Stars* without him the first night he was gone, but it wasn't the same. Stella seemed a little whiny, and I felt out of sorts. We moped around the second night too. Surprise and alarm ran through me when I realized how much Stella and I missed him while he was gone. This arrangement was only temporary, and we couldn't get too attached to him or his peaceful house.

So on Thursday evening, I decided we needed to get out. Isabella had mentioned Palm Springs held a street fair and closed the main street to vehicles every Thursday night during the winter. And best of all, it was free.

So we went over to check it out. We found a place to park by the art museum and wandered around the closed-off street, gazing at the booths and enjoying the crowd. A decent live band played cover songs, and I'd just pulled out a small container of animal crackers for Stella when my phone rang. I looked at the cracked screen and noticed it was Titus.

"Hello?"

There was a pause. "Where are you?"

My shoulders relaxed when I heard Titus's deep, gravelly voice. "We're at the weekly street fair on Palm Canyon Drive."

"Are you there alone?"

I nodded and smiled when Stella pointed to a vendor selling glow-in-the-dark rubber balls and toys. "I'm with Stella. We needed to get out, and Isa told me about it last week. How's Max doing?"

"He's good, and growing so damn fast. I just got home, and the house is too quiet. Where'd you park?"

"In the art museum parking garage."

"Okay. I'll call you when I get there. Meet me in front of the Marilyn Monroe statue."

He hung up before I could tell him we were fine and he didn't need to come. I slid my phone back into my purse and started wandering back toward the statue. Stella and I noticed it when we walked out of the parking garage.

The twenty-five-foot-tall statue of Marilyn was modeled after the iconic photograph of her standing above the grate with her white halter-top dress blowing up behind her. I'd always loved the playful sexiness of that photo, even though my parents would have called her a whore or a harlot.

We sat on the grass near the statue, eating her animal crackers and enjoying the balmy evening. I looked up and saw Titus getting out of the back of a car and walking toward us.

"Hi. You got a ride over?"

He grinned down at us. "Yeah. I figured you could give me a ride home."

Stella and I both stood, and he palmed her little head and turned us around. "I've never taken a photo in front of Ms. Monroe before. Say cheese." He positioned us for a better angle, then deftly held out his phone with his long arm and took a few photos with the button on the side.

"You're good at taking selfies. Do you do it often?" I asked innocently.

"Yeah, I do, little smart ass." He smirked. "Fans sometimes ask me to take pictures with them. It's usually faster to just do it myself."

We walked around the outdoor art installations in front of the art museum. Next to the Marilyn statue was a big pit with large metal babies in it. They were faceless and on all fours, as if crawling around.

"The babies creep me out. What did you think of them?"
I asked Stella as we wandered over to the vertical car statue
behind it.

She shrugged indifferently. But Stella did seem to like the
1950s vintage car installed on its tip to look like it was driving
vertically into the reflective pool below it.

Titus gazed up at the statue. "I like this one too, but Marilyn
is still my favorite."

I grinned. "Of course it is."

"Have you eaten yet?"

I offered him the bag of animal crackers. He raised an eyebrow and took a few, then guided us over to the food trucks.
"Stay here. I'll grab a couple of plates of shawarma."

Before I could protest, he strode off. Stella and I found a
place to sit and wait, and Titus came back a few minutes later
with two heaping plates and napkins hanging out of his front
pocket. He handed one to Stella and me.

Taking the plate in both hands, I looked up at him. "I'll pay
you back."

He shook his head and handed me some napkins. "Shut up
and eat."

The smell of cooked, seasoned meat and onions wafted up
at me, and my stomach growled. I used the plastic knife to cut
off a few manageable bite-sized pieces for Stella, then we dug
in.

"Oh, God," I groaned with my mouth full. "This is so good."

We were all quiet as we inhaled our food. Titus finished first,
wiped his fingers and mouth off, then pulled a can of seltzer
water from his back pocket.

"Something to wash it down with." He popped the can and handed it to Stella first.

She grabbed the can with both hands. Taking a big gulp, she let out a burp, sighed, and handed the can to me.

She grinned happily. "Thanks."

"Yes, thank you. That was delicious." I wiped my fingers, then leaned down and wiped around Stella's mouth.

Titus grabbed another napkin, poured a little seltzer water on it, and worked on Stella's hands. "That's one of my favorite food trucks in Palm Springs. Let's walk up the street a little, then head back before it gets too dark."

Glancing at him out of the corner of my eye, I cleared my throat. "I'm glad you met us. How'd things go in Vancouver?"

He stood up, and we started walking. "Good. Trixie, Max's mother, let me take him the entire time."

"Is Trixie her real name?"

"Yeah. She's a little hard and bitchy. But a decent mother. We were never together."

"How'd you end up with a child, then?"

He rubbed the back of his neck. "It's pretty typical. I got injured and felt sorry for myself, then acted like a fucking moron. And she was happy to make a player feel better. Even an injured one."

Stella tugged my hand and pointed to a booth with a display of puppets. "Look, Mommy."

"Those are neat. Look but don't touch, okay?"

She nodded and walked over to the display.

I glanced back at Titus. "So you're saying she had sex with you because she felt sorry for you?"

"A pity fuck?" He grinned. "She's a hardcore puck bunny, and my partners usually come back for more. I like to make it good for both of us."

My face heated, and I swallowed. Somehow, I knew he wasn't exaggerating. "Okay. Not a pity fuck. What's Max like?" I blatantly tried to change the topic.

"Max is a laid-back little kid unless he's hungry or wants something. And he likes balls and all kinds of sports."

When Stella finished looking at the puppets, we turned back and started walking toward my car. The evening air felt pleasant and cool, and the twilight gave everything a soft glow.

Titus helped buckle Stella in, then got in the passenger seat. Even after he adjusted his seat back as far as it would go, his knees hit the dashboard.

"Aren't you going to demand to drive?" I asked.

"No. It's your car. I can prove my masculinity in other ways."

"Like making sure your partners always come back for more?" I drawled. Then my eyes went wide, and I slammed my palm against my mouth. "I didn't mean to say that out loud."

He barked out a laugh. "But you did. And yes." Turning sideways a little, he studied me. "I'm glad you feel comfortable enough to let your snarky side out a little."

"You're one of the few people." Relief flooded through me when he seemed to let my comment go.

"What do you mean?"

I glanced in the rearview mirror at Stella. "My father told me once he was going to beat it out of me. Then I told him he could try, and things went downhill from there." I sighed, remembering what had happened next.

Titus reached over and gently squeezed my thigh. "Then he's a fucking idiot. I think a quick-witted woman with a few thorns is a lot more interesting than a doormat."

"Good to know."

Chapter 4

Before Stella woke up that morning, I sat on the back patio working on a website design. I looked up when the door opened and saw Titus walking out, holding two cups of coffee.

He put one in front of me. "It's black. How do you like yours?"

Smiling up at him, I picked up the cup. "Black. Thank you."

Titus glanced around out and sat next to me. "It's nice out here. What're you working on?" He still made me a little jumpy and nervous, but it wasn't from anxiety anymore.

I turned my computer toward him. "A website for a pest control company in Midland, Texas." Their landing page showed a logo of a big, bug-eyed cockroach and their name, Critter Gitters, underneath.

"Catchy. Where'd you learn to do this?" He motioned to the website.

"Most of it is self-taught. I took graphic design in high school and finished two years of college. But then Stella came along."

"Do you want to go back?"

Taking a sip, I thought about it. "Maybe. I'd have better credentials and make more money. But I don't know if I'd make *that* much more money." We talked and drank coffee together in peace until he had to leave for practice.

After Stella and I ate breakfast, we sat down and wrote letters and colored a shamrock to send to Nana in Weston, Florida. My grandmother had dementia and lived in a memory care facility there, so I doubted she even knew who I was anymore, but I didn't want to lose that connection. It'd been several years since I'd been able to visit, and I missed her every day.

Titus came home that evening, changed into sweats, and sat at the kitchen bar working on his laptop. While we talked, I dragged a stool over to reach a high, out-of-the-way cupboard where I kept my meager stash of food. I grabbed pasta and red sauce and jumped down.

"Do you want some spaghetti?" I asked.

"What's that?" He tipped his chin up to the cupboard. "What?"

He pointed. "That. Why do you keep food clear up there?"

I tilted my head, not understanding. "That's where I store my dried goods. And I put our perishables in the fridge in the back of the vegetable drawer to keep them out of your way."

He leaned back in his chair and studied me carefully. "Abigail, why do you have your own stash of food?"

I felt like a naughty child when he called me by my full name, and embarrassment and something else curled in my stomach. "Because I need to keep it somewhere, and Stella and I have to eat."

Titus wiped his hand down his face. "You don't need to buy your own fucking food. You can eat whatever the housekeeper buys, and add anything you want to the list on the fridge."

"Thank you. I didn't know that, and I asked if I could help around the house or make meals, but you said no." I rubbed my damp palms against my shorts. "My parents had me pay for our food, rent, and utilities." I glanced up at him. "I didn't want to assume or take advantage of you."

"Fuck me," Titus muttered. "I'm sorry to disparage your parents, but they are complete *trous de cul.*"

I sucked in a breath, then let it out. "It's okay. I know they can be assholes."

"What other French words do you know?" he asked curiously.

Setting the bag of spaghetti down, I leaned against the counter. "Mostly just the bad ones," I admitted. "A couple of my best friends speak French. Their dad is French." I tilted my head. "But I had to look up what *p'tite cocotte* means. Why do you call me a little casserole?"

He grinned. "It also means little sweetie or little tart. But I like casserole better." His face got serious. "You and Stella eat whatever the fuck is in the fridge or cupboards. And if you need anything, including toilet paper, toothpaste, deodorant, or fucking tampons or panties, for Christ's sake, put them on the list. Okay?"

There was no way I'd be putting underwear or tampons on that list, but I nodded. "Okay. Thank you."

I looked down at the spaghetti, thinking about how worried I'd been over the past year that Stella might go hungry. I'd used food stamps and an infant food program for the first two years after

Stella was born, but my parents forbade me from using subsidies while I lived with them.

My father had seen the voucher and gone into a rage. "No one living under my roof is going to use government handouts," he'd raged while ripping up the food voucher. He'd also screamed that I didn't need the money anyway since my grandma only cared about me. I didn't know what he'd been going on about. Shaking off the memory, I turned back to the stove.

My shoulder blades itched, and I could feel Titus watching me as I put a pan of water on the stove to boil.

He stood. "There's some hamburger in the fridge. I'll brown it, and we can add it to the spaghetti sauce. Unless you're vegan or vegetarian."

"We're not. But meat is expensive so we don't eat it a lot."

"Isa said she told you I'd pay you a monthly salary to help watch Max."

Turning to him, I put up my hand. "I don't expect you to pay me when he's not even here. I'm good at stretching my money."

Titus looked up at the ceiling and sighed. "It doesn't surprise me that you and Isa are best friends. You're both stubborn as fuck, and so damned frugal."

My back went up. "I'm not stubborn, but I am frugal because I've had to be."

He folded his arms and nodded. "I get it. But I'm going to pay you."

Shaking my head, I put my hands on my hips. "I can't let you–"

"Half. I'll pay you half until he gets here, alright? And I'm not arguing about it anymore." I opened my mouth, but he shook his head. "If you need anything or have any questions or concerns, talk to me. Alright?"

I sighed, but relief slid through me. "Okay, and thank you. But promise you'll talk to me as well if something bothers you."

"Deal, *p'tite cocotte.*"

"Little casserole," I muttered, but my lip quirked.

We started drinking coffee together most mornings, and he asked me about Seattle, how Stella was doing with her schoolwork, and my odd website jobs. I asked him about hockey and his childhood. Titus didn't ask about mine.

We also started eating dinner together regularly, and when he left to visit Max or play his away games, we missed him.

Sometimes, Stella carried around the little stuffed animals he'd given her, and she always slept with one or both of them. It touched me that this big, scarred, tattooed hockey player didn't even know her at the time, but he'd still gotten them for her. It was more than her biological father ever gave her.

When I got up the nerve to look at the email with the get-to-know-you questions Isabella sent us that morning, I didn't think they were too bad—at first. Then I skimmed through the ones about our sexual preferences, past partners, favorite positions, and sexual fantasies and stopped cold. Oh, shit, I did *not* want to talk with Titus about that.

I heard the garage door open, and he walked into the kitchen a few minutes later.

I smiled sickly at him. "Hey, how was practice?"

"Good." He raked a hand through his hair and set his bag on the counter. Then he sighed. "Where's Stella?"

"She's taking her afternoon nap. You seem tired, and a little annoyed. Aren't you excited about making it to the playoffs?"

He filled a glass with water and drank the whole thing. I watched his thick, muscular throat swallow and had to look away.

He set the glass down. "I've been to a lot of playoffs. And Connor and the other owners just fired Coach Bailey. He's been on suspension, and I've been helping out as an assistant coach."

This was news to me. "They fired their coach? Right before the playoffs?"

"*Oui*. He played mind games and sabotaged some of the younger players. And he was an all-around fuckhead, even to Isabella. It was past time for him to go, and I just helped him along."

I frowned. "Isabella didn't say a word. He sounds like a jackass."

"Speaking of Isa, she sent me a list of questions she wants us to review before the hearing. They're supposed to help us get to know each other better."

Blushing, I opened my laptop and turned it around to show him her email. "She sent it to me too."

He grinned. "From your red face, it appears you've read through them."

"Yep." I smacked my lips.

"Tell you what. We'll save the more interesting ones for another day. Let me grab some food and we'll get started."

I let out a long exhale. "Okay. There's leftover chicken and roasted potatoes in the fridge. And brownies."

"Sounds good." He heated his food, and we sat at the bar and started in on the questions.

I scanned the first one. "What's your favorite color?"

"Black."

I stopped. "Black? Really?"

He shrugged and took a bite of chicken. "It hides blood and other bodily fluids better. What's yours?"

I stared at him. "Mine is green."

"Why?" He took another bite.

He had straight white teeth and a nice jawline. I liked watching him, but I needed to stop.

Clearing my throat, I lowered my eyes to the screen. "Stella has green eyes, and I love all the trees and foliage in the Northwest."

"You have green eyes too. With hazel mixed in. I've never seen eyes like yours."

"My mother said they're a mark of the devil."

He shook his head. "She sounds fucking crazy."

I nodded. "She probably is." His comments warmed my heart, which was odd because he'd just called my mother crazy.

"You have beautiful eyes." He ate a potato and stared at me. "Don't let her get in your head."

"Okay."

He watched me shift uncomfortably and his eyes crinkled. "Half of my childhood was spent near Victoria. Someday I'll take you and Stella to the Canadian Gulf Islands. Talk about green."

"We'd love that. I've only been as far north as Orcas Island in the San Juans. Okay, next question. Where were you born?"

"In Montreal. My parents moved to Calgary when I was nine, but they moved back to Montreal a few years ago to take care of my *grand-mère*. I'm an only child. Where were you born?"

"Tacoma. Then my parents moved to Seattle. I'm an only child too." I studied the questions. "What's your favorite memory?"

He grinned. "That's easy. The first time I stepped onto the ice after Vancouver drafted me."

"That must have been amazing. How old were you?"

"Nineteen. And it was mind-blowing. I can still hear the crowds cheering."

"I can't imagine being so good at something, a professional team drafts you at nineteen. I'd like to come watch you if you ever get tickets." He didn't respond right away, and I worried that maybe I'd overstepped. I looked back down at my screen.

"It'd be nice to have you and Stella come watch me. But have you ever been to a hockey game?" he asked as he ate.

"No, I've seen a few on TV, though. Do they allow young kids?" The thought of watching Titus play made my heart race.

"Yeah, and they think it's good practice to get them hooked early. But it can get a little intense, and some players are hotheads. Make sure you bring earplugs."

Smiling, I reached over and plucked a potato off his plate. "Okay. I want to watch you play."

He grinned. "I'll get you tickets then. What's your favorite memory?"

That one was easy. "The first time I held Stella. When the nurse laid her in my arms, I was shaky and tired, and… well, anyway. The room was so quiet I could hear her soft, little sounds."

Titus set his fork down. "Were your parents there?"

"No." I looked back at my computer.

"Was Stella's father there?"

I shook my head and hoped he'd go on to the next question.

"Does he support her?"

"No. And he's not her father, he's her sperm donor." I hadn't meant to sound so bitter. Laying my palms on the counter, I started to stand.

Titus squeezed my hand, then let go. "When you're ready to tell me, I want to know about that stupid fucker."

I let out a breath and nodded. "Okay." I grabbed some water and sat back down. We went through a couple more questions but took a break a few minutes later. He could tell my mind had drifted, and Stella was up from her nap. She walked in, dragging her yellow blanket behind her.

As I cut up a few grapes for her, Titus heated some chicken and potatoes and slid the food onto her plate. I froze and stared at his large, scarred hands preparing food for my little girl.

He glanced over at me. "You okay?"

"Yes." My heart thumped hard in my chest. "Thank you."

"For what?"

"For helping me take care of her."

"You don't have to thank me." He winked at Stella, who smiled back. "We're a team, and she's *ma p'tite puce*."

Clearing my throat, I blinked a few times to get my emotions under control. He didn't know my parents had rarely helped with Stella, and whenever they did, they complained loudly in front of her.

"I'm almost afraid to ask what *p'tite puce* means."

He handed Stella a piece of brownie, and they grinned at each other. "It means little flea. I've heard you call her 'little bug.' Don't worry, it's a good thing."

Chapter 5

Later that evening, as we watched an episode of *Pawn Stars*, Titus turned to me. "Are you coming with me to Connor and Isabella's party tomorrow night?"

Isabella had invited me, but I didn't know if Titus wanted to go. "Yes. Isa and Connor said Elodie's babysitter would watch Stella too."

"Good. Connor's little girl is sweet, so I think Stella will like her."

"When Isa first told me about Connor, none of it was good."

Grinning, he turned to me. "Yeah, she hated his guts. Then she became good friends with half the damned team, and it drove him fucking nuts. That's when Isa started the team-building Wednesday night parties."

"What for?"

He smirked. "She thought the players needed to 'bond' as a team, or some bullshit like that. Connor dubbed the parties 'Whiskey Wednesdays' because most of them bring whiskey as their potluck side dish. Or ketchup-flavored potato chips since they know she hates them."

I wrinkled my nose. "Whiskey? Yeah, if you're a masochist and like pouring fire down your throat. I'd try a ketchup-flavored potato chip though."

Stella sat between us in her purple pajamas. "Look, Chumlee." She patted Titus on his stomach.

He turned back to the TV and put his arm around her, pulling her a little closer. "It is. He's goofy."

She nodded. A few minutes later, Stella slumped against him and fell asleep.

"I'll carry her to bed," he whispered, picking her up. I followed them into her room and watched him tuck her in.

We walked back out to the kitchen together, and Titus opened the fridge and pulled out a beer. "You don't like whiskey. What do you drink?"

"Maybe white wine? I don't drink much, though. It's–"

He held up a hand. "Let me guess, too expensive."

I grinned sheepishly. "Yeah."

"Another group is coming to the party tomorrow night. Isabella has some good friends who live in Palm Springs not far from here, and they have a Martini Monday party every week. I've gone a few times, and they're an entertaining group."

A sick feeling slid through me as I imagined Titus going to parties with other women. Had he hooked up with anyone I'd be meeting tomorrow night?

I didn't have any right to feel jealous, but there it was. He wasn't a monk, and he had a son and a baby mama, for hell's sake. He was also a successful professional athlete, hot, muscular, and larger than life. And when he spoke French, my ovaries melted.

Clearing my throat, I ran a hand down my thigh. "We, uh, never talked about seeing other people."

"Other people?" He straightened.

"Yeah, like if you want to see other women while Stella and I are living here."

His eyes narrowed. "I don't. What made you think of that now?"

I started busying myself by straightening up the kitchen and putting the popcorn bowls in the dishwasher.

"Abigail," he prodded.

Sighing, I turned to him. "I was thinking about you at those parties. If I'm going to run into someone you've been with, I'd like to be prepared."

He crossed his arms and studied me. "I haven't hooked up in a while, and I'll be introducing you to most of the team tomorrow. Some of them are forward little fuckers."

I cocked my head. "They know I'm your 'girlfriend,' right?"

"Most of them."

My brow furrowed. "Then it doesn't matter."

"What do you mean?"

I rubbed the back of my neck. "While we're living with you and you're working on getting custody of Max, I'll make sure I behave like your girlfriend. And we're on the same team, so it doesn't matter if someone's interested. I'm with you."

Titus relaxed and nodded. "Alright. I'll do the same."

My heart swelled at the thought, and I turned away to hide my emotions. "Are they nice?" I asked as I wiped down the counter.

"Who?"

"The Martini Monday crowd, and your hockey team."

"The Martini crowd are great people. Isa loves them, and you'll fit right in. They're a little fucking crazy, but it's the good kind."

"I'd like that." The picture he painted of Isa's friends seemed idyllic, and I also wanted that.

"My teammates are only assholes sometimes. Jackson is Connor's cousin. He's a decent guy."

"Isabella talks about him and has mentioned a few of her Martini Monday crowd."

"Rudy's the other center and also plays forward. He's a nice guy too, and a fucking brick house on the ice."

"Is that a good thing?"

"Yeah," he grinned. "Mikael's our goalie from Sweden. He's brutally honest and blunt as hell. It's probably a Scandinavian trait." Titus sounded like a proud, exasperated uncle when he talked about the younger teammates.

Sighing, he shook his head. "And then there's Wyatt. He's a brilliant forward, but he acts like a fucking prick sometimes. Be careful around him."

I nodded. "Don't worry, I will."

Isa stood in Titus's kitchen making pancakes the next morning. "So, how's it going with you guys? Are you getting to know each other?"

"Isa, the questions you sent us. Some of them are..."

"Explicit?" Isabella supplied, her spatula tapping on the edge of the frying pan.

"Very," I admitted, heat rising in my face.

She smiled sneakily. "I know! But you both promised me you'd go over them together. That means *all* of them."

"But what's the purpose here?" I asked.

"The best way to *really* get to know someone is to talk about uncomfortable, intimate things. Titus told me once," she said, sliding a perfect golden pancake onto my plate, "that he loves S.E.X., and he even likes it a little rough. I've also heard he's fantastic at it." She glanced at Stella. "He and Connor are similar in that regard. And I like doing *that* with Connor. A lot."

My heart fluttered in a confusing mix of apprehension and curiosity, and I squirmed a little in my seat. "That's overly informative. Thank you."

She smirked. "Joke all you want. We'll talk in a month or two."

Memories of Kyle's careless touches and then his sharp betrayal—and my father's harsh words and fists—flashed like warning signs. But Titus wasn't like them, I already knew that deep in my soul.

The bright sun streamed through the kitchen window, casting a warm glow across the bar where I nursed a cup of coffee. Isabella flipped another pancake, then slid it onto Stella's plate and topped it off with fruit and whipped cream.

"Oooh, cakes," Stella cooed.

Isabella smiled at her. "That's right, Stella Bella. Cakes for breakfast."

My heart squeezed a little whenever she spoke to someone besides me.

Isabella turned off the stove and came to sit beside me. Her eyes were earnest, her voice softer now. "You're twenty-three. It's been over three years since you've—"

"Since Kyle left," I finished for her, the name causing my mouth to tighten.

"Not all men are like Kyle. Or your psycho father. You deserve to know what it's like to be with someone who cherishes you and makes S.E.X. fun." She looked up at the ceiling. "And so hot it'll burn your eyebrows off."

I let out a shaky breath, trying to imagine a reality where intimacy wasn't a power play, or didn't leave me feeling worthless or wanting. Could Titus be different? My mind conjured up his hard, muscular body and tattoos, and the sweet way he played with Stella. Hell, I even loved it when he called me a little casserole in French.

"Come on," Isabella said suddenly, pulling me to my feet. "We'll find something beautiful for you to wear tonight."

True to his word, Titus deposited more money into my account than had ever been there at one time. I cried when I saw it, then paid off my credit card and the last bill at Stella's old daycare.

Shopping was a blur of cheery, colorful clothing stores. Isabella held up several dresses until we found a green satin one with a V-neckline that showed a little cleavage.

Stella watched us both curiously while we laughed and chattered together as we shopped. When a couple of store clerks tried to talk to her, Stella ignored them.

"Abby," Isabella declared when I walked out of the dressing room in the green dress. "That's the one."

"I like it too," I mumbled, staring at myself in the mirror. The color brought out the natural highlights in my hair and made my eyes look almost beautiful. I also got my hair trimmed and styled while Isa took Stella to lunch, and the added layers framed my face and tamed my curls into beachy waves.

When we finished shopping, we strolled along Palm Canyon Drive, soaking in the early afternoon sun. Isabella pointed out the bar where she'd taken the hockey team for karaoke night.

I read the sign. "The Cockpit. Is that an airplane thing or a penis thing?"

She grinned. "It's a gay bar, so a penis thing. This area is full of hip bars." She pointed to several others along the same street. The area had a nice modern, retro vibe.

We continued to window-shop and even splurged on a thick, sweet date shake. It tasted almost like caramel but with big chunks of chewy dates, and Stella loved it. We gazed around at the mid-century shops and signs. Everything seemed so colorful and cheery, and the brilliant blue sky warmed my soul a little.

"This town differs from any place I've ever been, with this 1950s Hollywood flavor to it." Stella hummed next to me, licking her spoon, and kicking her legs back and forth.

"It really is, isn't it? I didn't know what to think when my dad told me he planned to move here." Isabella looked around and sighed. "I need to get back and start getting ready for tonight."

Early that evening, I showered and carefully did my hair and makeup, then slipped into the green dress. The fabric shimmered and flowed around my body.

"What do you think?" I asked Stella.

She glanced up from the coloring book Isabella had gotten her.

"Good." She went back to coloring. Okay, maybe I'd get a better reaction from Titus.

When we walked into the kitchen a few minutes later, Titus stood at the sink. "We're ready," I told him.

He stared at me, then sighed and hung his head. "Fuck."

His expletive stung. Even no reaction would have been better than that. "Is that what you're going with? 'Fuck'?"

Setting his water glass down, he put his hands in his pockets. "What I meant to say is you look very nice."

"Thank you." I glared.

"You do look nice, and so do you, *puce*. Are you ladies ready?"

"We'll find out, won't we?" I picked up my small bag, feeling annoyed and a little hurt. "Stella's car seat is in my car. It's a pain to move, so I can drive."

Titus shook his head. "We'll take mine. I bought a car seat before you came."

His thoughtfulness threw me, and I didn't know what to say. I felt Titus's gaze on me as we buckled Stella in.

His eyes met mine for a fleeting moment before he looked away, a frown creasing his brow.

When we got in, he stared at me but didn't start the car.

"What's wrong?"

"Nothing. But stay close to me tonight."

I realized he was worried about me, and my annoyance died. "Alright. And if anyone asks, I'm your newish girlfriend, and Isabella introduced us. We keep it simple and as close to the truth as possible."

Titus looked at my face and hair, then down at my dress. "Stay where I can see you."

I shifted nervously, his comments making me self-conscious. "It's just a dress."

"It's not only the dress, sweetheart. And you look beautiful. Just stay close, okay?"

"Don't worry, I'll be fine." I liked him calling me sweetheart too much, and taking in his furrowed brow and the tight set of his jaw, I felt an unwanted flutter in my chest. His protectiveness made me feel a little too warm.

Chapter 6

My stomach fluttered as Titus's eyes skimmed down my length, and his lip quirked. I thought he might be silently apologizing for swearing the first time he saw me dressed up.

On the drive over, he pointed out a fun neon carwash sign with a bright pink elephant to Stella. Then she pointed out a McDonald's sign to him.

Glancing at her through his rearview mirror, he chuckled. "That's a good one too."

Connor lived in an exclusive area with large, gated grounds surrounding enormous, sprawling modern homes in Palm Desert. Intimidation rose through me when we drove through the gates.

"That's Javier's house," Titus said, pointing to the much smaller caretaker cottage. I unbuckled Stella, and we knocked on the door to the tiny home.

"Yay, they're here!" I heard a child yell from inside.

An older lady answered the door. "You must be Abigail Carver and little Stella. Come in. I'm Lena Jenkins, Elodie's backup nanny and babysitter." The cheerful woman had on a blue caftan and smelled like lavender.

Stella stayed behind me and wouldn't look at Lena. But when Elodie came to the front door, Stella slid out from behind me. Elodie took Stella's hand. "Javy has a one-eyed cat, and her name is Shawnda. She's a little scared of people. But guess what?"

Stella stared wide-eyed at Elodie, who kept chattering away. "She loves me now. We're going to make cookies tonight, and watch a princess movie, and play games."

The smile that spread across Stella's face made my heart lighten. "Make cookies?" she asked.

"Yes!" Elodie squealed, and Stella followed her inside.

I realized I needed to find other kids for her to play with. A few minutes later, Titus and I headed over to the main house, with Stella practically pushing me out the door. Connor's home glowed with life, and laughter and music spilled out into the evening air.

We walked in, and Titus rested his hand lightly on the small of my back. Slow, hot shivers slid down my spine.

"Abs, You look smoking hot. Thanks for coming a little early. Will you help me set up the bar?" Isabella grabbed my hand and pulled me with her.

Heat crept into my cheeks, and I glanced back at Titus–and noticed him studying my ass. His eyes flicked back to my face, and I raised my eyebrows at him. He shrugged and winked at me.

Javier Cruz, Isabella's dad, stood out on the back patio hanging up lights with Connor's cousin, Jackson.

"Hey, Mr. Cruz. It's so good to see you again." We hugged and caught up a little. Isa's dad always smelled like cut grass and kindness to me.

Isa handed me a glass of wine. "Here. You might need a little liquid courage tonight." As more people arrived, Isa and Titus introduced me to his teammates.

Jackson grinned down at me. "Isa, do you have any other friends like Abby you could introduce *me* to?"

I blushed, and Isabella laughed. "No. And you're too young. You need to focus on hockey."

Rudy, the red-haired center, pushed his way in. "I'm a little older than Jackson, so I'm next in line."

"Abigail, you are the one who is too young for Titus," Mikael, the Swedish goalie, said in his thick accent. "He is an old, grumpy man who swears and grunts at everyone."

I moved closer to Titus and put my hand on his stomach. "He only swears and grunts at me a little. And he doesn't scratch himself in public anymore, so I know he can be trained."

Titus pinched my side, and I laughed. His abdomen was firm and warm under my palm, making me want to feel him without his shirt. I suddenly pulled my hand away like I'd been burned.

He put his arm around my shoulder. "She's mine, asshole. Fuck off."

Mikael shook his head. "He makes my point for me."

I also met Isabella's other friends. Laurel seemed sweet, and she was beautiful. Her boyfriend, Sebastian Mendoza, was also one of the best-looking men I'd ever seen, but he didn't smile or talk much, and glared at a few players when they tried to get close to Laurel.

"Abby, you need to come to our Martini Monday parties. You seem crazy enough to fit right in if Titus is your boyfriend," Martina, Laurel's roommate, said as she handed me a martini glass full of a bright pink concoction. "And I'd love to drag you to karaoke night at The Cockpit."

I took the glass from her because I didn't know what else to do. "Thank you. What is this?" I asked, taking a tentative sip.

She grinned. "It's a prickly pear martini."

The drink had a botanical, citrusy taste, which was a pleasant surprise since I didn't like sweet drinks much. "Hmm, this is good, thank you. I've never done karaoke before."

"We'll have to indoctrinate you, then."

I never had many girlfriends besides Isa and Claudette. "That sounds good. I've only been to a bar a few times."

She smiled happily, like this was great news. "Don't worry, we'll rectify that."

I glanced around for Titus, like I'd done all evening. He stood talking to a tall, stunning blond woman. Jealousy coursed through me. She looked gorgeous in a blue halter-top dress. I turned away so I didn't have to watch them together.

When Martina walked off to get another drink, one of the hockey players slid in next to me. "Hey. My name's Wyatt." He was handsome and had tattoos circling his biceps. His name also rang a bell, but I couldn't place him.

I switched my drink to my other hand and shook his outstretched palm. "It's nice to meet you. I'm Abigail." Then I remembered his position, at least. "You're a forward, right?"

His eyes slid down to my chest, and he leisurely grinned back. "Yeah. And you're Isabella's friend?"

"Yes, we grew up together. I guess you know her from her internship." He didn't let go of my hand, and my stomach lurched when he pulled me closer to him.

"I do. It's loud in here. Let's find a quieter place to talk."

He started pulling me by the wrist, and panic flared in my chest. My father used to grab my wrist sometimes and drag me behind him.

"Hmmm, it's not that loud." I tugged but didn't want to make a scene. "Let go."

He didn't let go. I instinctively tugged harder, and when he stopped suddenly and turned around, my drink splashed, sloshing liquid on us both.

"Fuck! Why'd you do that?" he snarled.

He stepped toward me, and I flinched back as if trying to shield myself from a strike. Panic crawled up my throat, and I cowered there for several seconds, gasping for air.

An arm reached around me and took my glass, passing it off to Martina. Then Titus was there, yanking Wyatt's hand off my other wrist and gently folding me into his arms. I wheezed and tried to breathe.

"It's alright, you're safe. Use your diaphragm and take deep breaths. That's it, I've got you." He rubbed my back and rumbled soothing words into my ear. I slowly wrapped my arms around him and let out a small sob.

"I'm sorry. He wouldn't let go. I'm so sorry."

Titus growled viciously in his throat, but his hands continued to rub my back. Mortification crept in as my breathing returned to normal. The room had gone silent.

"Oh, God. I'm sorry." I hid my face in his neck.

"You have nothing to apologize for." Titus pulled me to his side and faced off against Wyatt. "If you *ever* lay a finger on her again, I will end you."

Wyatt's face had gone white as he stared at me, trembling in Titus's arms. "I didn't mean to scare her. I didn't know–"

Isabella broke in. "Wyatt, just go. Maybe you'll learn not to be such an asshole from now on."

"Look, I had no idea–" Titus growled again, and Wyatt held up his hands. "Okay. I'm gone." He turned around and strode out.

"I'm taking Abby outside for a few minutes," Titus told Connor and Isa. Connor nodded and glanced at me with pity. I hated when people felt sorry for me, and shame and embarrassment crawled through my belly.

The cool night and the scent of desert jasmine drifting through the garden comforted me a little, and we found a private patio at the far end of Connor's enormous pool. Voices faded, replaced by the soft rustling of palm trees. It was a peaceful spot, and my stomach started to unclench.

I felt Titus's heavy gaze on me. "Abby, you flinch sometimes when someone makes a sudden move near you. Like you're expecting to get hit."

My throat tightened, and I fought against memories clawing their way to the surface. Staring out into the night, I admitted the truth. "You already know why. My father has a nasty temper, and he got violent sometimes."

Fear and shame spread through me like a virus. I knew my father's behavior wasn't my fault, but on some subconscious level, I still felt responsible for it.

"Shit," Titus exhaled. "Has he always been like that?"

I jerked my shoulder. "It got worse when my grandfather died, and Nana changed her will and cut him and my mother out. At least that's what I've been able to piece together. He left me mostly alone through elementary school. And when I was in middle school after a particularly bad fight, I told him I'd call the police and report him if he kept hurting me. My mother didn't talk to me for a month after that, but he stopped hurting me. Until I had Stella and eventually had to move back home." I covered my face. "I didn't have anywhere else to go."

He gently wrapped his arms around me. "Getting yourself and Stella out of that situation took guts and courage."

His words wrapped around me like a warm blanket. "I'm not strong, and when you growled at me, you scared me the first time we met. I might have even peed a little."

Titus's lips twitched. "Seeing you with Stella on your hip and your black eye and bruised face knocked me on my ass. I wanted to rip the asshole's head off who did that to you."

I squeezed his hand. "I know. You told me."

"I'd love to have you and Stella at my hockey games, but they get a little violent sometimes." He searched my eyes. "I don't want you to be afraid of me."

"We want to come. And I know there's a world of difference between playing hockey and hitting your child."

He nodded and settled me against him. "Okay."

"When Isa called and asked me to be your fake girlfriend to help you get custody, I thought she'd concussed herself riding her skateboard." He chuckled, and I smiled at the sound. "But I'm so glad she did. We're safe here with you, and Stella is happy."

My brain struggled to find the right words to express my feelings, so I turned and wrapped both arms around him as far as they would go, my sternum pressing into the side of his muscular arm. It was an awkward hug, and I quickly let go. "So thank you."

He searched my eyes, then brushed a strand of hair away from my face. Over the past three years, my life had been chopped into little bits of happiness I'd stolen in between my parents' cruelty. I also craved happiness and wanted to be both safe and happy. But it was almost too much for my battered soul to comprehend. So I'd settle for safe.

Chapter 7

Isabella came over for lunch a few days later. Setting her backpack down on the counter, she went to the fridge and grabbed the water pitcher and sandwich fixings. She always seemed perfectly at ease in Titus's house, and I wished I felt as comfortable.

"Have you heard from Claudette lately?" she asked.

"No. I planned to call her this week." Claudette was our other best friend. Besides working at a tech company, she also owned an online "adult boutique toy store" called the Cherry Box. Her parents ran an import business, and her father was French. I adored her parents and secretly wished they were my own.

Isa started making sandwiches. "I just talked to her this morning, and she's selling the Cherry Box. She got a promotion at work and is moving to Berlin next month."

"Wow! Good for her. She's always wanted to live abroad. What's she going to be doing?"

Isa shrugged. "I've never really understood what she does." Claude was some kind of computer genius.

"Me neither. Who's she selling her online store to?"

Isabella grinned and smacked my arm. "You!"

I froze, knowing I'd misunderstood her. "Pardon?"

"You," she repeated. "She wants to sell the business to you. She called me first to get my opinion and see if you'd be interested."

My mind couldn't process what Isa was saying. "Me? Why?"

Isa put her hands on her hips. "If you still lived with your parents, there's no way you could buy the Cherry Box. And live. But think about it, this would be *perfect*. You could work when Stella goes to bed or before she wakes up, and when she's napping."

I smiled a little. "Knowing my parents would loathe the idea makes me want to do it even more." Then I remembered my bank account balance and my budding fantasy came crashing down. Thanks to Titus, I had a little over two thousand dollars to my name, but my car needed an oil change and new tires.

"Isa, I can't afford to buy a pack of gum right now, let alone a successful online business." My shoulders slumped. "I'll call her and thank her for thinking of me though."

"Claude wants you to buy her out slowly. She rambled on about taxes, being single, and not having any write-offs. And she's willing to take payments based on your sales."

My mind spun with possibilities and potential issues. Claudette didn't keep any inventory and drop-shipped most of her products directly to her buyers. She'd explained her business to Isa and me one day a few years ago before I got pregnant.

We'd been celebrating her birthday, and I made a red velvet cake and Isa brought two bottles of cheap wine. While we ate cake and got drunk, she told us about her sex toy business.

"Okay, I'm a little scared because it sounds almost too perfect. Did she really say I could pay her off over time?" We eventually called Claudette and put her on speaker while I fed Stella lunch. "Claudette, are you moving to Berlin?" I asked incredulously.

"Hell, yes! My dad tried to talk me into moving to France, but once he heard what my employer is going to pay me, he suddenly thought Germany sounded wonderful."

Isa leaned over my shoulder. "We're so excited for you." She cut up an apple and put a few small slices on Stella's plate while we talked.

"And jealous," I added.

"Girl, I hear you're living with a French Canadian hockey player. That beats living with your fuckwad parents any day."

I smiled. "It does. Stella adores him, and she's a good judge of character. She loves you and Gabriel too."

"She does love me, so I agree. What'd you think of him when you met him?" Claudette asked.

"The first day was a trainwreck," I admitted. "It's a lot better now. Tell me about the Cherry Box. I want to buy it, but I'm destitute. How can this be good for you?"

Claudette discussed taking a percentage of the net sales over time until the business's appraised value had been reached. While we talked, Stella finished lunch and hopped down to play in her room.

"Let me wash your hands first, bug." I wiped Stella down and she took off.

"You'd be helping me with my tax issues," Claudette finished.

Isa rolled her eyes. "Gee, I wish I had that problem."

"Just wait. As a professional single adult who doesn't own a house or have any write-offs, I am getting royally fucked. And you will too once you start working."

"I think people call that a first-world problem," I told her.

"Yeah, yeah. So what do you think, Abs? Is it something you want to do?"

"Absolutely because I'm not an idiot–most of the time. It's perfect for my situation, but I feel like it's some made-up dream, and I'm suddenly going to wake up. Like Isa introducing Stella and me to Titus."

Claudette got quiet for a moment. "Abby, she told me about your dad hurting Stella, and I know that fucker hurt you too."

Isa nodded. "When I met her at the airport in Seattle, she had a black eye and bruised ribs."

Claudette swore viciously. "Abigail, I'm going to say this one more time and then I'll shut up about it. You need to get the police to press charges. I know you think it'll just set him off, but that psycho asshole has never needed an excuse to hurt you. Your father is crazy, and he needs to be stopped."

A knot formed in my gut, and I wiped my sweaty palms on my jeans. "I will. If they show their faces here, I will. But I just want them to stay away, and Stella is... she's happy, and talking, and doing so well."

"You should get to feel happy and safe too," Isa said quietly, grasping my shoulder.

My eyes got glassy, and we were all silent for a few moments, lost in thought. Claudette finally cleared her throat. "Hey, I want to visit you guys in sunny Palm Springs before I leave next month."

We talked a little more about the Cherry Box, then started making plans to have Claudette come to Palm Springs. But their words haunted me.

On Sunday afternoon, we went to a Thunderbirds playoff game. Stella and I had seats next to Isabella, Connor, and Elodie. We made our way through the crowded arena, both of us gazing around with big eyes. The ice rink gleamed under the bright lights, and loud, upbeat music played through the speakers, promising an exciting, fast-paced game.

Isabella pointed down at the Thunderbird bench. "It feels weird not sitting by the team doctor and the players," she yelled.

Connor squeezed her shoulder. "Do you miss it?"

"Yes. I don't miss worrying about someone getting hurt–or the blood. But I miss the rest."

I watched the players skating around the rink to warm up. With their bulky pads and helmets, it was difficult to pick them out without looking at their jerseys. But I found Titus right away. He moved so naturally on the ice, he looked like he'd been born knowing how to skate.

Elodie and Stella gazed around curiously and stuffed pretzel bites in their mouths. They both wore giant, fluffy earmuffs to protect their hearing, which were much better than the cheap earplugs I'd brought.

Elodie had on a little Thunderbirds jersey with Jackson's number on it, and Connor and Isa wore nice Thunderbird pullovers.

I'd thought about getting a Thunderbird shirt but decided I'd splurged enough for the month.

"This is the first hockey game I've ever been to," I admitted.

Connor grinned. "You're in for a few surprises, then. Just don't freak out if you see a fight or a few injuries."

I stared at him with wide eyes. "Titus warned us about that. I think it'll be fine." I glanced at Stella and hoped I was right.

The game started, and Titus dominated on the ice. Between the players, the crowd, the music, and the announcer, the game was so loud we couldn't talk during most of it.

The players on both teams were fast, but Titus stood out. Isa told me he and Connor were in a class all their own. And after watching him play, I believed her. I also wondered why he wasn't playing on one of the professional teams. He didn't talk much about it, and I worried his injuries were still causing him grief.

He was on fire tonight, though, and every time he scored, the crowd chanted "Spar-tan! Spar-tan!" They yelled as they stomped their feet.

"Is that his nickname? Spartan?" I asked Isa after the first period when things quieted down a little.

"Yes. They call him The Spartan because he's that good. And Connor's nickname is The Hammer." She wiggled her eyebrows, and I laughed.

Stella ate up the excitement, clapping her hands and giggling when a few players got checked up against the boards. I was finding out my sweet girl might be a little bloodthirsty.

"Look, Mommy. Tie-Tie!" She squealed when they showed his face on the giant screen with his stats.

Stella stood on her seat during a break to get a better view. At one point, Isa grabbed my arm and pointed up to the giant screen. They'd captured Stella as she clapped her hands and pointed down to the ice. Then she and I were up on the screen together. Stella waved excitedly, and I smiled at her antics. The camera eventually zoomed over to take in Connor and Isabella.

I looked down at the bench and noticed Titus grinning up at us. For some reason, I quirked my eyebrow and finger-waved to him. He shook his head, but he still smiled when he headed back out on the ice.

By the end of the game, exhilaration and exhaustion coursed through me, and my throat hurt a little from cheering so loud. I could only imagine how Titus felt after every game.

The Thunderbirds won handily, and I turned to Connor. "Wow, he is kind of a Spartan, isn't he? Titus scored three of their five points, and two in the last half."

Connor winced. "They're called periods, not halves. And there are three. We also score goals, not points. Players can accumulate points for either goals or assists. So goals and points are different."

I looked at him blankly. "Okay."

Isabella grinned. "This is her first hockey game, McCoy. Give her a break."

She wanted to wait outside the locker room so we could congratulate the players and talk to Jackson and Titus. Stella and I stood awkwardly off to the side.

Wyatt came out first. He was one of the best players on the team besides Titus and Jackson, and he'd scored one of the other two goals. I still didn't like him. He noticed Isa and Connor, then looked over at me. I stepped in front of Stella, blocking her from

Wyatt's view. His lips tightened, and I thought I saw regret flash in his eyes before he turned and walked toward the parking lot. I didn't care. He'd grabbed me and hadn't let go when I asked him.

Jackson came out next, and Elodie ran up and threw her arms around his waist. "You played so good!"

Jackson hugged her and talked with Connor about the game, then made his way over to us.

"Hi, Stella Bella." Stella didn't answer him, but at least she didn't hide behind me. Jackson pulled a jersey out of his bag and held it out to me. "I have something for you. My jersey got ripped during the second period, and instead of throwing it away, I thought I'd give it to you since you aren't wearing any Thunderbirds swag."

I smiled and took the jersey. "Thank you, that's so sweet and thoughtful."

"You probably need to wash it first, but the tear is on the bottom."

"This is going to be worth big money someday." I grinned and rolled it up, tucking it under my arm.

"How'd you two like the game?" he asked.

"It was so exciting. And Stella loved it."

Stella nodded next to me. It was progress. Jackson smiled down at her. "Elodie loves the games too. Except the one where I got this." He pointed to a scar across his cheekbone. It looked a lot like the scar on Connor's face.

I grimaced. "Ouch. I'm glad you didn't lose an eye."

"That's what Isa said."

Titus walked up and put his hand on Stella's shoulder. "Did you like the game, *p'tite puce*?"

She bounced up and down and wrapped her arms around his leg. "Yeah!"

Titus glanced at me, then saw the jersey rolled up under my arm. "What the fuck is that?"

I wasn't fazed. "And hello to you, Spar-tan. The nickname fits, by the way." Pulling it out, I held the jersey up and turned it around so he could see Jackson's last name and player number emblazoned on the back. "Jackson gave it to me since I don't have any Thunderbird gear. I thought it was very nice."

Jackson grinned. "I'll see you guys later. Bye, Stella Bella."

I waved goodbye as Titus glared at the jersey. His spiky, dark blond hair made him look like he'd just rolled out of bed, and those tattoos on his muscular arms made my thighs clench. I needed to keep my greedy eyes to myself.

Stella wrapped her arms around both of our legs, and Titus smirked down at me. Just then, a couple of photographers who'd been taking photos and videos of the players as they walked out zeroed in on Titus. They snapped shots of us together, and I shifted nervously. I took Stella's hand and started backing away.

"We're going to take off. Thank you for the tickets, that was a lot of fun." I glanced at the photographers again.

Titus turned to them. "Okay, you got what you came for. You're making my girls nervous."

They grumbled a little but finally backed off after snapping a few more shots. Titus watched them leave, then turned back to me. "I'm starving. Let's go eat." He glanced over at Connor. "You guys up for Goody's? I feel like a ribeye steak sandwich."

"Yay! They have chicken nuggets," Elodie cheered.

Connor nodded. "Sounds good. We'll meet you there."

I held up my hand. "We'll see you at home."

Titus shook his head. "You're coming too."

"Stella ate most of Elodie's pretzel bites, so I don't think she's very hungry."

Titus cocked his head and studied me. Then he glanced at Stella, who looked up at us with her inquisitive, green eyes, but she didn't say anything. Even at her young age, Stella seemed to understand that sometimes I had to say no to things because I simply couldn't afford them.

I had three dollars and some change in my wallet, and I'd promised myself I wouldn't charge anything on my credit card again until I had a way to pay it off. I was ashamed to tell Titus that.

He glanced at Connor and Isa. "We'll meet you there. If you get there before us, order me the ribeye sandwich, Stella the chicken nuggets, and Abby a cheeseburger. We made those the other night, so I know she likes them. We need to have a little talk."

Connor shook his head. "Good luck. I've had that same talk with Bella."

"Peas in a pod." Titus's lip quirked.

I shifted nervously as they walked off, and Stella leaned into me, reading my body language. "Titus, go on. We'll see you at home. You don't need to feed us."

He stepped into my space and slowly wrapped his muscular arms around me. Then he laid his chin on top of my head. I froze at the unexpected contact. It felt good to be held, and he smelled like soap and pine. I wanted to melt into him, but I couldn't.

"Abby, I want to go out to lunch or dinner with you guys sometimes. Or take you to a movie, or maybe ice cream. But I hate that worried, pinched look in your eyes every time I bring it up."

"I'm sorry–"

"Don't fucking apologize. You two are mine; my girls–for as long as you live in my house. And we're a team, just like you said. I'm paying, so stop worrying about money all the fucking time."

I stiffened in his arms. He had *no idea* what it was like to agonize about whether you had enough money to feed your child. Or if you could afford your next rent payment, or whether you should pay the childcare bill or put gas in your car so you could go to work–because you couldn't afford both.

Frustration rolled through me, and I struggled in his arms. "I can't. I need to go." He immediately let go and stepped back. "Abby, talk to me."

My throat closed, and I fought to keep my composure. "You don't know, you don't understand. I can't just 'stop worrying about money' when it's how I feed–" I stopped and glanced down at Stella. I needed to just shut up, but I was so *mad*.

"Okay, sweetheart. It's alright, we don't have to go. I can text Connor and cancel our order." He held up his large, beautiful hands.

Stella took my hand again, and I looked down at her. She stared up at me with what was probably the same pinched, worried expression Titus said I'd had on my face. I straightened my shoulders and sucked in a breath, then let it out slowly.

"I... I'm sorry." I squeezed Stella's hand so she knew I was also talking to her. "You've never been anything but kind and generous to us. I didn't mean to take my worries out on you."

He watched me carefully. "You should be sorry." His voice sounded mild, so I knew he was joking. "But you can make it up to me by coming to eat with us. And letting me take you and Stella out sometimes. Deal?"

I sighed, my shoulders slumping. "Okay, and thank you. Watching you play was amazing, by the way. Stella cheered her lungs out."

We walked toward the parking lot with Stella between us.

"Thanks." He grinned at me. "And just so you know, you're not wearing Jackson's fucking jersey."

Chapter 8

When we walked into Goody's, Connor sat at a large booth with drinks and a number placard on the table in front of him.

"Isa took Elodie to the bathroom to wash their hands," he told us.

I looked down at Stella. "That's a good idea. Let's go do the same thing."

We walked into the bathroom, and Isa and Elodie were finishing up at the sink. Isa smirked at me. "Did Titus get you 'straightened out' and tell you to stop worrying about money because they're both worth close to a hundred million?"

I stopped short. "Titus is worth a hundred million?" I felt sick to my stomach all over again. I knew he was rich, but this was... so much worse.

She nodded. "They've invested well. You look like I feel every time I think about it, so I don't. Titus played with Connor in the professional league for years. I don't think they know what it's like not to have money."

I propped Stella up, and we washed our hands together. "I think I'm breaking out in hives."

"You're not—it's just nerves. I can see why Titus might give you hives sometimes though. But I like them both despite their money. Well, I love Connor, but you know what I mean. They're decent and kind, even if they're a little clueless about how the rest of us live."

We smirked at each other in the mirror. After our talk in the bathroom, I decided to let it go, and we sat in the restaurant for almost an hour laughing and talking about the game and our kids while we ate greasy, delicious comfort food.

Titus had a half day off the next day, and when Stella went down for a nap, he pulled Isabella's list of questions out again.

Taking my hand, he dragged me over to the couch. "Alright. Let's continue. What's your favorite food?"

I relaxed a little, hoping all the questions we covered today were like this. "Crepes. With strawberry sauce and real whipped cream."

He looked at my mouth like he was imagining me eating crepes with whipped cream. "My *grand-mère* would approve. Mine is a thick steak with a side of poutine and a good whiskey."

"What's poutine?"

"French fries topped with cheese curds and brown gravy. It's a Canadian dish." He looked back at the list.

"Is that a real dish, or are you just trying to gross me out?"

He reached over and tugged my ponytail. "Don't knock it until you try it."

We discussed food preferences, daily routines, and our childhoods. "What's your most embarrassing memory?" he asked.

"Mmm. Probably starting my period in middle school and having the cutest boy in my grade notice it."

"What'd you do?" he asked.

"The boy loaned me his hoodie, and I wrapped it around my waist and walked home. He said he had two older sisters, so he understood. It was horrible, but I made a good friend that day. What's your most embarrassing memory?"

He winced. "I walked in on my parents having sex. I was thirteen at the time, and my hormones had just hit hard. So the timing was piss-poor."

"Eek. That's... unfortunate."

He nodded. "What's your best childhood memory?"

"Hmmm, probably summer camp. For some reason, my parents thought it was a Bible camp, but it was actually a YMCA camp. I spent four weeks with other kids my age and no parents. Best summer ever. What about you?"

"Winning the junior hockey league championship in Calgary." His grin looked a little mean. "We beat Connor's team. What's your worst childhood memory?"

Swallowing, I fought back sudden nausea. Why hadn't I anticipated this question? "I'll have to think about it." I didn't have to think about it. The memory was seared into my brain. "What about you?"

"When I broke my collarbone and couldn't play hockey for almost six months. Abby, come here."

I didn't look at him as I slowly scooted over.

He patted his lap. "Right here. We need to get used to touching each other." I crawled into his lap, and he stayed quiet while I adjusted to being this close to him. After I stopped squirming and relaxed against him, he wrapped his arms around me.

Stroking his hand gently through my hair, he kissed my forehead. "Tell me."

Slowly, I relaxed into him and laid my head on his chest. Then I gathered my thoughts as he pulled me closer.

"When I was seven, I brought a pack of playing cards home. You know, the standard face cards. My friends and I had been playing some game, and I didn't think anything of it."

Titus ran his hand down my back. "What happened?"

Shuddering, I leaned into him a little more, taking comfort from his hard, warm body. "My mother found them in my bag, and she told my father a few days later when he came home in a terrible mood. They said face cards were evil and had Satanic symbols. Looking back, I realized my mother sometimes saved things like that so she could deflect my father's anger."

He squeezed me. "That's a shitty thing to do, especially to your child. What happened?"

I sighed and rubbed my palm on my thigh. "He whipped me with his belt."

Titus sat silently, waiting for me to continue.

I turned my head, and looked out into the room, not seeing it. "He hit me on my back, my bottom, and even my legs. I remember trying to crawl away from him, but he stepped on my back and kept whipping me, screaming Bible verses, and calling me a whore. I didn't even know what a whore was back then." I felt something wet on my chin and realized tears were dripping down my face.

"I'm so fucking sorry," Titus murmured in my hair. I'd stopped talking and sat quietly on his lap. "Finish it, *mon coeur*."

Sighing, I dropped my head to his shoulder. "He whipped me for what felt like hours, and by the end, I was bleeding and only half conscious. My mother finally stopped him. It was the only time she ever stopped him. And you know what the worst part is?"

He shook his head.

"He wasn't always a monster. When I was younger, he played and joked with me sometimes. But I think that made it worse later on when he got violent and started resenting me. It felt like a betrayal, and I never knew what to expect from him."

We sat for a few moments, and I soaked up his warmth and comfort, both of us lost in our thoughts.

Eventually, I sat up and wiped my face. "I should have told you my worst memory was when I got lost at the mall as a kid."

He squeezed me. "No. Don't lie about something like that. Let's take a break and make dinner. Stella will be up soon, and we can work on these fucking questions later."

We grilled pork chops, and Titus pulled out a bottle of wine and poured me a glass. When Stella woke up, we ate an early dinner and watched a movie together. I read Stella a couple of books, then Titus came in and we tucked her in together.

"The installers are coming tomorrow to install the fence and pool cover in the backyard," he told me after closing her door and walking back to the kitchen. "I'll be gone over the next few days for the two away games in Colorado, and then I'm going to see Max. Will you two be okay?"

"Yes. How are the team's chances of winning?"

He rubbed the back of his neck. "Honestly? Not good, but they've done a lot better than I thought they would. This team is so new, and they haven't dealt with the pressure of being in the playoffs or having a longer season." He grabbed an apple from the fridge, and I picked up my wineglass, then we sat on the couch facing each other. "It takes a toll. *Merde,* the fact we even made it to the playoffs is a fucking miracle. We were playing like shit until January."

"Your teammates seem nice. Except for Wyatt."

He smirked. "They're young, but they work hard and aren't complete assholes. Except Wyatt."

Titus was gone for almost a week. They won one game and lost one in Colorado, and then he took off to see Max for a couple of days before he came back home. He called a few times to check in with us.

Stella and I talked to him on speaker the night before he planned to come home while we made macaroni and cheese for dinner.

"More cheese, Mommy," Stella instructed.

"I'll never say no to more cheese, bug."

He sighed. "That sounds a lot better than the frozen chicken dinner I'm heating up right now."

"And I put a crunchy corn flake topping on mine, but we'll save you some. Are you at your condo? Where's Max?"

"I'm flying out early tomorrow morning, so I took him back to his mom tonight."

"You sound a little off. Are you alright?" I asked.

"I heard from my attorney today. The judge is pushing back our hearing date, and it's the second fucking time he's done it."

Relief flooded through me, and then guilt followed close behind. The only reason Stella and I were here, tucked away safe in his beautiful home, was because Titus wanted custody of Max.

"I'm so sorry. I know you're looking forward to having Max here, but think of it as a silver lining. It'll give us a little more time to get our stories straight so we can avoid going to jail for perjury."

He grunted. "We're not going to fucking jail, *p'tite cocotte*. Don't worry. What have you two been up to this week?"

I'd been working with Claudette to take over the Cherry Box, and we'd painted a wall as a surprise for Titus. But I didn't want to tell him either of those things.

"Oh, just hanging out with Isabella and Elodie. And Stella went in for a wellness checkup."

Titus had slowly been converting the office on his side of the house into a bedroom for Max. He'd planned to paint one wall a nice, soft blue color, but he hadn't gotten around to it yet.

A couple of days ago, I enlisted Isa and Connor to help me. Titus said he got the idea from Elodie's room, so I figured those two knew what he wanted. Luckily, Titus had already picked out the color he wanted.

"I'll pay you in babysitting if you'll help me paint the wall," I'd told Connor.

He grinned. "It's a deal."

So we painted the room, and that evening Elodie stayed with us while Connor took Isabella out to a poolside restaurant in Palm Springs a few of their friends had been raving about.

Titus seemed quiet and tired tonight, and I could sense his frustration.

"Hey," I told him. "We have a little surprise for you when you get back."

"Really? Is it leftover mac and cheese?" I could hear a faint smile in his voice.

"That, too. The installers are done with the fence and pool cover. Thank you again for getting it installed."

"It's for Max too. So what's the surprise?"

"Uh-uh. You have to see it firsthand. Are you one of those kids who ransacked the house before your birthday to find all your presents?" I asked.

"No. I told my parents what I wanted, and they got it. Now, what's the surprise?" We talked until the mac and cheese was done.

"Ketchup, Mommy," Stella requested when I pulled it out of the oven and dished her up a plate.

Titus chuckled. "I've never met anyone who loves ketchup more than her. I'll have to bring her a bag of ketchup-flavored potato chips."

My phone beeped, and I noticed my battery was almost dead. "My phone battery is messed up, so I might lose you."

"Your phone looks like it'd been run over a few times. I'm surprised it even works."

I shrugged because it was true. "Hey, I'm just happy to have one. When are you coming home?"

"Tomorrow. I'm going to let you go so I can call my parents before it gets too late. Tell Stella I'll bring her some ketchup potato chips."

After hanging up, I smiled a little as I returned my phone to the charger. Titus made me feel less alone in the world. Under his stoic exterior, he was thoughtful and even-tempered. Even when he got bad news, he didn't take it out on us. I liked so many things about him besides his gorgeous face and beautiful body. And those tattoos.

But I gave myself a stern talking-to as I ate. I needed to lock my feelings down and keep my relationship with him platonic. Having feelings for Titus could make things awkward between us and potentially jeopardize Stella's safety and stability. I couldn't do that to her.

Chapter 9

Titus came home while Stella and I were out on our usual morning run the next day. If the weather was warm enough, I'd put Stella in her stroller with the squeaky wheel and run around the neighborhood for a couple of miles.

Today, she wanted to get out and walk on the way back, so I stopped and unbuckled her. In Seattle, the weather was typically rainy and cloudy for most of the year. But here, the dazzling blue skies and sparkling sunshine made me feel light and cheerful.

We'd also met a few neighbors on our outings. Most of them were walking dogs or shuffling along, taking in the beautiful weather too. "Hi, George." I raised my hand at the older gentleman walking toward us. He and his mother lived three doors down in an immaculate white mid-century modern house with a turquoise blue door. I'd never met his mother, but George walked her little dog every day.

"Hello, Ms. Abigail, Ms. Stella." He smiled and tilted his full white head of hair at us. "It might get in the low seventies today."

George had on nice slacks and a button-down shirt, and he looked like a gracefully aging movie star.

"That warm? We'll have to plan something outside today, won't we Stella? How's your mom doing?"

George's smile dimmed a little. "She's losing her memory, and some days she knows it. I think that makes it worse for her."

"I'm so sorry, George. My grandmother suffers from dementia too. What's your mother's favorite cookie?"

He smiled. "She likes snickerdoodles. I used to tell her those were my favorites too, just because I knew she liked them."

Stella started tugging on my hand. "You're a good son, George. Enjoy your day."

When we walked inside, Titus sat at the bar, his rolling suitcase beside him. "I wondered where you were."

Stella ran over and hugged Titus's thigh. "You back."

"I missed you too. Have you been out walking?"

"Uh-huh." She turned to me. "I go potty."

"Holler if you need help."

"'Kay!" Stella ran off to the bathroom.

"How come you're all sweaty?" he asked, gazing down at my shorts and gray tank top.

"I just got done with a run."

"That explains your legs." He grinned and eyed my thighs.

I blushed and resisted the urge to fidget. "Sometimes I do wall Pilates and a little yoga. But I'm not very consistent."

"Consistent enough. Thank you for painting Max's wall." He stood up. "I'm going to hug you now."

My heart did a lazy somersault in my chest, and only a little of it was because he was thoughtful enough to warn me first. "Okay, but I smell like a boys' locker room."

He wrapped his arms around me. "Trust me, you don't."

"I'll get you all stinky and damp!"

He squeezed me harder. "You smell like you. Only a little saltier." He sniffed my neck and goosebumps erupted across my skin. "The wall was a nice surprise, and it looks great."

"Connor and Isa came over and helped, and I traded a little babysitting. You're welcome, *mon petite* Canuck."

His eyebrow raised. "Your little... Canadian?"

Laughing at the pained look on his face, I shrugged. "Hey, you call me your little casserole and Stella your little flea. You're lucky it's Canuck."

"Good point." He grinned, took my hand, and pulled me into Max's new bedroom. "Give me your opinion about furniture before I have to head to the arena."

A couple of days later, I knocked on George's door. His mother's little dog yapped inside, and it took a minute for him to answer.

"Hello, is everything alright?"

"Hi, George. I made snickerdoodle cookies for your mom and stuck a couple of extras in there for you."

He smiled and put his hand to his chest. "Thank you, Ms. Abigail. That is so thoughtful. She'll love these."

"It's no problem. Let us know if we can do anything for you." I started to turn away, then stopped. "George, I think I told you my grandma has dementia."

"Yes, you mentioned it."

"She was the most important person in my life until Stella came along, and I love her more than my own parents. That's a story for another day." George studied me curiously as I stood there awkwardly on his front step. "What I wanted to say is, I understand. And if you ever need anything, or just... someone to talk to I guess, I'm around."

He smiled sweetly. "You too. Thank you for the cookies, that was very thoughtful."

My circle of friends and loved ones had never been very big, and I wanted to change that if I could. Titus and George seemed like good places to start.

Claudette and I communicated several times a day over the next couple of weeks as she taught me how her online business worked. Luckily, I had some website design and maintenance background, but I needed to learn so many other facets of her business.

She also had a virtual personal assistant named Edna, who lived in Indiana and helped with ads, bookkeeping, and several other miscellaneous tasks. I hadn't met her yet.

"Claude, I can barely afford toothpaste. How can I justify having a virtual personal assistant?"

"You can't afford *not* to have one. She only works a few hours a week, but she makes them count. And sometimes two heads are better than one. Like double penetration."

"A sexual innuendo, how nice. And how does that even work?" I shook my head, even though she couldn't see me through the phone. "Alright. I trust you." I waved at Stella as she walked into the kitchen rubbing sleep out of her eyes. Titus had left for the arena already.

"I need to get back to work soon, but I told Edna we'd have a Zoom meeting so you two can meet."

"That sounds good. Is there anything else I should be doing?"

"Yes. You can look through the website and get to know all the products. Are you and that hot French Canadian hockey player fucking yet? Maybe he can help you figure out how some of them work, and which ones are your favorites."

My face got hot. "No! Geez, you're worse than Isa."

Claudette sighed loudly. "Abby, Kyle was a selfish asshole. And I'm ninety-nine percent sure he was also a selfish lover. You need to find out what it's like to have sex with someone who's actually good at it. And I bet Titus is more than just good."

After I'd gotten over my anxiety and fear when we first moved in, I came to a startling and unpleasant realization that Titus oozed testosterone and sex appeal. He reminded me of a French Canadian version of Charlie Hunnam. And sometimes when he used a French name or phrase... Oh God, I needed to reign in that train of thought.

"Thanks. Your advice is about as useful as a white crayon. I'm a single mother, and I don't date."

Claudette scoffed. "Who said anything about dating? I'm talking about screwing. Boinking. Having sex. Copulating. Good, old fashioned fucking. Do you know who's probably a pro at it? That hot as hell hockey player you're living with."

"I can't think of him like that."

Stella looked up from her coloring book. "Mommy, I hungry."

"Okay, love. What sounds good today? I've got eggs or oatmeal. Ooh, we have fresh strawberries to put on waffles."

She smiled. "Yum. I have that."

"I'm just saying you need a good lay. Now put me on speaker," Claudette instructed.

I switched my phone to speaker and set it on the counter. "Can you hear us?"

"Yeah. Hey Stella, this is your favorite Aunt Claudette. How are you?"

"Good." She kept coloring, her little tongue sticking out.

"Listen, don't let Isabella sneak into my favorite aunt spot, okay? She may have Elodie and a one-eyed cat. But I've got two-day shipping. And I sent you a surprise that'll be there tomorrow. Okay?"

"'Kay. I have waffles too."

Claudette hummed. "With strawberries. I heard. I'll let you ladies go, but call me when you get my present!"

I met Edna, my new virtual personal assistant, the next day on a Zoom call.

"Your business is the most interesting one I work with, that's for sure." She pushed up her designer glasses. "I also have some ideas to increase profitability and expand when you get your feet under you."

She lived in Indiana, except in the winter, and worked with three other online business owners. She was a retired marketing manager with a friendly Midwest competence and briskness, and I liked her right away.

"When I can get a handle on the business, I'd love to hear your ideas. Can I ask you something?"

"Absolutely."

"It seems like you don't really need to work. Why are you doing this?" I could see her beautiful, gleaming kitchen in the background, and she wore a couple of diamond tennis bracelets and an enormous diamond ring.

"My husband will never fully retire. And I got bored, but I like to travel. I started helping my niece, and it took off from there."

"That makes sense."

She looked at me carefully. "Can I ask *you* something?"

"Sure."

"Why are you taking over Claude's adult toy store? You seem so young and... wholesome."

"Are you saying I'm not young and wholesome?" Claudette interrupted.

"You're young, but you've never been wholesome. You like sex too much, and I'm not saying that's a bad thing."

"Fair enough."

Blushing, I wiped my palm on my thigh. "I like sex too. I just haven't had a lot of it. But enough to have a little three-year-old named Stella. And I'll be helping my friend with his little boy when he gets joint custody. I need something with a flexible schedule, and with enough potential income to support us."

Claudette interrupted. "She lives like a pauper, so that shouldn't be too hard. And her parents are scary, self-righteous fucktwits. Satan will probably kick her dad out of Hell when he gets there. She needs financial stability."

Edna's eyes went hard, and she straightened. "I'm a churchgoer, and it ticks me off when people use religion as an excuse to be assholes."

I raised my eyebrow at her use of the word asshole in the same sentence as churchgoer. I already liked Edna.

She took a deep breath. "Claudette looks at the business as a hobby, but I think you could really grow it if you wanted. Do a wedding or anniversary registration. Have a monthly toy box pairing with a spicy book and hit up the book clubs. Maybe even work with a few romance authors. Things like that."

"Wow. You've put some serious thought into this." I leaned forward. "Okay. I'm going to figure this out, and then let's see if we can work on some of your ideas."

Edna smiled. "It's only eleven in the morning here, but I feel like a margarita now. I may have to come visit you in Palm Springs sometime."

I grinned. "It's only eight here, and I feel like a margarita too. We may need to call a mandatory Cherry Box meeting in Palm Springs. You'd love it, especially between January and April."

The next afternoon, Claudette's surprise for Stella came via UPS. It was a kids' street hockey set containing two goals, two hockey sticks, and a couple of pucks. Claudette hadn't skimped on a cheap set either.

"I be like Tie-Tie," Stella kept saying. She bounced up and down as I put the goals together.

After we set it up, we played in the cul-de-sac in front of Titus's house. He drove up not long after we started and parked his

Bronco then came out to see what we were doing in the middle of the street.

Stella smiled happily and waved her hockey stick. "Look!"

"I see. Where'd you get it?"

She grinned. "Claude."

Titus stopped grinning. Stella ran after the puck, and Titus turned to me. "Who the fuck is Claude?"

I grinned and walked up to him. "My friend from Seattle."

He narrowed his eyes. "What kind of friend?"

"One of my best friends."

"Abigail," he growled, leaning into me.

I started laughing and patted his arm. "Her full name is Claudette, and I'm taking over her online business."

He folded his arms and rocked back on his heels. "You like messing with me."

"Yeah, I do." It tickled me that he didn't like other men giving me things for some reason. I didn't examine my feelings too closely.

He picked up one of the hockey sticks from the curb. It looked so tiny in his hands, it was comical. "Are you always going to be a little smart-ass with me?"

I walked over to stand next to Stella and crouched down to get ready to play him. "Not always. Sometimes I need to sleep."

He laughed and gently tapped the puck over to Stella. She whacked at the puck with her little stick but missed it. Then she missed it again.

Titus straightened and came over to show her how to hold and swing the stick. "Put this hand here at the top of the stick, and this one a little lower."

"Here?" she asked.

"Just a little lower. There you go. Now bring the stick back like this, and swing it forward."

Stella took another swing and barely moved it. "I try again."

One thing I loved about her was that she didn't get frustrated easily and had an easy, if quiet, temperament.

I stepped back and took a few photos of them together to send to Nana with our next letter to her. She would have loved Stella, and probably even Titus. She'd been my oasis growing up, and I'd missed her with a fierce ache when she started losing her memory.

Stella tried a few more times, and Titus tweaked her stance a little. She eventually hit it and started cheering with her hands over her head, like she'd seen some of the hockey players do.

Titus cheered with her, and we played and goofed around until it got too dark. I never regretted having Stella, but I did regret who her biological father was, especially now as I watched the two of them together.

Even after we went our separate ways, I hoped Stella would remember Titus. A heavy lump settled in my throat, but I swallowed it back.

Chapter 10

I felt almost like a teenager, furtively watching porn on my laptop after my parents left for work. Only it was me studying the Cherry Box website when Titus left for the arena.

The site sported a sensuous pair of red lips licking two plump cherries. The landing page enticed the viewer with just the right amount of spice and sensuousness and encouraged shoppers to have fun and enjoy their shopping experience.

Claudette's personality was written all over it. Sitting in Titus's cheery, sunny kitchen while Stella ate her lunch at the kitchen table, I went through Claudette's notes. Then I started looking through the product offerings.

The last time I'd gone through the website was with Claudette and Isa, and we'd all been laughing and drunk on cheap wine. Now, as I clicked through it, sober and in the light of day, my mouth hung open.

Claudette said her monthly subscription boxes were the biggest money-makers, and I could see why. Whoever designed them had a good eye; they included a few tried-and-true, quality adult toys, along with some lesser-known titillating implements and fetish pieces. As I scrolled through, the site made me feel both anxious and horny.

I also began to feel overwhelmed and in over my head. Could I make a go of this business? Did I have enough confidence and grit to figure it all out? And what the hell was an anal hook or a spreader bar?

Stella jumped down from her chair, and I slammed my laptop closed, my heart racing.

"All done," she informed me. She precariously picked up her plate and took it over to the kitchen sink. I looked down and noticed her shoes were on the wrong feet again, and her shirt was inside out.

Stella found out that Elodie picked out her own clothes and dressed herself the last time they played together, and suddenly Stella wanted to do everything for herself. I felt both proud and a little melancholy that she was growing so fast.

"Do you want to straighten up your room or do schoolwork first?"

"I want to play ponies." She could be quietly obstinate when she didn't want to do something, which irritated my parents to no end.

"That sounds fun, but we have to do the not-so-fun things first."

Stella slumped. "Okay."

We worked on her colors and numbers for a while, and then she straightened her room by shoving her dirty clothes under her bed.

I walked in a few minutes later to check on her progress. "Nice try, bug. But the hamper is where your dirty clothes go." She sighed loudly, then pulled her clothes back out. I hid my smile at her sass.

She finally got to play ponies, and I went back to the kitchen and opened my computer again. Last week, I reviewed the simple sales contract Claudette's attorney sent me and looked through her business accounts and statements.

It had taken me a while to decipher the statements, but I pushed my anxiety and doubts aside and mentally straightened my spine. Isa told me last year that Claude had given her a monthly subscription for her birthday, and each month she received a Cherry Box. I'd have to ask her about the experience at the Monday Martini party that night.

That week, Laurel's neighbor, Scott, held the Monday Martini party at his house. His place looked like someone with great taste lived there, and he had a beautiful backyard with a sparkling pool and spa.

"You need to come to karaoke night with Martina sometime," he told me. "She's DJing now at the Cockpit, and it's far and away our biggest money-making night." Scott was one of the bar's owners.

Martina smiled and patted his arm. "Thank you for the plug. I'm always looking for new victims."

Slowly, I began to meet all the beautiful people Isa hung out with in Palm Springs. I even found out Harley Emerson, the gorgeous tall blond woman Titus had been talking to at Isa's party, was Damien Andreasen's fiancé. I liked her a lot more after learning that little tidbit.

Titus introduced me to several other people. "Abby, this is Ezekiel Deegan. He goes by Zeke, and he's Damien and Sebastian's business partner." Zeke and Titus were the biggest men in the room. He grinned and shook my hand.

I smiled. "My friends call me Abby."

"And my friends call me Zeke. Or something worse if I piss them off."

"Titus calls me 'little casserole' sometimes. I'm not sure which is worse."

"Really?" He turned to Titus. "I can think of a thousand better nicknames for her."

Titus smirked and pulled me into his side. "She's *ma p'tite cocotte,* you ugly fucker. And quit flirting with her just to fuck with me."

Zeke snorted. "Shit, man. There's your favorite word again."

Isa and Connor walked in not long after, and I grabbed her hand and dragged her out by the pool to get some privacy. "Okay, I need to know what you think about the monthly boxes you got."

Her lips curved up into a dreamy smile. "I need a drink first."

Scott's Martini Monday theme that week was casino night, so he served traditional old-fashioned cocktails with a poker chip stir stick. He'd also set up a poker table, but I was more interested in getting Isa's thoughts and input about the Cherry Boxes, so when the men started a poker game, the women followed us outside.

Isa turned to them. "You can't tell anyone about what we're discussing tonight. Abby hasn't told Titus yet, and she doesn't want it getting out yet."

Harley pointed at Martina. "She's the one with the big mouth around here. And she's Sebastian's cousin."

Martina took a sip of her old-fashioned and shrugged. "I should be offended, but it's true." She leaned closer. "I'll swear myself to secrecy. But in return, you all promise to come to karaoke night. I always make better tips when my hot friends show up."

Laurel patted her thigh. "They come to see you. But we promise."

Isa turned back to me. "Alright, we've sworn them to secrecy. I'll give you my thoughts, but I also want to get their opinions."

I nodded. "Okay. God knows I need the help."

So Isa told them about the Cherry Box and me buying the store. By the time she finished, everyone seemed intrigued and had hopped on their phones to pull up the website.

"I need sex and orgasms tonight," Harley muttered as she scrolled.

Laurel stared at me. "You're going to buy and run an online adult sex toy store?"

My face went hot, and embarrassment and anxiety crawled through me. "Yes. Claudette said I can do it from home so I don't have to take Stella to daycare."

Laurel grinned wide. "Oh, my god. This is so fabulous."

Harley nodded absently as she scrolled through her phone. "I love that you're thinking outside the box. Pun intended. These monthly boxes look intriguing." She glanced up at me. "Do you have a shibari box?"

"I don't even know what that is."

She grinned and waved her hand. "I didn't either, until a few months ago. It's Japanese rope bondage, I'll tell you about it sometime."

Martina flipped furiously through the products. "Wow. I want to be a tester if you ever need one." She held her screen up to Laurel. "Have you ever seen a dildo like this?" She scrolled again. "Or peppermint anal penetrating gel? Or multiple vibrating–"

Laurel interrupted her. "Alright, I get the idea."

Martina started chuckling. "Some of her shop owner reviews on the products are hilarious. Listen to this. *'Warning: Stretch out and hydrate before using this monster dildo vibrator. I am not bluffing, ladies. I slid this thing inside me, put the suction cup in place, and turned it on to a medium setting. For the love of GOD, do NOT start on medium. My legs went airborne like a dead cow with rigor mortis. My back froze up, and I orgasmed so long and hard, I think I blacked out. After finally prying the thing off me, I lay there in a stupid, happy daze for a good five minutes. My back and glutes are still sore two days later."*

I laughed so hard I snorted, and Harley had tears in her eyes. Ramone and Jonathan, Laurel's best friends and neighbors, studied us suspiciously from the other side of the pool.

"What are you all laughing at over there?" Jonathan asked.

Laurel waved at them. "Don't mind us. We're just gossiping."

A tall, muscular man with midnight hair and expensive clothes walked out and stood next to Jonathan.

Laurel pointed at him. "That's Iz. He's the other owner of the Cock Pit."

I glanced over and had to look again. He was at least as big as Titus and sexy as hell.

"Make him say something." I poked Martina, but she just glared at him. Then I noticed him staring back at her.

Laurel waved. "Hi, Iz. Glad you could join us. How'd the bar do last week?"

"Hello, lovely Laurel. The bar is fine, and Martina dominated and tantalized the karaoke crowd again. How was your week?"

"It was fine. My roommate is fine too."

He grinned. "Oh, I'm well aware of that. Tell her I'm dragging her out of here in about ten minutes."

She turned to Martina. "He said he's dragging you out–"

"I heard him," Martina cut in, still glaring at Iz, who just winked at her and walked back inside.

"Holy shit, his voice is something," Isa murmured.

Harley pointed to her phone. "Focus, people. You should have Cherry Box parties and sell subscriptions. Kind of like Tupperware or Pampered Chef parties, only more fun."

I shrugged. "Maybe. My experience with sex toys is almost zero, so I need to get a good grasp on them first, and really dive in and learn the ropes."

Everyone paused.

"Am I the only one who wants to make inappropriate jokes right now?" Isa asked.

"No," Martina and Harley answered together.

Martina leaned forward and smirked. "I'm sure Titus will be ecstatic to have you 'get a good grasp' on his 'product' and have you 'really dive in' when you–"

"Okay," Laurel interrupted. "We get it."

"What?" Martina asked, looking around. "Everyone else was thinking it. I just said it."

My face flamed. "Titus doesn't know, and I'm not exactly sure how to tell him this is the business I'm buying."

Harley patted my shoulder. "You'll figure out the best time, but my advice is to do it soon. Secrets have a way of getting out."

Isa snickered. "Yeah, and I'd like to be a fly on the wall when it does."

Chapter 11

I studied the tall, voluptuous woman with sooty brown hair and purple tips. She was wearing skin-tight clothes and black stiletto boots, and looked a little like Morticia from *The Addams Family*–only without as much black.

We met Trixie and Max at a toy store on Davie Street, a retail area in Vancouver where locals liked to shop. She sauntered in twenty minutes late and didn't apologize. Shopping bags weighed down Max's stroller, and he sat inside looking resigned and bored.

The Thunderbirds had a few days off between playoff games, so at the last minute, Titus brought Stella and me to Vancouver with him. I was happy to meet Max, but the thought of seeing Trixie made my stomach tight and my hands clammy.

Titus introduced us. "Abby, this is Trixie, Max's mother. Trix-ie, this is Abigail."

I shifted nervously and raised my hand. "Hello."

She lifted her sculpted eyebrow and scanned me before turning to Titus. "She's what, seventeen or eighteen? Titus, honey, is she even legal?" Trixie laid her hand on Titus's arm, and I wanted to smack it away.

Instead, I moved to the side and gently pulled Stella forward. She leaned against Titus's leg and glanced up at the woman.

"Trixie, this is my little girl, Stella. And I'm twenty-three."

She looked down at Stella for a moment and pursed her lips. Then she turned around, bending at the waist to give us a front-row view of her ass in her skintight pants with the top of her black lace thong peeking out, then pulled Max out of his stroller.

She turned around and smirked. "This is Max, Titus's son."

Max's blond hair had been gelled into spikes, and he wore designer clothes and little Adidas shoes. He was a solid kid for an eighteen-month-old, and he bowed his back and wiggled to get out of Trixie's arms. When he spotted Titus, he let out a loud, happy grunt and started thrashing even harder. "Dada!"

Stella backed up a little and watched as Trixie finally let the struggling toddler go. He flung himself at Titus, who scooped him up and gave him a big hug.

Stella patted my leg. "Who is he?" she whispered.

"That's Max. He's Titus's little boy, and we're going to hang out with him for a couple of days."

"Oh." Stella's eyes went wide when Titus set Max down in front of her.

"Max, this is Stella and Abby," Titus told him.

He bounced on his toes and giggled as he pointed to Stella. He didn't glance at me.

I leaned down. "Hi, Max. I'm Abby, and this is Stella. She's mine."

Max finally gazed at me, then turned back to Stella. "Mine."

Titus put his hand on Stella's shoulder, but Max reached over and pulled it off.

Then he stared at Stella again. "Mine."

Titus grinned and glanced at me. "Yeah, buddy. I get it."

Trixie rolled her eyes. "Jesus Christ." She dug through the bottom of the stroller under a few shopping bags, pulled out a backpack, and tossed it at Titus. "Do you want the stroller too? And when are you dropping him off?"

Titus stood and slung the bag on his arm. "We're leaving around nine on Saturday morning, so we'll drop him off at seven." He turned to me. "Do you want to keep the stroller?"

"How long do you want to shop?" I asked.

"I don't *want* to shop at all. But let's get some lunch while we're here. Maybe an hour, tops."

I looked at Trixie, trying to keep my gaze from dropping to her ample cleavage. "It looks like you need it to carry your bags. We'll be fine, but thank you."

Trixie eyed me and cocked a hip. "Suit yourself." Turning to Max, she patted his head. "See you in a few days. Can Mommy have a hug?"

He shook his head, still staring at Stella.

Trixie sighed and kissed his head. "Love you, Maxie. Be good." She strolled off without looking back or saying goodbye, her lush hips swaying.

I turned to Titus. "She's... nice."

He smirked. "No, she's over the fucking top and sucks the air out of a room. But she loves Max." He tucked a strand of hair behind my ear. "You good?"

Nodding, I looked down at the kids. "She doesn't like me, does she?"

Titus shrugged. "Probably not. You're everything she isn't. You hungry?" He stared at my mouth.

"I could eat." I gazed back, trying to decipher what he meant.

After lunch, we found a park and let the kids play in the brisk spring sunshine. I took a few photos to send to Nana in our weekly letter and tried to include the Vancouver skyline. By the time we made it back to Titus's apartment, we were all worn out.

Titus kept a black Jeep SUV with tinted windows at his Vancouver condo. It now sported two child car seats.

I looked back at the little ones and grinned. "You might need a minivan. I think you could even pull it off."

Titus glanced back at the two kids and shrugged. "If it'd be easier to maneuver these guys around, I don't care what we drive." He sat up a little straighter. "Speaking of vehicles, how's yours holding up?"

My smile died, and I looked out the window. "Fine. Do you have extra diapers and supplies at your place?"

"Yeah." Titus studied me but didn't bring my car up again.

That weekend, Stella patiently played with Max. He became her shadow and followed her around everywhere. She'd point things out and name them, and he jabbered back at her.

The first night when we tried putting him in his crib, he threw a fit.

"You need to sleep in your crib, and she needs to sleep in her bed," Titus patiently told him.

"No, mine!" He called Stella "mine" like it was her name, and I didn't know what to think.

We tried to reason with him, and Stella watched quietly from the doorway. Finally, Titus sat in the large rocking chair in the corner of Max's room and rocked him to sleep, laying him down in his crib.

But when we woke the next morning, Max lay curled up, sleeping next to Stella with his little arm around her waist. I looked down at him and shook my head, admiring the kid's tenacity.

At breakfast, they sat next to each other with Max in his highchair. "Want one?" Stella asked him, holding up a strawberry slice.

"Uh-huh." Max clapped his hands as Stella put a couple of strawberry slices on the little plastic plate on his tray. He ate them, and Titus stood up to give him more.

"No." He held his palm up to Titus.

Stella grinned at Titus and slid another strawberry piece onto Max's plate. He clapped his hands and shoved it in his mouth.

Titus smirked. "You're enjoying this, aren't you?" She nodded, and I tried not to laugh.

On our last evening in Vancouver, we were heading out with the kids to get dinner when a beautiful woman walked into the condo foyer. She wore a black coat cinched at her curvy waist, and her long, shiny brown hair swept around her. I recognized her from a couple of online photos with Titus, and my insides clenched. Did she live in his building, too?

When she saw Titus, her face lit up and she grabbed his arms. "Titus? Oh my God, I haven't seen you in so long! And is that little Max? He's getting so big. How's your season in Palm Springs going?"

"Hello, Carla. Yeah, this is Max." He turned to us. "And this is Abby and Stella." Carla's eyes swept over me, and her smile slipped as she stepped back.

The silence grew awkward, so I shifted the diaper bag on my arm and held out my hand. "It's nice to meet you."

Her smile grew again as she eyed the diaper bag. "Oh, you're a nanny." She turned back to Titus. "I'd love to get together with you later tonight." She glanced down at the kids. "After everyone goes to bed, why don't you come over to my place for a whiskey and a soak in my hot tub again? It'll feel good on your back." She wiggled her eyebrows at him.

My heart squeezed, and I took a step back, wishing I could become invisible. Turning away, I looked down at Stella so they couldn't see my face. I didn't know if I could hide what I was feeling right then. Stella held the ends of her jacket up to me, and I knelt and zipped her up. Then I zipped Max's coat while Titus and Carla talked.

"She can babysit. She's the nanny," I heard Carla say.

I took Stella's hand and walked toward the front entryway. Max followed us, and I took his hand too. Titus turned to me, and I pointed to the door. "We'll be outside."

His eyes narrowed, and he searched my face. "I'll be right out. Give me a minute."

I nodded and took the kids outside. We walked to the parked Jeep, Max chattering the entire way. Titus caught up with us as we got to the vehicle. He beeped the locks, and I opened the back door so the kids could climb in.

We buckled them up, got inside, and he turned to me. I gazed out the window at the passing cars.

"Abigail."

"Where do you want to eat?" I asked, still staring out the window.

"*Cocotte*, look at me."

I steeled myself, plastered what I hoped was a calm expression on my face, and turned. "Yes?"

He leaned over and took my chin. "I'm not going to Carla's tonight while you watch the kids."

"Okay. But if–"

"No." His eyes drilled into mine. "And if the roles were reversed, just remember, I'm not that magnanimous. Now let's go eat."

Carla and Titus had history, and the thought made me want to throw up. But at least for tonight, I wouldn't be in his condo watching our kids while he was somewhere in the building with Carla. In a few months when Stella and I left, and he came here alone, there was nothing to stop it from happening. The thought burned like acid in my throat.

I nodded and kept my face neutral. "Alright." But for the rest of the day, I was quiet.

When we dropped Max off the next morning, he patted Stella's cheeks and hugged her for a long time before finally letting go. Trixie stood behind them, tapping her foot, but she didn't pull him away.

When we boarded the chartered jet for the flight back, I breathed a little sigh of relief. Max didn't care about me, but he'd thoroughly bonded with Stella. And even though it stung to see both Titus's baby momma and his... whatever Carla was to him, we'd made it through the weekend in one piece.

The Thunderbirds made it through three rounds of playoffs over the next two weeks. Stella and I went to most of the home games, and her love for hockey and Titus grew.

Titus also gave us matching jerseys with his number nineteen and his last name printed across the back. The jerseys probably cost more than any article of clothing we owned.

He grinned wide when we came out to the kitchen to model.

"I love it!" Stella exclaimed.

"She wasn't even this excited at Christmas." I scowled jokingly.

Titus shrugged. "That's because you didn't give her a hockey jersey with my name and number on the back."

"Humble much?" I rolled my eyes, but my lips twitched.

When we wore the jerseys the first time, Jackson came up after the game. "You and your mom look great in your Thunderbird jerseys, Stella Bella." He grinned at me. "But you'd look even better in mine."

"I think Titus hid it," I admitted sheepishly. "I washed it and left it to dry in the laundry room. But the next thing I knew, it was gone."

Jackson smirked. "Figures. He's gotten a little possessive of you two."

I tilted my head and started asking him what he meant, but Titus walked out of the locker room. He saw Jackson talking with us and walked behind me, pulling me back into his chest.

Jackson nodded to him. "That game was better than the last one. Nice save there at the end."

Titus grunted. "My back hurts, and I'm fucking starving,"

"Did you steal the jersey I gave Abby?" Jackson asked, not mincing words.

"No, asshole. I threw it away."

Jackson laughed and pointed at me. "See?" He waved at Stella and took off.

My heart sped up, and I turned around. "You threw it away? Why?" Could Titus maybe like me as a little more than a roommate? My mind spun with the possibility.

"Because I wanted to. Do we have enough pot roast left over from last night? I just want to go home, eat dinner, and watch an episode of *Pawn Stars*."

I rolled my eyes and smirked at him, then let it go. "Yep. I made enough for tonight, and there's some pie and ice cream too."

He sighed and cupped my neck before letting me go. "Fucking perfect."

Chapter 12

Later that week, Titus pulled Isa's dreaded questionnaire out again. I'd just tucked Stella in for the night and walked back to the kitchen. He poured me a glass of wine, grabbed a beer, then tilted his chin to the patio.

"Let's go through a few more of Isa's questions. We're running out of time, and I'm curious as hell about some of your answers to these more explicit ones."

My stomach dipped, and I laid my hand on my cheek. "Oh, God. This is going to be excruciating. I deeply and sincerely regret promising her we'd go through all of them."

He grabbed my hand and grinned, leading me out to the patio. "I don't. And it's okay, it won't kill you."

We sat down on the outdoor loveseat, and I put my wineglass on the coffee table. Then I grabbed one of the throw pillows and held it to my stomach. "That's the problem. It seems like whatever doesn't kill me gives me high anxiety and questionable coping skills."

The thought of sitting out here in the soft evening light, discussing sexual preferences and past experiences with him, sent my pulse skittering. But I trusted Titus with my secrets and my feelings. He knew more about my heartaches and past trauma than even my best friends did, and he still seemed to like me.

His mouth twitched. "I'm at least ten years older, and I've been an unattached professional athlete most my adult life–with a faulty moral compass according to my very religious *grand-mère*. I should be more worried than you."

His description of himself intrigued me. I set the pillow down, took a deep breath, then blew it out. "Okay. Let's do this."

Looking down at his phone, he pulled up the questions. "How old were you when you lost your virginity?"

He wasn't messing around this time. "Nineteen. How about you?"

His eyes flew to mine. "Nineteen?"

"Yes. How old were you?"

His lip quirked up. "Fourteen."

"Wow. That's young. How old was the girl. Or boy?"

"I like pussies, so it was a woman. Probably nineteen or twenty, and she thought I was older. It's a cherished childhood memory. Was it a good memory for you?"

"No. It hurt, and he was... bad at it."

"What a fucking *trou do cul*." He shook his head. "Next question. Do you like having sex in the morning or evening?"

"Either? I guess I don't have a preference. What about you?"

His eyes slid over to me. "It depends. In the evening, if it's a practice or game day. Or the morning, if it's not. So I can take my sweet time and we can have multiple orgasms."

Holy mother. My womb spasmed a little. "Okay," I breathed.

He looked down at the questions. "Have you had sex in a public place, and how many times?" he continued.

"No! Have you?" Did I want to know all this about him? Yes, I did, I realized.

He laughed. "Fuck yes, and more than once. You'll have to try it sometime, and I'm always happy to help out."

Did he just say that? "What?"

"Besides a vibrator, do you use sex toys regularly?"

If my face got any hotter, it was going to start on fire. "Hmm, no. Do you?" But I'd be selling them online soon. I didn't bring that up.

"Depends on the definition of sex toy." He eyed me speculatively. I waited for him to elaborate, but he went on to the next question. "What are your favorite sexual positions?"

"I don't know." I cleared my throat and tried to push my lust and embarrassment down. "Maybe missionary, or... from behind?"

Leaning toward me, he put his arm on the back of the loveseat. "You've had anal sex? And you liked it?" He looked intrigued.

"What? No! I meant regular vaginal sex. Where I'm not facing him, and I don't have to see–" I stopped talking.

"See what?"

"Anything. I don't have to see anything."

My breathing sped up, and I shifted restlessly. Kyle had been a disappointing, selfish lover. And he'd chased his own orgasm like a sprinter in a hundred-meter dash. I should have seen it coming when he abandoned me a few days after finding out I was pregnant.

"What's *your* favorite position?" I asked.

Titus studied me, his eyes growing heavy. "Mm. It's difficult to pick just one. My favorite position might be from behind too. But standing in front of a full-length mirror so we can both watch my cock slide in and out. And I can pinch and roll her nipples while she watches."

"That's... very specific," I whispered hoarsely, seeing us in front of that full-length mirror. The picture he painted mesmerized me.

"I could be even more specific if you think you can handle it." His eyebrow rose.

My throat went dry, and I swallowed before answering. "I can handle it." I didn't know if I could or not, but I wanted to know.

He nodded. "Alright. Then I'd slide a hand down her soft stomach to rub and pluck at her swollen, sensitive clit. And maybe use my other hand to squeeze her throat just enough, until she begged me to keep fucking her. I'd work her clit, maybe finger her ass, and fuck her hard until she came all over my cock."

He leaned over and picked up his drink, taking a pull as he watched my face. "What's your most erogenous body part?"

I gulped, then shook my head as if trying to clear away the web of lust he'd woven around me. It took a moment to find my voice.

"Maybe... my breasts?" After his comment about pinching and rolling nipples, my own were rock hard.

His lip quirked. "You say that like it's a question. We might need to do a little research."

We needed to do research? I didn't touch his comment. "What's *your* most erogenous body part?" My breasts felt heavy and tender.

He leaned back and fingered a strand of my hair. "The tip of my cock, just under the head, or the glans. I like a soft, wet tongue there," he answered in a low, gravelly voice.

"Good to know." My vagina pulsed, and I knew my panties were soaked.

"How many sexual partners have you had?" he murmured.

"One. You?"

He raised his eyebrow. "A few more than one. But with the right person, one would be more than enough."

I stared at him and wondered what it would be like to be Titus's "one" sexual partner. "Okay," I croaked.

"Have you ever orgasmed with a cock inside you?"

I swallowed. "That's not one of the questions."

He shrugged. "The instructions say we can improvise and add our own questions. Have you?"

"No, and I think a woman being able to orgasm with a penis inside her is a myth. Like the Holy Grail."

He chuckled. "Or Excalibur?"

"Of course a man would come up with a sword metaphor." I straightened my shoulders and tried to gather my composure. "I think it's impossible without some serious help."

"It's entirely possible to come with a cock buried deep inside you. At least with a man who isn't a fucking *imbécile*."

My breathing sped up. "He'd have to know what he was doing."

"True. And maybe not be a selfish asshole. Would you like to try?" he asked softly.

"Try what?"

"Coming on my cock."

Lust shot through me, and my mind seemed to shut down. I forced myself to focus. "I... like you."

"I like you too. Do I hear a 'but' coming?"

"No buts. Let me finish."

He grinned. "Please do." He kept fingering the strands of my hair, and the soft tug on my scalp felt more erotic than any touch I'd ever received.

I stood up and shook my arms out, trying to dispel some of the lust and need coursing through me so I could string two words together. He watched me with a little smile. The smug bastard knew exactly what he'd done to me.

"Feel better?" he asked.

Sitting back down, I turned to him. "Not really. You know more about me than anyone, except maybe Isabella. I'm scared that if we do... this,"–I motioned between us–"and it doesn't work, it'll ruin everything."

His smirk died. "You and Stella are safe with me."

"I know. I trust you."

He sat quietly for a moment. "You can trust me with your heart too."

"I think you know what my parents are like. I'm scarred from that, and maybe damaged inside." His jaw clenched, but he didn't interrupt or contradict me. "I like you... so much. And Stella already loves you. If you make me come while you're inside me, it won't be a casual thing. For me, anyway. And I have so much to lose." God, my hands were sweating again. I rubbed my palms on my thighs.

"Come sit on my lap. I want you closer."

I slowly uncurled my feet and crawled over to sit on his lap. He pulled me into him, his hard length rubbing against the back of my thighs. But he didn't seem worried about it.

"Is that what I think it is?" I asked faintly, giddiness and vague alarm sweeping through me at his size.

"Yeah. Don't worry, I can control myself–for now. I fucking hate that you think you're damaged. You've been hurt, and you have scars. I do too, but they're mostly on the outside of my body."

Carefully, I relaxed into him and breathed in his scent. "I have a few scars on the outside too."

He held me close. "I'd like to see them sometime."

"I'll show you mine if you show me yours," I joked. His length rubbing against me made my insides flutter. Titus wanted me too, and it was a heady feeling.

"Are you willing to try this with me? Try being mine, and not just because of Max?" he murmured in my ear.

I held my breath until I became lightheaded, then let it out slowly. "Only if you can make me come with your cock inside me."

He cupped my cheek and grinned. "We'll take it slow. But I guarantee you, when you're ready I'll make you come so many times with my cock inside you, you'll be eating your words. And my cock along with them."

My breath came fast, and I shivered. "I'd like to try that."

"You're flushed and panting, and if I ran my finger across your pussy right now, I bet I'd find you wet and ready for me. Let's keep going. Do you like oral sex?"

The thought of him running his finger along my wet pussy made my vision dim a little. "Give me a minute." I buried my face in his neck and sucked in a breath. Which didn't help when his scent hit me again. "I've never had oral sex before. I tried to give it once, but he might have gone too fast and I gagged."

"He's a fucking idiot," Titus growled. "We'll have to do it right then, won't we? And when I go down on you, I'll taste and lick your sweet little clit until your pussy is red and weeping, then I'll shove my tongue into your cunt and suck your juices. You'll learn to love both giving and getting it."

"You have to stop now," I panted.

"We're going to take this slow, but when we get there, you'll come for me as many times as I can make you."

"You have a dirty mouth, Tremblay."

He leisurely eyed my flushed cheeks and heaving chest, and a slow, wicked grin spread across his face. "Lucky for you, I have a dirtier mind."

Chapter 13

That night, images of Titus's mouth working me between my thighs kept flashing through my mind. It took a long time to fall asleep, and when I woke up the next day, my eyes were dry and my head felt heavy.

After brushing my teeth and splashing water on my face, I walked out into the kitchen the next morning as Titus was getting ready to leave.

His lip twitched when he saw me. "You have circles under your eyes. Didn't you sleep well?"

"It's so nice of you to point that out. No, I kept having nightmares about gagging on large swords."

He chuckled and stood in front of me. "I'm going to hug you goodbye."

My toes curled, and heat flooded me. "Okay."

Wrapping his arms around my shoulders, he pulled me into his warm, hard body. I could feel his heartbeat beneath my cheek, and his heat and masculine pine scent curled around me. Titus rested his chin on the top of my head, and I heard him breathe in a few times.

"Are you... sniffing me?" I asked.

"*Oui*. You smell like sunshine and bedsheets. I'm going to kiss you now."

My head fell back, and I gazed up at him. "Yes," I whispered.

He grinned, then leaned down and brushed his lips across mine. Moving slowly at first, he leisurely nibbled my mouth, then licked across my lips. I gasped, and Titus slipped his tongue inside. Standing up on my tiptoes, I pressed against his mouth. He palmed my head and angled his lips to deepen the kiss. My heart slammed in my chest, and lust rushed through me. I met his tongue, wrapped my hand around the back of his neck, and kissed him back.

Whimpering in his mouth, I rubbed my breasts against his chest. He slid his thigh against my center, and I ground myself against him. He pulled back and I panted for air as my head spun. Titus kissed like he played hockey–expertly and aggressively.

He leaned his forehead against mine, squeezed me, then let out a breath and stepped away. I swayed toward him, instantly missing his heat and wanting his mouth back.

"I need to go. Tell Stella we'll play street hockey when I get home this afternoon."

My hand drifted up to my swollen lips when he walked out. I tried to stay busy and keep my mind off Titus's mind-blowing kiss and filthy mouth that day, but I was distracted and wet all day while Stella and I drew pictures for Nana and went to the library to pick up more books.

Titus and I kissed and made out on the couch after Stella went to bed over the next few evenings. But he kept his promise to go slow, and I went to bed alone every night with a deep ache between my legs.

On Wednesday, we went to the team party at Connor's house. The Thunderbirds had a tough playoff game on Sunday, and Isa wanted to have one last Whiskey Wednesday in case they lost and the team was done for the season.

"Are you sure it's alright if Stella hangs out with you and Elodie?" I asked Javier when I dropped Stella off at his little caretaker's cottage.

Javier smiled. "Of course. They get along, and we have big plans."

Stella looked up at Javier. "Where's the kitty?"

"The last time I saw her, she was on the couch. We haven't fed her dinner yet. Do you want to help?"

Stella rocked on her toes and smiled. "Uh-huh."

Elodie took her hand. "Come on. I know how to feed her by myself. I'll show you." Stella went inside with Elodie and didn't look back.

I watched her go, feeling abandoned for some reason, and Javier squeezed my shoulder. "It's okay to feel a little conflicted when kids start becoming more independent. Go have a nice evening. We'll be right here."

Titus held my hand as we walked over to Connor's house. He introduced me to a couple of players I hadn't met, his hand on the small of my back. When we walked into Connor's kitchen, Wyatt stood drinking a beer and talking to another player.

"Don't fucking touch her or talk to her, got it?" Titus growled.

Wyatt straightened and put his hand up. "Hey, I didn't know she was going to freak the fuck out, and no one told me she was living with you. That's a big commitment for you, isn't it Tremblay? Did you finally decide to take a puck bunny home?"

Titus growled and started forward, but Jackson stepped up to Wyatt and smacked him on the side of the head. "Shut the fuck up, dumbass. Abby is the furthest thing from a puck bunny, and you know it. Why are you always trying to antagonize everyone?"

Wyatt turned on Jackson. "Quit fucking hitting me, asshole."

Jackson pushed his shoulder. "Then quit being a little prick."

Everyone in the kitchen stood still while Titus stared at Wyatt for another few seconds, his eyes narrowed. He finally glanced down at me. "You okay?"

"I'm good." Turning to Wyatt, I looked him up and down. "Seriously?"

"What?" he snapped.

"You were the sperm who won?"

A few of the players laughed, and Wyatt's face went red.

Isabella wiggled her eyebrows and grinned wide when Wyatt stomped out. A few minutes later, she dragged me out to the pool patio. "Did you two finally decide to pull your heads out of your asses?"

I flicked her arm. "That's kind of hard to do since my head was never up there."

She rolled her eyes. "Spill, Carver."

"I like him, okay? I couldn't help myself, and I tried not to. He's patient and sweet, and Stella adores him. We're taking it slow."

Isa smirked. "He's sweet to you and Stella. He isn't sweet to anyone else."

Grinning, I patted her shoulder. "I'm okay with that. Titus said you guys usually play games at these parties. What kind of games?"

She smiled knowingly. "Whatever games you want."

"Have you played poker?" I asked.

"Not yet, but we can play tonight."

After we ate barbeque, Titus, Connor, and a few others started a game of pool. So Isabella rounded up a few people and pulled out Connor's custom-made poker set. She set a fifty-dollar fixed limit, and we decided on Texas Hold 'em.

Wyatt sat down at the table, but Jackson frowned and turned to me. "You okay if he plays?"

I stared at Wyatt. "Yeah, if he can behave himself."

Wyatt held up his hands and smirked. "I can behave, it's just more fun not to."

I leaned back and looked at him. "Some people suck the fun right out of a room. Try not to, okay? I've got a three-year-old and I don't get out much."

He stared at me, then nodded as Isa dealt the cards.

Mikael, the Swedish goalie, looked down at his hand. "Why is this game named after one of your states?"

"Because it started there," Rudy replied. "I wrote a report about poker in high school. Poker likely started in New Orleans, but Texas Hold 'em originated in a little town called Robstown, Texas. And in the 1960s, a few Las Vegas casinos picked it up."

Mikael picked up his hand and studied it. "Your country has a strange fascination with poker."

If he only knew. My parents' aversion to playing cards spurred me to learn every card game I could find. I quickly scanned my hand, and in less than two seconds, had a strategy. Then I watched everyone's faces carefully.

Rudy nodded. "The longest poker game was held in the basement of a theater in Tombstone, Arizona called the Bird Cage. Guess how long it lasted?"

Mikael shrugged. "A week?"

Rudy shook his head. "Eight years. It was finally shut down in the late 1880s."

Mikael glanced up at Rudy. "See? A strange fascination."

Jackson studied his cards with a slight frown. "I heard Wyatt Earp and Doc Holliday played there."

I could tell them a little more about that card game, but I kept my mouth shut.

"Alright. Mikael, you're the small blind. Care to make a bet?" Isa asked.

We played for almost two hours. Rudy went out first, then Isa and Wyatt, and finally Mikael. Jackson and I were the only ones left.

"You've played this game before," Mikael accused me.

"Yes, I have."

He turned to Isa. "Just once I would like to win a game at these parties, *vänen*."

Isabella smirked. "We can't all be winners."

Mikael scowled. "We can all be winners once in a while. You and your friend are 'win hoggers.' Is that a saying?"

"No," Wyatt and Isa answered together.

"It should be," Mikael muttered under his breath.

I ignored them and studied Jackson carefully. He was a good player, but he had a couple of tells. He frowned when he had a

few cards with some potential, and he didn't show any emotion when he planned to bluff.

Flicking a glance at him, I thought he planned to bluff. My
poker face ranged from a look of vague confusion to dumb,
frustrated concentration. Claudette told me I looked like an
airhead. Which was exactly the point.

I had a pair of tens and was hoping for another pair. Jackson
studied me. "Check," he murmured. Isa burned a card and
turned up the last one. It was a ten. Jackson threw his hand
down and smirked. "I've got a pair of jacks."

I twitched when I realized he hadn't been bluffing. but I
carefully laid my cards down. "Three of a kind."

Rudy and Mikael laughed, and even Wyatt chuckled a little.

Jackson's smirk turned to a frown, then a grin. "Well, damn.
Nice hand, Goldilocks."

"Why do these guys think it's okay to give them cute little
nicknames?" Connor asked Titus rhetorically. I didn't know
they'd been standing behind me, watching.

Titus grinned. "I have no fucking clue." Connor and Jackson both snorted.

I grinned happily up at him. "I won."

"I saw. Are you ready to get Stella and head home, *p'tite
cocotte*?" I nodded and collected my winnings. Titus turned to
Isa. "Thanks for having us, *choux*."

Isa grinned. "It was a fun night. Except she cleaned us out,
which usually happens when we play poker. She used to beat
Liam and his friends all the time."

Titus raised an eyebrow. "Who the fuck is Liam?"

"My older brother. But he's not the one you should worry about," Isabella replied. Titus tilted his head, but she just raised her eyebrow.

We said goodbye and walked outside, the cool desert evening bathing us in soft shadows. Titus took my hand, and we walked slowly, enjoying the quiet.

He also had a French nickname for Isabella. I didn't know how I felt about that. "What does *choux* mean?" I asked.

"Cabbage."

"You call her cabbage. I suppose you're going to try to tell me not to worry, it's a good thing."

"Yes." He took my hand. "How'd you learn to play poker when your parents banned playing cards?"

"I learned to play every card game I could find as a big 'fuck you' to my parents. Claudette and her family taught me how. They didn't know why I wanted to learn at such a young age, but Claudette's mother agreed and told us every woman should know how to play poker and pool."

We continued walking. "And do you know how to play pool?"

"I'm passable." I shrugged modestly.

"And you played poker with Liam?"

"Yeah. Liam and his friends thought it would be funny to clean us out." I smiled at the memory.

"Let me guess. It didn't work out quite that way."

"Nope. Liam thought it was hilarious. His friends, not so much."

We picked up Stella, and she hugged Elodie and Javier goodbye. Then she tried to hug the cat, who swatted at her and ran away.

"Did you have a nice time?" I asked.

"Yeah. I want a kitty."

Oh boy. There was no way I could get an animal when we were two steps away from being homeless ourselves.

I sighed. "We can visit Javier's kitty, alright?"

She gazed at me but said nothing else. When we got home, Titus answered a few texts and phone calls, and I read to Stella and got her tucked in.

"I love you, little bug." I kissed her goodnight and turned off her light.

When I walked into the kitchen, Titus leaned against the counter, looking down at his phone. He glanced up at me, his jaw tight.

"What's wrong?" I asked carefully. A hundred scenarios, each worse than the last, went through my mind.

"The hockey media put out a few stories about us."

"Okay. Is that bad?"

"Not for me since it'll help my case in Canada—if we can get it before the fucking judge." He studied me. "But somehow they found out we're living together. I don't want your father coming after you and Stella."

My stomach dropped and my hands clenched. "He doesn't follow hockey news, so I doubt he'll see it. For some reason, he thinks I'm going to hell in every religion, and it's his job to beat it out of me."

Titus leaned in and ran his hands down my arms. "But if he googles your name, it might come up. I'm going to have Zeke and Damien put in a home security system. And your phone is shit. You need a working phone, especially when I'm out of town."

I thought about the money I'd won at poker. And he was right, if my father came after me, my phone needed to work. "I won two hundred dollars tonight, and I got two new website jobs this week. I think I can find a decent refurbished phone online."

Titus shook his head. "No. You're getting a *new* phone. You'll also need it when Max gets here."

I pulled back. "This isn't *The Price is Right*. I can't just 'get a new phone' or 'a new car.' It doesn't work like that."

He leaned in. "Bullshit. From now on, when you need something that will help keep you safe or improve your life, it *does* work like that."

"Remember when I asked for your opinion? No? Me neither."

He growled and folded his arms. "You and I need to come to an understanding. And all your sarcastic little comments? They just make my dick hard."

A shot of lust speared through me, and I bit my tongue to keep my next snarky remark to myself.

Sucking in a breath, I folded my arms. "What understanding?"

Titus watched me. "You and Stella are mine, and I want to keep you longer than a few fucking months, or just while I work on getting custody of Max. I'm also getting you a new phone."

My heart flipped over in my chest. "What?" I whispered hoarsely.

"This can't be a surprise to you. We fit. We're good together, and you're a fantastic person and mother and funny as hell." Titus put his hands on his hips. "We get along—when I don't want to throw you over my shoulder and spank your sweet ass. You're also hot as fuck, and we've been mentally stripping each other almost since you got here."

My temper started to simmer. "I don't mentally strip you." I looked at his abdomen, then my gaze slid lower. "Okay, maybe a little."

He grinned. "Maybe a lot, but I don't mind. And I appreciate your honesty."

"Yeah? Here's a little more honesty for you. There are trillions of nerves in the human body, and you're getting on every single one of mine."

Smirking, he stepped in front of me. "Good. I'd also like to work on your erogenous zones."

"Really? Because I'd like to–"

Titus leaned in and kissed me, but didn't start sweet and slow this time. He cupped the back of my head as he plundered my mouth, and I let out a little moan as I grabbed his shoulders and pulled him closer.

He pressed his thumb to my chin, opening my mouth wider. Then he slid his tongue inside. My emotions whipped from irritation to white-hot lust in seconds, and my mind was having trouble adjusting. But my body wasn't.

Running his mouth down the side of my neck, he carefully bit my collarbone. "*You* taste like sunshine."

"Your lips feel so good," I murmured, wrapping my arms around him.

"I want to strip you bare and spread you out, then suck and lick you until you come."

The image played through my mind, and a shiver rippled through me.

"Breathe, or you're going to pass out." He grabbed my hips and lifted me onto the counter. Then he opened my legs and stepped between them, pulling me into him.

I shamelessly rubbed against his hard chest, then wrapped my legs around his waist and softly rocked myself against his length.

"Do you want me, Abigail?" he asked, burying his face in my hair.

"Yes," I whispered against his neck.

"Good. I want you too." But he unwrapped my legs from around his waist and stepped back. Then he put his hands on my thighs. "When you're lying in bed tonight, I want you to think about me buried deep inside you." Then he leaned in and kissed my forehead. "*Bonne nuit.*"

He knew damn well I wouldn't be sleeping well that night.

Chapter 14

My blood pressure slowly rose, and I walked around in a needy daze over the next few days. Titus would sometimes run his fingers along the nape of my neck as I stood at the kitchen counter or sat at the bar. Then he'd brush by me sometimes and trail his palm along my lower back. Small, barely-there touches that were driving me slowly out of my mind. I vibrated like a tuning fork whenever he got near me.

When he came home from the arena in the evenings, we fell into the habit of making dinner together and sharing our days. Titus grilled steaks that evening, and we planned to eat out on the back patio. Stella and I brought out plates and a salad, and I handed Titus a beer. The smell of sizzling meat filled the air.

I gazed around. "It's so lovely and peaceful out here. We need to do this more often." Soft lighting illuminated the palm trees, and a few crickets chirped in the bushes.

"We do." He took a pull from his beer. "I'll heat the pool this weekend. It's about time we opened it for the season. Do you have a swimsuit?"

"Of course. Both Stella and I have swimsuits." I'd found them at a yard sale for three bucks a piece, but we had suits.

He turned the steaks and smiled at me. "We'll have to start using the spa too. It'll be a fucking relief not to use it as an ice bath."

I shivered. "I don't know how you stand it. I stuck my arm in to test it, and I was cold for the rest of the day."

"The first two minutes are miserable, but after that, it gets better."

The steaks were delicious, and I hummed softly as I ate my first bite. "This is so good." He watched me moan and savor my food, his cheek twitching.

After we cleaned up and watched a little TV with Stella, we walked to her room together to tuck her in.

"What do you want to read tonight?" I asked her.

"The monkey book." She did her usual nighttime ritual of fluffing up her pillow a little, then crawling into bed with her yellow blanket and her little moose.

Grinning, I pulled out *The Grumpy Monkey* and handed it to Titus. "I think you should read tonight."

He looked down at the front cover. "Are you trying to tell me I'm grumpy?"

Laughing, I patted his arm. "No. I'm just teasing you." I held his gaze. "You're one of the most even-tempered men I know. You just hide it well sometimes, like when you're playing hockey or talking with your teammates."

He grinned and curled his hand around the back of my neck. "That's most of the time."

"I ready," Stella said, a little loudly.

Titus didn't break eye contact. "Okay, Stel. I'm coming." He leaned in and grazed my forehead with his lips before he sat on the bed and read Stella her book.

She started dozing off, and we kissed her goodnight and walked out.

"Do you want to watch TV or sit out on the back patio before you go to bed?" I asked, stopping at the kitchen bar.

Titus came up behind me and slowly wrapped an arm around my chest. Then he pulled me into him, leaned down, and kissed my neck, then bit it.

I whimpered and went limp. All the sexual tension building over the past few days seemed to flood my system at once, and I instinctively rubbed against him.

He growled low in my ear, and ran his nose along my earlobe. Chills erupted down my spine, and my body sagged against him. He'd been teasing and priming me, and my body craved his touch.

Carefully, he slid his hands up my stomach, and I could feel his callouses. His thumbs brushed against the undersides of my heaving, swollen breasts, and I held perfectly still, breathing loudly, afraid he'd pull away again and say goodnight.

After stroking my breasts until my nipples were hard and aching for his touch, he ran a hand up to my throat and just laid it there. When I instinctively arched back and rubbed against him, Titus nudged my legs apart and lodged his thigh against my center, holding it still.

I needed more. His warm hand on my neck made me want to feel his bare skin against me everywhere.

"Please don't make me go to bed aching and wet again," I begged softly.

He chuckled low and started rubbing his thigh against me. "Tell me what you want."

Was he really going to make me talk right now? "More."

"Tell me exactly what you want."

My mind blanked as his thigh rubbed across my clit, but I needed more friction. I moaned softly, and he stilled.

"No, don't stop!"

"Then tell me."

Struggling to think, I reached back and grabbed his neck.

"I need you to... touch me. On my breasts. I want your skin on mine."

"That wasn't so hard, was it?" He murmured in my ear. When he rubbed against me, I felt his long, thick length.

He didn't move fast enough, I reached down and grabbed his thigh. "Do I need to get Stella's crayons out and draw you a picture?"

Titus chuckled. "And you want me to spank you too. Good to know."

"I never said that."

"Your sass did. Don't worry, I'll make sure it's a good thing."

He turned me around, then lifted me up on the counter as if I were a small child. Sliding my thighs apart, he pulled me to him. Then he finally slid his big hands under my t-shirt, up my ribcage to my breasts. I pushed against his warm, calloused palms.

I gasped. "Holy mother."

"Are you praying?" he chuckled. Pulling me more firmly into him, he palmed my butt. "Wrap your legs around me."

When I circled his waist, I felt how much there was of him.

Breathing his scent in, I laid my forehead against his chest.

"Do you want me, Abigail?" he asked, just like he had the other night.

"Yes." I sighed softly, worried he was going to send me to bed again.

"And do you want my cock?"

I froze, and need and want slammed through me. But I'd felt the size of his shaft.

Banging my head softly against his chest, I tightened my arms around his neck. "Yes. I want your cock like I want my next breath, but I'm worried you'll get stuck inside me with that thing. You're massive."

He barked out a laugh. "I'd love to get my cock stuck inside you. All night. But I promised you we'd go slow."

"We don't have to go slow."

"Yes, we do. And when we get there, you're going to fucking beg me to shove my 'massive' cock into your wet, tight little cunt."

"Oh, God," I whimpered.

"But we'll do other things tonight, and I'll show you how my mouth and tongue feel on your sweet, wet pussy. It makes my dick hard to think I'll be the first to eat you out. Now hang on."

I tightened my thighs around his waist and held on. He walked us into his bedroom with me clinging to him. Soft light filtered in from the backyard through the French doors. Titus laid me across his massive bed and knelt over me.

"I've had countless filthy fantasies about you stretched out on my bed, taking my tongue and cock like a *bonne fille.*" Like a good girl. My pussy clenched tight in need.

"You have?" I asked breathlessly.

He brushed a strand of hair off my cheek, the light touch tingling. "Fuck, yes. You look so sweet and innocent, but your sharp little tongue makes me want to fuck you long and hard."

Leaning in, he captured my mouth in a deep, wet kiss. Then he ran his nose down my throat and kissed the hollow in my neck. Sliding my hands under his shirt, I ran my palms up his back. His scars, muscles, and taut, warm skin felt so wonderful under my fingertips.

He knelt up to pull my shirt over my head, and I grabbed his shirt and tugged it off too. He undid my shorts and pulled them down my legs along with my panties, then he got rid of my bra. Lust and anticipation coursed through me, burning away any embarrassment.

I'd imagined so many times what he would look and feel like above me, nestled between my thighs. He was so much better in the flesh. My body had never felt this kind of craving or hunger, and my pussy clenched in want. I ached for his touch.

His hands skimmed up my torso, and he ran his thumbs across the swell of my breasts. Then Titus bent and slowly licked and sucked on one of my nipples. Lust and need burned every thought from my mind as he leaned over me, his muscular thighs caging me in.

"That feels so good." After fumbling with his button, I slid his zipper down and pushed my hand inside. His soft, warm skin over his long, thick shaft felt so big in my damp hand. When his hips pumped against my hand, my heart jumped and need burst through me.

Titus switched to my other breast, and my hips shifted restlessly. He sat up and pushed strands of hair off my face. Feeling precum at his tip, I slid my finger across it, then brought it to my mouth to suck off.

His eyelids lowered and his breathing sped up. Titus trailed his finger through my slit, then he brought it to his mouth and sucked. My vision narrowed, and I moaned softly.

He bent down and kissed my stomach, and I froze as his thumb rubbed along my clit.

"Your pussy is soaked. I'm going to taste and suck on you until you're mindless and begging, and then make you come all over my face."

My legs squeezed together involuntarily, but Titus patiently pried them wide open. "I'm going to get you addicted to having my tongue on your clit."

When he leaned in and gave me a long, firm lick, stars exploded behind my eyelids. Then he sucked on me in earnest, and my neck arched back. He repeated the process several times, and my head started thrashing.

"Holy fucking... son of a...." My vision blurred and sharp spears of lust shot through me. "That's so... Oh, God!"

I felt him chuckle as he slowly and thoroughly worked me over with his firm, beautiful mouth. Babbling nonsense, I prayed out loud he wouldn't stop. Titus bit the inside of my thigh, then slowly slipped a finger inside me. He used just the right amount of pressure and movement.

My hips arched up to meet his tongue, and my head thrashed. I broke out in a sweat as a cataclysmic orgasm steadily built inside me. The man knew his way around a woman's clit, and he stroked, licked, and flicked me into a hot ball of need. When he slid a second finger inside and fluttered his tongue against me, I locked up and orgasmed on a long, high moan.

By the time I came down, my center pulsed with each heartbeat, and endorphins swam through my system.

I felt wetness on my cheeks and realized a few tears had slipped out.

Titus crawled up my body and cupped my face. "Are you alright?"

Nodding slowly, I looked up at him in wonder. "That was... I didn't know it could feel like that." I grabbed his thigh and squeezed. He still had his jeans on. "Can I try that on you?"

He laid on his side and propped his head in his hand. "Is that a trick question?"

I blushed. "The only time I tried to give oral sex, it didn't go well. But after what you just did with your mouth and tongue? I have a feeling it was him and not me. You're a wizard."

"I think you just quoted *Harry Potter* to me." He smirked and ran his hand along my cheek, then slid down and cupped my breast. "Your tits are beautiful." He ran a finger in between them. "I plan to fuck them one day soon."

"How does that work, exactly?" I murmured as I pressed into his hand.

He swiped a thumb across my nipple. "First, I'll suck, bite, and lick them until they're swollen and throbbing, and soaked. Then I'll lap in between until you're nice and wet, and finally drizzle a little massage oil right here." He ran a finger between my breasts, then grasped one and pushed it against the other. "I'll put my cock there, push them nice and tight, and fuck your tits until I shoot my come all over your neck and chin. It's called a pearl necklace."

Titus slid his hand up and grasped my neck, then squeezed me just tight enough to send my blood pumping.

My eyes widened and my pussy spasmed as I stared blindly at him. "I'd like that," I whispered. "But tonight, will you teach me how to…"

"Suck my cock?" he finished softly.

"Yes," I whispered.

He grinned and cupped my cheek. "If you insist."

Chapter 15

Titus leaned over and kissed and nibbled on my neck, then slowly pulled back and knelt above me. I'd fantasized so many times about what his body would look and feel like without clothes. His shoulders were thick, veined, and muscular, and the intricate tattoo on his chest drew my eyes, with the crossed hockey sticks, the number nineteen, and a red and black maple leaf.

I reached up and ran my fingertips over it, watching his nipples harden as I trailed my fingers across his skin. His chest and abs were hard and defined, and I traced down the ridges to the V above his waistband. When I got there, Titus rolled off the bed and slowly stripped out of his jeans. He stood naked, and my mouth watered while my heart pounded.

"You're huge," I blurted out.

He grinned and grasped my hand. "We'll make it fit." He leaned in and his grin faded.

"Unless you've changed your mind?"

"No way. Have you?" If anything, his thick length, tattooed body, and challenging smile made me even more wet and needy.

"*Non.* Would you like to feel my cock, Abigail?"

"Yes," I whispered, getting to my knees. He guided my hand to his shaft, and I felt his soft skin and the hardness underneath. He let go and let me explore, and I wrapped my hand around him as far as it would reach while he gritted his teeth and groaned.

Then I used both hands to explore, staring at his shaft. I stroked him, mesmerized by his size and the precum seeping out of his tip. I leaned over and absently licked it off, and Titus drew in a harsh breath.

Sucking his tip into my mouth, I swirled my tongue around his length. After learning his feel and taste, I drew him further inside and hummed in pleasure around him. His texture was like nothing I'd ever felt.

He growled softly, and I looked up to see him clasp his hands behind his neck, his biceps bunching.

I wondered if I was doing something he didn't like. Pulling back, I gazed up. "Am I doing it wrong again?"

"Fuck, no," he groaned. "Nothing about having your hot, wet mouth around my cock will ever be wrong. Keep exploring. I'm trying not to grab your head and shove myself down your throat."

Reassured, I grinned and sucked him back in my mouth. He was big, so I wrapped both hands around his base. His hips jerked, and I realized he wanted more friction. I squeezed and pumped him with my hands while I sucked and licked his tip and length.

"*Mon Dieu,* your mouth feels like I'm fucking wet satin."

His words made my body heat again, and I tightened my hold on him. Feeling brave, I brought him to the back of my throat, then pushed my head down on him.

"Fuuck, that's it. Loosen your throat. Don't force it. Just open up and relax."

His quiet, gruff instructions sent lust rolling through my insides. I'd just had a mind-blowing orgasm, but he oozed testosterone and my body responded. A strand of saliva and precum caught on my lip when I pulled off for a moment, and my eyes watered. But I latched back on. Power and lust coursed through me as I gave him this.

Titus brought his hands down and held my face, stroking my cheeks with his thumbs. His hips started thrusting a little harder and his fingers tightened. "I'm going to come, and it'll be more than you can swallow. You need to pull off."

Shaking my head, I tightened my lips around his shaft. His precum tasted salty and sharp, and I felt him harden even more inside my mouth.

My lips were stretched and sore, and my jaw muscles ached. But I loved the feel of him inside my mouth, and the heady thought of making him lose control.

"Fuck, I'm coming," he warned.

My hands were still wrapped around his base, and it was a good thing. He held my shoulders and threw his head back. I pushed my head closer and took his cock down my throat as far as I could go, then tried to swallow all his come. But he was right, it was too much. I pulled off and pumped his length, then watched while he finished orgasming. Some of his come landed on my breasts and stomach.

He groaned and threw his head back as he finally came down. Then he reached over to rub his semen into my breasts.

My vagina spasmed. "You're making a mess."

"I'm marking you."

That idea made me shudder. "I love oral sex. Can we do it again tomorrow night?"

"Fuck, yes." He brushed my hair out of my eyes. "You're a beautiful, hot mess. Let me get a towel."

I followed him into the bathroom, and when I saw the mascara streaks on my cheeks and under my eyes, I started and looked up at him. "I look like a crackhead. I need to go take my makeup off and go to bed."

He took my chin in his hand and kissed my mouth. When he pulled back, he studied my face and grinned. "You look like you've been thoroughly mouth-fucked, and you enjoyed it."

"That was the best not-quite-sex I've ever had." I didn't tell him it was the first time I'd ever orgasmed in front of another person before.

He shook his head and sighed softly. "You're a fucking unicorn too."

"What do you mean?"

He didn't answer. "After you get cleaned up and ready for bed, come back so we can talk."

My stomach dropped, and I started to panic a little inside. I hated those words. Whenever someone told me they wanted to talk, it never boded well.

By the time I got ready for bed and checked on Stella, my mind had conjured up all kinds of worst-case scenarios. Did he want us to leave? Had I ruined our friendship by getting intimate with him? Questions swirled around in my head.

I cleaned up, took a fast shower, and changed into one of the secondhand kimonos I usually slept in. At the thrift shops in Seattle, they were easy to find for a few dollars. This one was sage green with cherry blossoms. It was also my favorite, and I picked it to give me courage.

When I walked back into his bedroom, Titus sat on the edge of his bed facing away from the door, massaging his back. I noticed a wicked-looking scar running along his lower spine.

Crawling onto the bed behind him, I ran my fingers down his back. "What happened?" I asked as I pushed his hands away and massaged along the area where he'd been working.

"I got checked by three players. I beat the shit out of one of them a while back, and he recruited a couple of his team-mates. One of them weighs almost three hundred pounds, and they messed up my back and knocked me out. The fuckers." He groaned when I worked his tight muscles. "Where'd you learn to do that?"

"Claudette's older brother went to massage school one summer for fun. Then he practiced on us and talked me through what he learned. Lay down so I can work out your kinks."

He mumbled something about my friends' fucking brothers, then stretched out on his bed.

I wanted to bend over and bite and nibble on his perfect ass. His back was just as gorgeous as his front. "Do you have any lotion or oil in your bathroom?" I asked, clearing my throat.

"Yeah, I have some virgin coconut oil in the cupboard." Grabbing the oil, I arranged his arms and legs where I wanted them. I warmed the oil in my palm, then slowly worked out the kinks and knots in his back. The feel of his warm skin and hard muscles and the sweet, tropical smell of coconut oil made my insides tighten again.

He let out a groan as I worked him. "That feels so fucking good. Tell me about this guy who taught you how to massage."

"Gabriel is Claudette's older brother. He's pretty much my brother too, just like Liam."

"Does he think of you as his sister?" He sounded skeptical.

"Yes. I think so. We were roommates for two years after Stella was born. He and his teammate swam for their college swim team, and they invited me and Stella to live with them. They're the only reason I was able to keep Stella away from my parents for so long."

"You lived with two male athletes for two years." He sounded almost resigned.

I poked him in the side, then went back to working on his back. "Yes, and don't make it weird. Not all men are perverts."

"I hate to tell you this, but we are."

"It was me and an infant, who turned into a toddler. They were both..." I choked up a little when I thought about Gabe and Elias.

"Tell me about them."

Working on his lower back with my forearms and palms, I told Titus about those two years. "We lived together in a little rented house in a questionable neighborhood of Seattle. They weren't around a lot with school, practice, and swim meets. But when they were, we made meals together, and they hung out with me and Stella. I think our neighbors thought we were a throuple, or a threesome, or something."

Thinking back on it made me a little melancholy. They'd been my guardian angels in so many ways.

"And were you?"

I pinched his thigh, and he grunted. "No! I already told you. And I'd sworn off men at that point. Gabe even learned to change diapers, and they helped with Stella whenever they were around. They both loathed Kyle, and my parents, and tried to protect me when they could."

"So nothing happened between you?"

"No, and sometimes Elias brought girls home."

"You lived with them for two years," he murmured, like maybe he didn't believe me.

I poked his beautiful, firm ass cheek and then ran my hand across it. "None of the naughty things you're thinking about right now ever happened."

Working through his oblique muscles, I worried about him being in constant pain. His back felt so tight. Methodically, I kneaded through the knots, then massaged his thighs and calves.

"Tell me about Kyle," he murmured.

My hands stilled for a moment. "We were both young, but I stepped up and he ran. And kept running. I don't want someone like that coming and going from Stella's life, so I've never pursued it. I think it would do more harm than good."

He nodded. "I agree." His hamstrings were thick and corded with muscle, and his glutes were a work of art. By the time I finished, I was sweating a little, and not just from exertion.

Titus rolled over and sat up. "Thank you. That felt so good." When he saw my kimono for the first time, he froze. "Is that what you wear to bed?"

"Yes. They're comfortable, and I can get them cheap at the secondhand stores where I live."

He scanned my body. "Where you *used* to live. When we first met, you reminded me of a character in a Japanese hentai film. It's anime porn. With your big, beautiful eyes and curly blond hair, you're a dead ringer, and seeing you in that gives me obscene ideas." He reached over and stroked my thigh. "Even more than usual."

"Japanese anime porn?" I grinned. "Is that even a thing?"

"Absolutely. I wouldn't recommend googling it though."

"Just by saying that, you know I'm googling it now. Which character?"

"There's no fucking way I'm telling you that. Maybe someday we can watch one together."

Thinking about watching porn with him did strange things to my body. I wouldn't even consider it with anyone else, but I felt safe with Titus. And maybe a little bit happy.

But he'd said he wanted to talk, so I screwed up my courage and studied him carefully. "What do you want to talk about?"

Titus pulled back the covers, then picked me up and set me in his bed. He turned off his lamp and got in beside me, pulling me into him like he'd done it a thousand times before. Maybe he wasn't going to kick me out.

"We're going to start fucking, and I plan to do it as much as I can get away with, in every conceivable position, and on every viable surface. So much more than 'not quite sex,' or making out in the kitchen."

I started panting a little. "Okay."

He kissed my hair and ran his hand up my leg. "You've gone through more shit than most people do in a lifetime, and I have to remind myself how young and innocent you are."

"I have a three-year-old child. I'm not innocent."

Rolling me on my back, he half-covered me and slid his thigh between my legs. "Yes, you are, and I like it. Are you on birth control?"

Turning my face to the side, I looked out his window. "No."

"Do you want to get on birth control, or do you want me to use condoms?" He reached down and grasped my chin, turning my face back to his. "I'm good either way." Titus studied me carefully in the dim light.

My cheeks flamed. How could I tell him I hadn't been able to afford birth control? Just like I couldn't afford a new phone, or decent clothes for Stella. My eyes suddenly filled with tears, and I got angry at myself. Then I started struggling.

"I need to go," I rasped out.

He instantly let go of me, but his deep voice stopped me. "Talk to me. What's going on in your beautiful, troubled mind?"

My body locked, and I wrapped my arms around my middle. "I can't do this with you. I like you too much to drag you into my dark, shitty life." I sobbed once, then sucked it all inside.

"Tell me what you're thinking. Isn't your life good right now? Aren't you and Stella happy here?"

"Yes!" I burst out. "Yes. But nothing good lasts, and my father is going to come after me. I don't want his poison to get anywhere near you." Gasping for breath, I realized I'd started crying, but I needed to get it all out. "And I'm taking advantage of you and... and mooching off you. Like I've done to everyone I love or care about. I'm so sorry. I'll help you with Max any way I can. But you deserve better than me."

Before I could escape, he rolled out of bed and picked me up, then sat down on the end of the bed and held me while I cried. The vitriol and neglect my parents had spewed at me and Stella came pouring out of me as I sobbed in his arms. I felt empty and worthless sometimes, even though I knew in my heart I hadn't deserved their treatment.

Titus let me cry all over him, and he gently rubbed my back and murmured soothing words in my ear. "It's alright, love. I've got you and Stella. That fucker is never going to touch you again."

I cried a little more, then hiccupped, and finally settled down.

"Tell me what you're thinking," he murmured.

I laid my head in the crook of his shoulder and wrapped my arms around him. "Most people ignore signs of abuse and neglect in outwardly functioning families. But when the kids start talking, they're labeled as troublemakers, or they're just acting out or causing problems."

"What do you mean?"

"A counselor at my school almost got fired for trying to help me because the school administrator and my father were friends. That's when I learned to keep my mouth shut."

Titus squeezed me and rubbed his chin along my forehead. "Do you have any other family?"

"My grandma was wonderful. And according to my parents, she had lots of money. She wanted me to come live with her. But then she got dementia, and I lost her too."

"I'm sorry, *gentile fille*. You and I are a team, and if that worthless fucker comes near you or Stella again, he'll have to get through me. We're going to talk, and you're going to be honest with me. Why aren't you on birth control?"

Sighing, I sat up. "I couldn't afford it, and there wasn't a reason to worry about it."

"You can now, and there's definitely a reason. I'm depositing more money into your account tomorrow."

"Titus, I can't–"

"You can and you will. And for fuck's sake, stop arguing every time we need to spend ten cents to make things better for you and Stella."

He paused as if he expected me to argue again. But I'd just realized something. Titus cared about our safety and happiness, and maybe he even *wanted* to help us. So I stopped arguing and jerked my chin. "Okay."

"Okay," he repeated cautiously. "And tomorrow will you make an appointment with a gynecologist? Whatever you decide about birth control, I bet you haven't had a check-up in a while."

I nodded. "Alright." I didn't want to tell him the last time I'd been seen by a doctor was just after Stella's birth.

"And for hell's sake, please get some runners that aren't about to fall apart. You have fucking holes in the tops of your shoes."

"Alright," I said a little louder, pinching him again.

He chuckled and rolled me over onto the bed, landing on top of me. "You pinch like a *p'tite fille*."

Rolling my eyes, I tried to pinch his side again. "That's because I *am* a girl, Tremblay."

Thrusting his hips into me, I felt his hard shaft against my center. My insides clenched, and I moved against him.

Smirking, he leaned down and bit my earlobe. "Oh, I know."

Chapter 16

The next morning, I woke when someone put a hand on my shoulder. I instinctively kicked out, but Titus easily dodged my foot. He stood by the side of his bed, dressed for practice and holding his hand up.

"It's just me, sleepyhead. I said your name a few times, but I must have worn you out last night." He grinned and didn't mention my reaction. I let out a long breath.

"What time is it?" My hair hung in my face, and I swiped it back.

"Still early. We're watching film this morning before practice. You look delicious lying there in my bed, but Stella is starting to stir. Do you want me to feed her before I take off?" He eyed my legs, then his gaze slid up to my breasts that were spilling out of my low neckline. His lips curled.

I sat up, then my head tipped over and I plunked my forehead on his stomach. "No. I've got it."

"Uh-huh." His hand rested on my neck. I pulled my head back and squinted up at him. Titus took in my face, then leaned down and slowly cupped my jaw and nibbled on my lips before pulling back. "Okay. Don't forget the gynecologist appointment. I'll see you after practice."

It was all so... domestic. And hot. A shiver of lust wound through me as I thought about what we'd done last night. Then I remembered Stella was stirring, and shot up, hustling to my room before she could find me in Titus's bed.

Later that morning, my phone rang. I looked down and noticed it was a number I didn't recognize, but it was from the same area code where my parents lived. Adrenaline hit my system and dread filled me.

I'd blocked both my parents' numbers when I left Seattle with Isabella, and I hadn't heard from them since. Letting the call go, I noticed a few minutes later the same number popped up again. Staring down at that number flashing on my cracked screen, I knew in my gut it was my father.

When Stella and I went for a run after breakfast, the morning was overcast and a little dark. After a while, I stopped to let Stella out of her stroller so she could walk. I watched her tuck her moose into the stroller and cover him with her blanket.

"Hello, Ms. Abigail." I jumped and whirled. George, our neighbor, stood behind us with his mother's little dog. "I apologize. I didn't mean to startle you." His eyebrows creased, and he studied me.

"Hello, George. I'm a little jumpy this morning, I guess." We chatted for a minute. "Can we walk back with you?" I asked.

Smiling, he looked down at Stella. "Of course. It's my distinct pleasure to have the two loveliest ladies in the neighborhood out walking with me." We chatted about how his mother was doing on the way back.

We also ran into Vern and Bowen who lived a few houses down from Titus. They were probably in their mid-sixties and liked to take morning power walks in velour jumpsuits.

Vern spoke in a charming Georgia accent, and he pointed his finger at me. "I hear you made Ms. Mary Alice snickerdoodles the other day." Mary Alice was George's mom.

"I did."

He folded his arms and waited.

"Vern, would you like some cookies too?" I asked.

"Oh my, yes! I'm a traditionalist, so chocolate chip cookies are my favorite."

"It's your lucky day because Stella and I are going to make some when we get home. Would it be alright if I dropped a few off later today?"

Vern clapped his hands. "Oh, honey, that would be so sweet! We'd love to try your homemade chocolate chip cookies."

While we baked, I called Isa. "Hey, what're you doing today?" she asked. Her cheery voice helped quell my jumpy nerves.

"Making cookies, and I'm using your dad's recipe with the dash of soy sauce."

"Ah, so you're making chocolate chip cookies." I'd learned to bake with her dad in their small, peaceful kitchen. Most of my recipes came from him.

Popping a piece of dough in my mouth, I stuck a batch in the oven. "I need to schedule a gynecologist appointment. Do you have any recommendations?"

"Yes, I do. And it's about damn time. What type of birth control are you thinking?"

I paused in front of the stove. "How do you know I'm not already on birth control?"

"Because you've been living on a shoestring budget since your asshole parents tried to bleed you dry when you moved back in with them. And if you don't want another unplanned pregnancy, you better take care of it since we all know both you and Titus are fertile."

"You're hilarious," I said flatly.

"No, I'm just brutally honest. Do you want to meet for lunch today?"

"Yeah." I rubbed my forehead. "I got a couple of calls this morning from the same area code as my parents. It might've been spam, but I think it was my father."

She blew out a breath. "We're definitely getting together for lunch then, and take a screenshot of the phone number and send it to me."

We decided on a park not far from downtown Palm Springs with a covered pavilion in case it rained. Laurel met us there. I wore shorts and a t-shirt, but Laurel looked professional and chic in a pencil skirt and silk top.

"Hi, Laurel. I'd hug you, but I have sand all over me from playing in the sandbox with Stella."

Laurel grinned and hugged me anyway. "How's the Cherry Box coming?"

I smiled. She was an attorney, but she was also affectionate and kind. "Good. Claude's coming to Palm Springs soon to officially pass it off to me."

"If she's here on a Monday, make sure you invite her to our martini party. Harley, Martina, and I are big fans." She winced. "It's actually kind of stalkerish at this point. Her reviews and commentary are so good."

Isabella pulled out the mango chicken salad she'd made for lunch. "Abby, you probably already know this, but Laurel is an attorney. She works with one of the best family law attorneys in Palm Springs."

I nodded. "I do know that."

Isa turned to Laurel. "I'm shamelessly bribing you with lunch and asking for free legal advice for Abby."

Laurel smiled and patted Isa's hand. "You already told me when you invited me. And I'm happy to get out of the office." She turned her startling blue eyes to me. "You know the saying, you get what you pay for? Well, I've been a practicing attorney for less than a year. So my advice is probably worth about the cost of this lunch." Laurel's face turned serious, and she studied me and Stella. "What's going on?"

So Isa and I told her how I ended up living with Titus, about the upcoming custody hearing, and my father's physical abuse. I felt ashamed to have her know about all the scars and skeletons in my life.

As she listened to us talk, her eyes turned sad. I finished by telling her about the calls from the unknown number this morning.

Laurel laced her hands on the table and watched Stella play in the sandbox. "My father's name is Victor. He lives in New York, and the last time I saw him he came here looking for my two little brothers and stepmother." She glanced at me with troubled eyes. "He violated a domestic abuse protective order by coming, and when I wouldn't tell him where they were, he hit and choked me on my front doorstep. So when I say I understand what you're going through, it's not just a platitude or generic sympathy. Because I *understand*."

Her eyes shimmered, and mine filled with tears as well. I turned and watched Stella playing, and my heart somehow felt less burdened.

Laurel cleared her throat and reached over to clasp my hand. "You have three legal issues from what I can see. Regarding Titus and his upcoming hearing, I'm not an attorney licensed to practice law in Canada. But I can give you my educated opinion, and common sense tells me it's probably accurate. I also recommend checking in with Titus's attorney."

"I understand. How can I help him?"

Laurel leaned forward. "Start documenting everything. Take photos of whatever he's done to get ready for Max. If he's set up a room, made any changes so the house is safer, bought books, toys, clothes. Whatever. Also, document who his pediatrician will be here."

Isa raised her hand. "I can get Max signed up at the pediatric clinic where I'll be working."

Laurel nodded. She went through a few other items, and I pulled out my phone and started furiously typing up notes.

"Okay. Got it." Having something concrete to work on made me feel better.

"The second legal issue is your father," Laurel went on.

I carefully set my phone down. "If I never see him again, I'll die a happy woman. I don't want to do anything that will make him come after us."

"People like him don't give up unless you *make* them. He's probably a narcissist, and it sounds like he has some mental health issues too. You need to pull your head out of the sand and protect yourself."

I started shaking my head. "It'll just make him angrier."

She leaned forward and looked me in the eye. "You also need to protect Stella."

"I'm trying to."

"You don't have to protect her alone. Use the law, your friends, or any resources you can get your hands on. I'll also talk to Ramone and get back to you. He's not only my boss and one of the best attorneys I know, he and Jonathan are my family. I trust them."

"Okay. If and when I can help you or pay you back, please let me know."

She waved her hand. "We're friends, and this is what friends do. The third legal issue is child support for Stella. Why in the world isn't that deadbeat sperm donor of yours helping out?"

Isabella nodded vigorously. "He wasn't a bad guy when we were in high school. But I swear to God if I ever see him again, I'm going to throat-punch him."

Sighing, I rubbed my forehead. "I filed for child support when Stella was born, but he went off to college and hasn't been working."

Isa turned to me. "You could call your case manager and renew your request. Have you updated your address?"

I shook my head. "Not yet. But if Kyle has graduated by now, maybe he's close to getting a job. It's worth a try."

Laurel nodded. "I need to get back to work, but call me if you have any other questions. And you and Titus need to start coming to our Martini Monday parties on the regular." She smiled. "He's easy on the eyes, and his view on the word 'fuck' is hilarious."

Isa grinned, and they both started laughing. I shrugged, not getting the joke. I'd have to ask Titus.

He called me later that afternoon and let out a long sigh. "Will you turn the spa on? My back is acting up, and it's been a long, frustrating practice. I keep forgetting this team's median age is around nineteen."

"I'll turn it on right now."

"It's difficult being their assistant coach *and* their teammate. I don't know whether to encourage them or bang their heads together."

Hearing his deep growly voice always soothed me and gave me shivers. "Have you thought about doing one or the other?"

"Yeah. When the season ends, I need to get serious about where I go next. And there's Max to think about."

Were Stella and I in that equation? I was too afraid to ask, and my heart squeezed. I tried to shake off the sting his words caused and worked to keep my voice normal. "You'll figure it out."

When we hung up, I turned on the spa and then stood there, gazing into the clear water. Had Titus meant what he'd said about us being together longer than a few months? Or had he changed his mind and started getting tired of us? Maybe the reality of having two little kids under four years was sinking in. I needed to get my shit together and remember this could all be temporary, like most things that had been good in my life.

Titus studied me for the third time as we ate out on the back patio. Stella had propped Mr. Moose next to her and was pretending to feed him bits of potato.

I forked another bite of salmon, even though I wasn't hungry. "The spa should be hot by now. I'll clean up if you want to soak."

He shook his head and helped me gather the dishes. Stella disappeared into her room to play with her ponies, and I finished straightening up the kitchen while he took care of the grill.

Walking back into the kitchen, he took my hand and led me to the couch where he pulled me into his lap.

"What's going on?" he asked quietly.

He smelled like pine soap and his own masculine scent, and it comforted me and made me melancholy all at once. I didn't have the right to burden him with my thoughts and insecurities.

"How's your back?" I asked.

"A little sore. When Stella goes to bed, I want to soak in the spa with you. Now tell me."

My eyes drifted down to the scars on his knuckles. "It's nothing. I'm probably just being paranoid, but this morning someone called my cellphone twice from the same area code where my parents live." I didn't tell him about being hurt and feeling insecure.

His hand clenched. "You didn't answer it."

"No, but it scared me. Isabella and I met Laurel Payne for lunch. She's an attorney, and she gave me some ideas."

He ran his hand up my arm and curled it around the back of my neck. "Good. I think it's time to put the fear of God in them."

I smiled humorlessly. "My father used to say that exact thing before he hit me. He'd say he was disciplining me to 'put the fear of God' in me."

He squeezed me to him. "Bad choice of words. I won't use it again. You talked to Laurel, and I think it's time to get Damien and Zeke involved. I have a couple of simple cameras on the front and back doors, but we should beef up security here."

Laying my head on his shoulder, I breathed him in and basked in his warmth. "Okay. I won't argue with that."

His kindness and calming presence were a balm to my scarred heart. And maybe it was all temporary, but like the sun setting on a cold day, I wanted to absorb every second until we might have to leave him, and his rays and warmth would be gone.

Chapter 17

Titus sunk into the steaming spa and let out a low groan of pleasure, causing goosebumps to break out on my arms. "Fuck, that feels good."

Unwrapping my towel, I laid it on the deck, gingerly stuck my foot in, then eased myself into the steamy, bubbling water. I'd tucked Stella into bed not long ago, then changed into my swimsuit. Titus laid his head back on the edge and watched me with hooded eyes.

His mouth tipped up when he saw my purple polka-dot bikini. "I like your suit, but it reminds me how young you are."

It always reminded me of the polka-dot bikini song. "At least it's not yellow, and Stella likes it. Practice was rough today, huh?"

He grunted. "The next team we're playing is tough. If we do manage to pull out a win, it'll be a fucking miracle."

Sitting across from him, we sat in silence for a few minutes, relaxing and listening to the gurgling bubbles and the quiet evening.

I looked up at the sky and noticed the clouds had cleared out and the stars and a half-moon shone in the evening desert sky.

When I gazed back at him, he held his hand out to me. "I want to play with you out here in the water. Are you up for it?"

My heart thumped hard in my chest, and I reached out and put my palm in his. "Yes," I whispered.

He pulled me to him, parted my legs, and positioned me so I straddled his lap. Then he leaned in and licked my lips. "Did you get an appointment set up?"

"I did."

Leaning in, he ran his lips across my clavicle, then nipped at the crease of my neck. "I want to finger your sweet little pussy and get you ready for my cock."

"I don't know if I'll be able to take all of you, but I want to try." I rubbed myself against his thick length with just our suits separating us.

He gripped my legs and ran his hands up my thighs. "We're not fucking tonight, but I'm going to make you come again, and then I'm going to fuck your tits and paint them. For some reason, you make me feel like a goddamn animal, and I have an urge to mark you."

I swear my eyes rolled back in my head, and I started shifting restlessly against him. "You have a filthy imagination, Tremblay."

"Is that a problem?"

"No, I like it."

He grinned and reached behind me to untie my bikini top. Peeling it off me and setting it on the spa edge with a wet plop, he leaned in and leisurely licked and sucked on my nipples.

"I want to make you come against the jet first. And then you're going to come again on my mouth." My hips shifted restlessly as he suckled me for a few moments. When I was panting and needy, he set me on my feet and pulled my bikini bottoms off, then stripped out of his own suit. "We don't need these either. Have you ever used a pool or spa jet to masturbate?" he asked casually.

My face flamed, and I swallowed. "I didn't know you could."

His lip ticked up in a wicked smirk. "Good. I like being the one to corrupt you." He swung me around, pulled my legs apart, and found a jet.

My hips jerked when the water hit my clit. "Oh, shit!" I gasped and tried to pull back.

He chuckled and held my hips in place. "Is it too strong?"

"It's... I don't know."

He held me still until I got used to the pulse, and then Titus let go of my hips and sat in front of me on the edge of the spa, opening his thighs. "Can you suck my cock while you hold your clit to the jet?"

My pupils dilated, and I arched a little. "Yes."

He worked himself while he watched me. "Then come here," he growled softly.

Leaning over, I positioned myself between his thighs. Then I took his tip in my mouth, working my tongue along the edge of his head, just like he'd shown me.

"Fuucking hell. Your mouth feels so good," he growled, throwing his head back. "Now open your thighs and put your cunt back on the jet."

I sucked and licked him deeper into my mouth, then rotated my hips so my clit hit the pulsing water. Not long after, a hard climax hit me by surprise. I moaned around his cock and pulled off, panting. He leaned over and held me while I shuddered, my orgasm rocking through me.

When I stilled, he slid back into the water and held me in his lap, his thick length twitching along my slit. He didn't seem to be in a hurry as he ran his fingers through my hair, then down my chest and thighs.

Moments later, I started squirming against him again, and he reached up and palmed my breast, rubbing his thumb across the nipple.

"Are you ready to play some more?"

"Yes. Are *you* ready?" I leaned in and bit his nipple, and he jerked and chuckled.

Titus made me squirm and blush, but he also liked to make me laugh. So far, sex with him had been dirty, inventive, and... fun. I hadn't expected that. He stood, turned me around, and laid my back on the towel. Then he pulled my thighs apart, stepping between them.

His mouth trailed down my stomach to my clit, and he worked me with his fingers and tongue. My hips arched to meet his mouth as he flicked me over and over.

But before letting me come, he crawled up my body and kissed me long and hard, making me taste myself on his mouth. I slid my tongue inside and licked him, picking up my salty, musky essence.

He pulled back and sucked on my lower lip. "That's it. See how good you taste? When we fuck, I'm going to make you suck my cock after I come deep inside your sweet little cunt. Then you'll know what we taste like together."

The image his dirty mouth painted sent a white haze across my mind. I was already halfway to an orgasm. Crawling back down to my center, he licked my opening, then fluttered his tongue right on my clit. When he roughly shoved two fingers inside me, I went off like a bomb.

My back bowed, and I moaned. My orgasm seemed to last forever, and I sucked in big gulps of air when I realized I was holding my breath.

After I came down, Titus knelt over me and cupped my face. "Are you with me?"

"Yes," I croaked, grasping his wrist.

"Good. Open up and get me dripping wet so I can fuck your breasts."

Sitting up, I grasped his shaft and opened my mouth to pull it inside when he rose to meet me. I sucked on him again and slid around his throbbing tip. Then I wiggled my tongue into his slit.

He grunted and jerked back. "Shit. You're a curious little thing, aren't you?"

I smiled and licked my lips. He placed his palms just below my shoulder blades and brought my chest to his mouth. Then he ran his tongue between my globes, making me even more wet and slippery.

Shoving his cock in between my breasts, Titus pushed them firmly together. He knelt over me and rhythmically fucked my chest while he stared down at me, his thumbs brushing across my nipples. I arched my back, and my lids drifted closed.

"Open your eyes. You're going to watch me fuck your beautiful tits."

My eyelids popped open, and my insides clenched. The man rocked me with his pornographic mouth, and his words lit me up like a grease fire. I looked down and saw the tip of his cock sliding along my upper chest, so I tilted my chin down and tried to catch it with my tongue.

"You feel so good. I'm going to make a fucking mess of you again," he said through gritted teeth.

My breasts grew tender and swollen as he held on firmly and pumped himself between them. But the bite caused my pussy to clench in need. I swirled my mouth around his tip when I could reach it.

He let go of my breasts, expertly pumped his cock a few times, and then squirted all over my chest and neck. When he'd expelled the last stream across my chest, he let go of his length and slowly rubbed his semen into my skin.

When he finished, he wrapped his warm, wet hand around my throat and gently squeezed. "Now that you're soaked in my come and I've made you orgasm twice tonight, you need to know something," he murmured against my ear. "You're mine. We belong together. I never want to hear you say you're mooching off me or you don't deserve to be happy again. And when you're ready, you're getting into therapy to deal with what your shit-fucking, asshole father put you through. Because we need you."

I stared up at him, a few tears escaping. How had he known my darkest thoughts? There was no hiding from this man. Leaning down, he brushed his lips against my cheek and let go of my neck. Then he gathered me up, cuddling me close as we sat quietly for a few minutes in the swirling water before getting out and drying off.

Later that night as I listened to his steady breathing while he slept, I wondered if this beautiful, scarred, tattooed man could love me someday. Or if he'd regret ever laying eyes on me.

The next morning, I woke up under a furnace. Cracking an eye open, I noticed a thick, muscular arm wrapped across my chest, and a hand cupping my breast. A hard leg draped over my hips, and a heavy body lay half on top of me. Then it all came back, and I sucked in a breath.

"Morning, my little anime porn star," Titus mumbled. He lay on his stomach, half on the bed, and half on me. He squeezed my breast and ran his thumb across my nipple. It pebbled, but he sighed a little and let go.

I fumbled to wipe hair out of my face and turned to him. "I should have gone back to my room last night."

"No," he rumbled. A good portion of his face smashed into the mattress, and his dark blond hair was as spiky and messy as ever.

"No?"

"No. You sleep with me from now on."

"But Stella will–"

"We'll show her where she can find us. She's smart."

He opened an eye, leaned up on an elbow, and studied me. "Your hair is kind of wild in the morning. It makes me want to wrap it around my fist, then take my mouth and–"

I leaned over and put my finger across his lips. "Your mouth has gotten me into enough trouble. And I can't go around wet and needy all the time."

He slowly licked my finger. "Yes, you can."

I pulled my hand back and held it behind my back. "No, I can't. I don't have enough panties."

"Then don't wear them. You could wear skirts and dresses around the house. With no panties." He grinned as if picturing it.

"I have a three-year-old, and we'll soon have a two-year-old running around the house. That might be tricky."

"Just don't bend over–unless it's for me. And we'll manage since they have to nap and sleep sometime."

He gathered my hair in his hand and nuzzled my neck. "The team is only practicing half-day today, so this afternoon I want to take you and Stella to the phone store, and maybe the mall to pick up a few things."

I started to go tight against him, but he squeezed my thigh. "Don't freeze up on me. We'll start small, alright?"

Chapter 18

His idea of small and mine were worlds apart. Later that afternoon, I watched Titus kneeling in front of Stella, lacing up a small pair of jaw-droppingly expensive joggers. They were similar to the pair he'd picked out for me.

"Run over to the door and back to make sure they're comfortable, okay?" he asked her.

"So pretty," she cooed.

He grinned. "They are pretty, just like you."

Stella ran to the door and back, then jumped up and down next to him. "I like 'em."

I knelt and checked where her toe sat inside the shoe. Then Titus took them off and added them to the stack of clothes he'd already picked out for us. He looked at me and winked.

My armpits were sweating. "You promised we'd start small. This is not small."

He shrugged. "It's small. If you don't think so, I can show you what 'not small' looks like."

I held up my hands. "No, no. This is fine, and thank you. But we need to stop now because I'm starting to have a panic attack."

He walked over and palmed my neck. "Breathe. It's going to be okay. After we check out, we'll go get dinner and be done."

I laid my forehead on his chest and breathed in his scent and warmth. My brain told me not to get used to all this, but my heart soaked up his care like a thirsty puppy. Maybe I should learn to live in these moments while I had them.

Stella slid her little hand into mine. "Okay, Mommy?" I didn't know if she was asking if I was okay, or if it was alright for her to have the shoes, and my heart cracked a little in my chest.

"Yes, bug. Your new shoes look so comfortable, and I love the color."

She smiled and clapped her hands. "Me too."

We'd already gone to the phone store and picked out a new phone. Or Titus had picked one out. It was the newest release with the most memory, and he'd also thrown in a new cover, screen protector, and warranty. I now owned a phone that was probably worth more than all my other possessions combined.

"I go potty," Stella told me.

"Alright. I think I saw one over in the corner."

Titus pointed to the pile of stuff. "I'll get us checked out here."

By the time we came back, the young, perky saleswoman who'd helped us stood in front of the cash register, touching Titus's arm and smiling up at him. He tucked his wallet back in his pocket and looked around. When he saw us, he gave the woman a quick thanks and strolled over.

The clerk stared at his ass as he walked toward me, and when she reached us her gaze flicked up and she noticed me watching her.

She didn't seem the least bit ashamed to be caught checking him out. I couldn't blame her, it was a very nice ass, and this wasn't the first time I'd seen someone checking him out.

Titus took us to his favorite Mexican restaurant for dinner. He spoke to the owner in Spanish, then introduced us.

"Pablo, these are my girls, Abby and Stella."

"It's nice to meet you, *señoritas*." He turned to Titus. "How'd you get such a beautiful woman, *señor*?" he asked with a straight face.

Titus grinned and smacked his arm. "Sheer dumb luck."

Stella and I ordered a chicken burrito to share until Titus added a child's meal and two margaritas to our order.

I opened my mouth to protest, but he shook his head and pointed to me. "I used to go to lunch with Isa sometimes when she worked at the arena. She tried the same crap on me, always wanting to 'share' a meal. Or she'd order a salad, then eat half my damn food."

"Whenever Isa and I eat out together, we split a meal. Her mom was pretty sick for most of Isa's life, and the medical bills ate up most of Mr. Cruz's income. Isa learned to be frugal." I grabbed a warm, salted chip and scooped up some chunky salsa, shoving the whole thing in my mouth. "Mmm. God, that is so good."

Titus's lip twitched. "I love hearing you moan."

Blushing, I licked a little salsa off my finger and grabbed another chip.

He leaned back and watched us. "I didn't know about her mom until a couple of months ago. I wouldn't have given her a hard time about it if I'd known."

I helped Stella put a few chips on her plate, and the server dropped off our margaritas. I took a sip of the tart lime concoction with a little jalapeño salt around the rim.

"These chips are good, aren't they?" I asked Stella.

She nodded and grinned. "Yep."

"You like chips?" Stella pointed at Titus.

"I do, *ma puce*. But if I get filled up on those, then I can't enjoy my tacos as much."

Stella stared at him and stuffed another one in her mouth. She obviously didn't care if she filled herself up on chips.

He grinned at her. "You talk a lot more now."

Smiling, I ran my hand down her back. "We read every night and practice colors, numbers, and letters. I also need to get her signed up for preschool soon." Then I wondered if we'd still live with Titus in Palm Springs by then. I also hoped I could make enough money from the Cherry Box to afford preschool.

Which reminded me that Claudette was coming in a little over a week. "I forgot to tell you, Claudette and Gabriel are coming to Palm Springs next week."

The Thunderbirds were scheduled to play on Sunday, and if they lost they were done for the season. If they won, they played the same team again out of state.

Just then the server brought out our food, and Stella and I tucked in. After a few bites, I noticed Titus watching me. "What?"

"Is this the same guy you lived with for two years?"

"Yes."

He leaned back. "Why the fuck is he coming to see you now?"

"He's mostly coming to see Claudette, and probably me and Stella too, but Claudette's moving to Berlin soon." I put my fork down. "They're meeting here because I need to go over a few things with her before she turns over her online business to me."

His jaw tightened, but he didn't say anything else.

"What?" I asked.

He sighed. "Fuck. I'm a selfish bastard, and I like having you all to myself. It also pisses me off thinking about you living with another man." He leaned forward. "You living with *two* men makes my head want to explode."

His admission startled me, but my chest warmed. "We were friends, and nothing more."

"Maybe that's how you felt. But I've been living with you for a fraction of that time."

My stomach flipped over and I tucked my hands under my thighs. "What are you saying?" I asked quietly.

"This is more than an arrangement. I need you to say it."

I glanced over at Stella, who watched us carefully while she slowly ate. Sometimes I wondered how much she understood.

Clearing my throat, I mentally braced myself. "This is more than an arrangement for me too." My face felt as red as the salsa, and my heart thumped in my chest. "But no more puck bunnies."

He slowly grinned, then leaned across the table and palmed my cheek. "Not a problem. Why the fuck would I want that when I have you?"

God, this man. I laid my hand on his and squeezed.

We ate in silence for a few minutes. Finally, I sighed, patted my stomach, and sat back. "Claudette and Gabriel plan to stay at a vacation rental not far from your house. If you're around, I want you to meet them." I held his gaze, willing him to understand. "They're some of my best friends. Gabriel... saved Stella and me. I was so vulnerable and lost. And scared. In some ways, he sacrificed his best college years for us."

His lips tightened, but he nodded. "Okay. I'd like to meet them. What kind of online business is Claudette turning over to you?"

Looking down at my plate, I thought frantically about how to answer him. I didn't want to lie but now didn't seem like a good time to tell him about the Cherry Box.

"Toys, mostly. All the merchandise is drop shipped, so it keeps costs way down. I'll show you the website sometime." I turned to Stella. "How're you doing, little bug?"

"Good." She watched me with serious eyes as my conscience nagged at me.

Titus looked at my plate. "You can eat more than that. When you first got here, you were emaciated and skittish. I like seeing you fill out and enjoy yourself. There's also more of you to... hold."

I grinned, knowing that wasn't the word he'd been thinking. We finished up and headed home. I wasn't used to drinking a whole margarita by myself and felt a little buzzed. When we got home, Stella dragged her feet as she walked inside and whined when I asked her to change into her pajamas. She was tired, so I helped her, and we read a short story. She fell asleep before I finished the book.

Then I got myself ready for bed and nervously walked out into the kitchen. Titus wasn't out there, but his bedroom door stood open, and soft light spilled out.

He sat on the edge of his bed looking down at his phone and absently massaging his back again. Stopping at the threshold, I knocked on the doorframe.

"Did she conk out?" he asked.

"Yeah. We didn't even make it through one book. Thank you for the phone today. And everything else, especially Stella's little shoes. So again, thank you."

"You're welcome. But you don't have to thank me."

"Yes, I really do. Anyway, goodnight." I started to turn.

"Abigail."

"Yes?"

"You're not sleeping in the other room anymore."

"I'm not?"

"No. You're sleeping in here with me from now on."

"You want me to sleep in here with you?" God, I sounded like an idiot.

"Yes. We talked about it." His eyes scanned my face, and he grinned. "Are you nervous? I'd tell you not to be, but there'll be times when it might be smart."

My shoulders straightened and I dropped my hand. "I'm not nervous. And I didn't know if you were serious or not."

"I was dead serious. You're safe tonight since our big game is tomorrow and I need sleep. But you're in here with me from now on, alright?"

I nodded and started backing up. "I'll, uh, go check on Stella and come back."

"Abigail," he said my name again in his low voice.

"Hmm?" I turned back to him.

"I won't do much tonight, besides maybe spoon you and play with your tits a little. And rub my dick along the small of your back. I'll also take off your nightshirt because your skin is softer than silk, and I want to feel it against me."

The humor in his eyes cut through my nerves.

"But other than that, you won't do much?"

"Right. More or less."

Want and anticipation rolled through me. "Okay. I'll be back." I hurried to Stella's room. She didn't even stir. On the way back, I grabbed a bottle of massage oil from my bathroom.

When I walked back to Titus's room, I set the oil on the night-stand. "Before you spoon me and… do those other things, I want to work a few kinks out of your back. I noticed you rubbing it tonight."

Titus's eyes swept over me, and he smiled. "I won't say no." He stood and pulled his t-shirt and shorts off, and the view was as spectacular as I remembered.

Chapter 19

Titus's body felt so good under my hands as I methodically worked out his knots. After his massage, Titus did take my nightshirt off, and by the time we settled down to sleep almost an hour later, we were both breathless and sweaty.

Before the game the next night, nerves swam through my stomach for Titus and the rest of the players. This was a do-or-die game, and they weren't favored to win. I didn't know how they stood the pressure.

Javier offered to watch Stella overnight since the game started so late. She loved the hockey games, but loved being with Elodie just as much.

It took me longer than expected to drive Stella to Javier's house out in Palm Desert and get back to the arena, so I was late for the faceoff. Scooting into my seat, I sat next to Isa.

She patted my thigh. "Titus glanced up here a couple of times. He'll be glad to see you."

We settled in to watch. The team they were playing was considered the best in the league. Their players were fast and looked more experienced than most of the players on our team. I wondered if the Thunderbirds could pull out another win.

At the end of the first period, I noticed Titus searching the stands as he skated to the bench. When his eyes locked on mine, I gave him my usual little finger wave and a grin. His eyes warmed, and he shook his head.

I'd gotten smart and brought better earplugs, and I was glad I did because this game was *loud*. Titus and Jackson played so well together, and we stood and cheered for most of the game, my voice slowly going hoarse.

When one of the opposing players checked Titus against the glass to get control of the puck, I groaned helplessly and watched as he shoved the guy back and shook off the hit. The players skated fast, and the puck flew around the ice. This was a vital playoff game, and they all knew it.

Titus and Jackson fought and struggled to score, and Mikael and Rudy were "brick houses." But in the end, when the timer ran out, the Thunderbirds were down by one goal. We'd lost. I stared at the scoreboard, numb and a little in shock.

After the final buzzer, the crowd gave the team a long, standing ovation and started chanting, "Spar-tan! Spar-tan!" Titus finally skated around the rink and held up his hockey stick in salute. It gave me chills, and I thought the fans knew he probably wouldn't be back next year.

Isa's shoulders slumped, and she stared dejectedly out at the rink. Connor wrapped his arm around her and pulled her in for a long hug. "Hey, they got to the fucking *semi-finals* and did a hell of a lot better than anyone expected them to. Without Titus, and you forcing them to become friends, they would have gotten blown out this season. And it pains me to admit that after all the shit I gave you." Isa smiled and pulled him down for a long kiss.

The crowd slowly started filing out, and the players skated off the ice. It was heartbreaking to see their disappointment, especially the younger players.

We waited outside the locker room. A player I didn't know came out and started talking to Connor and Isa, so I stood against the wall.

A few minutes later, I sensed someone hovering close by. Glancing over, I saw a middle-aged man in a sports coat with a press pass around his neck watching me.

Straightening, I turned toward Isa, but the man stuck out his hand. "I'm Paul Roberts with the Pro Hockey News Blog. Can I ask you a few questions?"

I reluctantly shook his hand, then stepped back. "I don't–"

"Are you Titus Tremblay's girlfriend?"

My heart leaped. "I'm not comfortable talking with you–"

"What are his plans for next year? Is he coming back to Vancouver, or is he going to play for the new Seattle team?"

"You need to ask Titus." I started backing away, but the man followed after me.

"Do you two have any long-term plans? Are you going to get married? Would you move to Vancouver?"

I held out my hands to block him from coming closer. Then I stopped short. "Sir! I don't know, okay? You need to ask Titus. Now, quit crowding me."

I heard a growl behind me, and an arm wrapped around my shoulders. "You okay?"

Taking a deep breath, I looked up at him. "Yeah, I'm fine."

Titus searched my eyes, then nodded and turned to the reporter. "Why are you harassing my girlfriend, Roberts?"

Roberts threw up his arms in exasperation. "You and your agent keep giving me the runaround, and your fans want to know what you're going to do next year, especially now that the Thunderbirds' season is over."

"For shit's sake. I'll call you next week and give you an interview. But if you fucking come near her again, I'll end you. Got it?"

"Yeah. Can I print that?" Roberts asked. The man seemed to have a death wish.

Titus sighed and let go of me. "Take the 'fuck' out. Some kids follow me online." My lip quirked. Titus said fuck all the time in front of Stella and Max. We might have to work on that.

It was late when we made it back home. I cleaned up and got ready for bed, then walked out into the kitchen to see if Titus was still awake. My heart rate sped up when I noticed him sitting at the bar in cutoff sleep shorts, peering down at his phone. He didn't have a shirt on, and my eyes ate up his chest and tattoos. When I stopped at the end of the counter, he looked up.

I'd changed into a red silk tunic with a white blossom pattern, similar to the kimono. It was a little worn, but still soft and silky. He swiveled his stool around and opened his legs. "Come here."

He grabbed my hand and pulled me closer, then ran his hands up my thighs to my ass cheeks and squeezed. "You're not wearing panties, *ma bonne gentille fille.*"

Hearing him call me his "good, sweet girl" in French made my heart speed up and my center grow wet. I loved this man's dirty talk.

"It's a good thing I'm not because you would've just set them on fire."

He buried his face in my neck. "I know I said we'd go slow, but I need to fuck you like I need my next breath."

My heart rate tripled, and my nipples hardened. "I have an appointment tomorrow to see the gynecologist. I plan to get an IUD."

He let out a long breath, set me back a little, and palmed my cheek. "It's alright, I'm not a teenager. I can beat off in the shower to fantasies of you a little longer."

My pussy pulsed at the image of Titus all soaped up and wet, stroking his massive cock while he thought of me in the shower.

"Do you have any condoms?" My voice quivered a little, but I wanted him so much my insides ached.

"Yeah. But I don't want to rush you into anything you'll regret. I doubt sex was on your radar since you shied away from me the day after we met."

I remembered how I'd flinched when he reached over to grab his bag off the counter that first morning.

"I'm sorry. It was instinct." I started backing away. "I know you'd never hurt me, and it's alright if you need more time."

He stood and grasped my arms, carefully drawing me into his chest. "Fuck no, I don't need more time." He found my mouth, and his lips didn't just kiss me, they devoured me.

My body craved his touch, and I wanted to crawl into his arms and never leave. I let out a low moan as he sucked on my tongue, making my insides tighten with need.

His hard length pushed against my stomach, and he shifted, sliding his leg between my thighs as he backed me against the counter.

His shorts didn't provide much barrier, and I reached down to palm his thick, heavy cock.

Groaning low, he grabbed my waist and set me on the counter. "I fucking love this counter. It's the perfect height."

Opening my thighs wide, he pulled my center against his hard length.

I moved restlessly against him. "That's it. Rub yourself on my cock," he growled between kisses.

When he pulled the tunic over my head, my arm got caught in the sleeve. So he grabbed the collar on both sides and tore. The thin, worn fabric didn't hold up against his strength.

He threw it behind him and gazed at me, sitting naked with my legs spread on his counter. "Sooo fucking sweet." He bent and took a breast into his mouth.

When he swirled his tongue, and bit and pulled on my nipple, I cried out. "God in heaven, your mouth feels so good."

He switched breasts, and I panted and reached down to run my hand inside his shorts, palming and stroking his shaft. Titus groaned, then pulled back and scooped me into his arms.

The fast motion made me dizzy, and I clung to his neck as he strode to his bedroom. Tossing me on his bed, he crawled over me before I could even bounce.

"You're a sight, sprawled out on my bed. Do you need a long, thorough fuck, or a hard fast one?"

I shifted restlessly against his body. "I just want you inside me. Please."

He knelt between my legs. "Put your hands behind your head," he ordered.

Slowly, I brought my hands up and laced them behind me.

"Perfect. Now spread your thighs for me."

I opened my legs, a blush crawling up my chest.

"Wider. I want the outsides of your knees touching the mattress, and your cunt open and dripping all over my sheets." My muscles on the insides of my thighs groaned at the stretch.

"Do you know what these muscles are called?" he murmured, running his lips along the insides of my thighs.

I shook my head, unable to speak.

"The sartorius muscles, also known as the honeymoon muscles. And they'll get a nice, hard workout if I fuck you right." He nipped and licked me, then shed his sleep shorts and palmed his cock.

Titus leaned back on his heels and gazed down at me, open and panting for him. "You look fucking gorgeous, and your pussy is soaked." He leaned in and skimmed his mouth along my inner hip.

"Please. I want you."

"Tell me exactly what you want from me, Abigail. Use your words."

"On my center. Please." My damp and needy body quivered beneath him.

"Where, exactly, is that?"

"On my clit, damn it. I want your mouth on my clit."

I moaned when he leaned over me and swiped his tongue across me. Then he pulled back.

"No! Please, don't stop."

He crawled up and whispered in my ear. "Then tell me *exactly* what you want me to do, and where, and for how long. I need to hear your words and know you're with me. And then I'll make you come so hard you'll want to pass out. And I'll ruin you for any other man."

My head thrashed back and forth, and I panted in need and frustration. "I want you to suck, bite, and lick my clit with your tongue and teeth until I come in your mouth. And I need your fingers inside my pussy to help me. Then put your... length inside me."

"And do what, Abigail?"

His incessant questions finally pushed me over the edge. "Fuck me!" I wailed. "I need you to fuck me. To shove your massive cock into me over and over again, and make me come while you're inside me. Is that specific enough?"

He chuckled wickedly and kissed my nipple. "Yes, *gentille fille.* That'll do."

My head flew back when he drove two fingers deep inside me with no warning. "Oh God, yes! Please," I wailed. My wet, swollen center sucked in his fingers like a high-powered vacuum, the invasion almost throwing me over the edge.

"See what you get when you use your words?" he teased. Then he took his time licking and sucking on my clit while his fingers pounded inside me. My body shuddered as he worked me over, the pressure building inside.

When he flicked his tongue mercilessly against me, I orgasmed like an erupting volcano all over his beautiful, wet mouth. After I came down, he ran his lips across my stomach, leaving a wet trail there.

"I want you inside me."

"I know. You yelled it at the top of your lungs." Grinning darkly, he reached over to his nightstand and grabbed a condom out of the drawer.

I gazed at the blue packet with XXL stamped across it. "Can I put it on? I've never done it before."

His lip quirked. "Have at it."

I sat up and he handed me the condom, then palmed his hard cock and stroked it. His length mesmerized me, and my eyes followed his hand.

"Did you get distracted?"

"Uh-huh," I said, licking my lips. He grinned as I tried to rip the package open with my thumb and index finger. When that didn't work, I put it between my teeth and ripped a portion off. Pushing my hair out of my face, I worked the condom out of the small opening.

"It's slimy," I exclaimed.

"It's lubricated," he countered, his cheek twitching as he watched me fumble.

I took the rubber between my fingers like I was putting on a sock and turned to him. "Okay, I think I'm ready."

He grabbed my wrist. "You're killing me here. You can do it next time, alright?"

Taking the condom out of my hand, he quickly placed it over his broad tip with one hand and expertly rolled it down his length in a smooth motion.

I reached out and wrapped my fingers around his shaft. "It looks tight. Are you alright?" I ran my closed palm up and down his length.

Groaning, he grabbed my shoulders. "I will be in about two seconds." Pushing me down on the bed, he nestled between my thighs and brought his hot, hard head to my opening and massaged it against my slit. Need sliced through me. Then he pressed his cock just inside as he latched his mouth to my nipple. When he bit down I arched into him, and he drove inside.

My tight center resisted him, and I bucked. "It's too much," I gasped. But I arched up to feel him slide deeper. He thrust inside me again and gripped my knees, pulling them up to my shoulders.

"It's fucking perfect." He shuddered above me and stopped.

I slowly adjusted to his size, my clit pulsing. Skimming my hands down his back, I tilted my hips up, searching for something. "Please, I need–" He surged out, then slammed back inside. "That. I need that," I panted.

My insides clenched around his cock as if trying to keep him inside. He pulled my arms above my head and pushed my thighs even wider with his knees, then pounded into me hard and deep, bottoming out and hitting my cervix.

The room filled with sounds of his hips slapping against my wet center, his deep breaths, and my shallow pants. I wanted to drown in the feel of him slamming into me, his hands holding my wrists tight. The musky smell of our mingled sex swirled around us, and I tightened around him.

Titus let go of my wrists and grazed his hand down my flank. Then he reached in and rubbed circles against my clit. My heart seized at his touch, and a climax started to build again, but before I could come he pulled out and flipped me over on all fours.

As he surged into me again, my mind buzzed with pleasure, and starlight seemed to shimmer behind my eyelids. Titus reached up and pinched and rolled my nipple. When he went back to my clit, I started thrusting back on him, craving the pressure and friction.

When he leaned in and bit the back of my neck, I cried out as another orgasm crashed over me, and I contracted around him. Titus groaned low, then reared up, grasped my hips, and slammed into me before coming deep inside. I hung there, suspended against him, until he slowly came down. I was limp and quivering in his grasp, my breath sawing in and out.

Damp hair hung around my face, and I was slick with sweat. Titus slowly lowered my hips so my knees touched the bed again, and he leaned over me.

"You just came with my cock deep inside you," he murmured into my neck.

"I know. I was there," I teased weakly.

"You know what that makes you?"

I shook my head. "Ecstatic?"

"It makes you *mine.*"

Chapter 20

My overheated body pulled me out of sleep, and something heavy lay draped across my legs. I opened my eyes and tried to remember where I was. Titus spooned me from behind, his morning erection jutting against my backside. It was a nice way to wake up, and sighed and nestled into him.

He stirred, then curled his arm around my shoulder, drawing me closer. "Good morning." His deep, slumberous voice caused a jolt of lust. "You thrash around in your sleep. I contained you so I wouldn't get kicked in the balls."

"Sorry. I'm a restless sleeper."

"It gives me the perfect excuse to grope you all night." He pushed my hair aside and nuzzled the back of my neck. Then he slid his palm between my legs and pressed against my center. "Good. You didn't put your panties back on, *ma p'tite cocotte.*"

My insides clenched. Why did him calling me his little casserole in French make me so damn wet? I shifted against him. His arm lay under my head, and he curled it, rolling me to bring my lips to his mouth. I pushed back against his length as the bedroom door flung open and Stella skipped inside. I squeaked and stiffened.

She came to the side of the bed and patted my head. "Mommy, I'm hungry."

Titus uncurled his arm, and I turned to face Stella. It took me a couple of seconds to answer. "Hey, bug." My voice sounded like a croaky toad. I hadn't put on my tunic after we cleaned up last night, and then I remembered Titus ripping it off me in the kitchen.

He let go under the covers, then propped on his elbow. "How do pancakes and maple syrup sound?"

She smiled and tried to reach over me and pat his cheek. "Good. I'm starving," she reminded us, then turned and ran back out of the room.

Titus grinned, and I looked at him with wide eyes. "She almost walked in on," I whispered.

He shrugged philosophically. "Do I regret it? Yeah. Is it probably going to happen again? Yes. Let's go make pancakes." He leaned down and kissed my shoulder. "We'll lock the door when she goes down for a nap later."

Titus went to the arena later that morning, so Stella and I pulled out watercolor paints and made a couple of pictures for Nana. Then I wrote her a long letter, telling her about Titus, our lives, and even the Cherry Box.

I used to call her sometimes, but her nurse finally told me it confused and upset her to try and talk with me on the phone. So we compromised, and on her birthday and the holidays, I sent her a long recorded message. And through it all, I continued to send weekly letters.

We put it in the mailbox as Stella and I went out for our morning run. The stroller squeaked rhythmically as I ran along behind it, pushing Stella. The days were getting warmer, and I'd worked up a respectable sweat.

When we hit the two-mile mark, I breathed a sigh of relief and we turned and walked back toward the house. Walter, one of our neighbors, stood by his mailbox. He had a shaved head and a stocky, solid build, and worked as a respiratory therapist at the hospital. I'd only seen him wearing scrubs.

"Hi, Walter. How are Milo's eyes doing today?" Walter's little dog, Milo, was susceptible to eye infections. Stella had fallen in love with the fluffy dynamo.

"They're clearing up, and thank you for asking. I heard you made George and Vern homemade cookies."

I nodded, hoping he wasn't offended he hadn't gotten any. "I did. We plan to bake again today. Would you like me to drop off a few for you?"

He smiled. "Thank you. I'd love that. What kind are you making?"

"Oatmeal raisin?"

He winced slightly.

"Or maybe lemon cookies."

His lips puckered in a slight frown.

I tried again. "Peanut butter cookies sounded good too."

Walter smiled. "I *love* peanut butter cookies. I'll be around today, so drop them off anytime."

As we walked home, I wondered how I'd become the mother on the block who baked everyone homemade cookies.

At the Martini Monday party that week, I mentioned to the women I needed something to wear for the hockey team's end-of-season banquet.

Martina's ears perked up. "I have a few short, sparkly dresses I wear when I DJ karaoke that might work."

"Where is the dinner being held?" Harley asked.

"The Ritz-Carlton in Rancho Mirage."

She nodded. "Ah. Very chic place. Something almost black tie dressy, but more fun, if you know what I mean."

They dragged me into Laurel's bedroom while the men talked and sipped whiskey out on the back patio. And that was how I ended up in a beautiful, but very short, clingy gold dress.

Isa slapped my hand as I fidgeted with the hem of the gold cocktail dress as we walked into the hotel a few nights later.

"You look stunning, and the length is fine as long as you don't bend over. Or breathe."

I shoved her arm. "Thanks, you're a huge help."

After I dropped Stella off at Javier's house, Isa and I drove over together, which meant Titus hadn't seen my dress yet. When we walked in, I looked around and found him talking with Connor at the bar. They both wore custom-tailored suits, and looked hot as hell.

"When I tried it on at Laurel's house, the skirt seemed long enough. Why is it so short now?" I complained.

"Stop tugging at it," Isa hissed. "It's a perfectly reasonable length."

"Says the woman who wore a pantsuit," I shot back.

She snickered. "I didn't want to flash anyone."

"Bitch, you helped talk me into this dress. I should stick you in my trunk, then drive around to help your family look for you."

Her eyebrow went up. "That was a good one."

"Thanks." I smiled and tugged on the dress one more time.

"If you keep doing that, you could stretch it out and ruin it."

She had a point. I sighed and dropped my hand.

Rudy came over with an appetizer plate full of wrapped sausage wieners. "You two look nice."

Isa grabbed two wieners off his plate and handed one to me. I popped it into my mouth and licked barbeque sauce off my fingers. "Hmm, thanks."

Titus walked over, slid his arm around me, and handed me a glass of sparkling wine as he palmed my bare back. "I would love this dress if we were home alone, and I was getting ready to peel it off you. It gives me dirty ideas, which means it's probably giving a few other people dirty ideas too."

I raised my eyebrow at him.

He sighed. "And you look beautiful in it."

"You look beautiful too."

He grinned and reached over to take a sausage off Rudy's plate.

Rudy sighed and turned back to the buffet table. "I'll get more wieners."

It felt nice standing at Titus's side, surrounded by his teammates and their partners and spouses. I'd gotten to know most of them since we'd started going to the games, and they were so cute with Stella, especially since she'd fallen in love with hockey.

He glanced around and grinned. "It always surprises me that half these assholes can even get dates."

"Most of them are very nice young men who play hockey, and probably have anger management issues."

"You're stereotyping."

I put my hand on his chest. "I'm teasing."

A few minutes later, the presentation dinner started, and Connor and the new coach gave out awards and made brief speeches. Titus won MVP, which wasn't a surprise to anyone. He thanked his teammates, but they couldn't talk him into giving a speech.

The presentation wrapped up before dessert, and I headed to the bathroom. The bathrooms were located down a wide, dimly lit hall with chairs and conversation nooks positioned along the way.

A couple of tan, middle-aged men in nice golf shirts sat near the restrooms. When they saw me walking by, the one in a pink golf shirt smiled at me. I returned his smile out of habit and went into the bathroom. When I came out, the pink-shirted man stepped in front of me.

"Are you already with someone tonight?" he asked.

Cocking my head, I stepped to the side. "Yes." It was an odd question.

When I tried to walk around him, he reached out and took my arm. "I know you're gonna be expensive, but you look like you're worth it. Are you with anyone later? Say, in a couple of hours?" The smell of alcohol wafted off his breath, and his face looked flushed.

When he seized my arm, adrenaline hit me, but I tried to keep my head this time. Why did some men think it was okay to touch women they didn't know?

"I don't like being grabbed." My voice cracked, and I tugged on my arm. But instead of releasing me, he tightened his grip. I tried to back up. "Let go!"

I felt scared now, and his friend just sat there watching us with a look of mild curiosity. Someone yanked the man's hand off. The movement jerked me forward a little, but I got my balance and turned to see who was behind me.

Wyatt stood there, glaring at the man. "She's not an escort, you stupid, drunk asswipe."

My mouth dropped open, and I turned back to the man.

"You thought I was an escort?" I sputtered. "You have got to be kidding me! Are you always this stupid, or is today a special occasion?"

His eyes narrowed. "You smiled at me. And you're wearing that dress."

"You smiled first, you knuckle-dragging, inbred swamp creature. It's a knee-jerk reaction to smile back. As for my dress, you can go screw yourself."

"It's not a big deal, honey," the idiot replied.

My blood pressure skyrocketed, and my ears started ringing. I was heartily sick of being manhandled and afraid, and I poked him hard in the chest. "The way a woman dresses does not mean she's 'saying' yes, or inviting you to touch her. Even if she's an escort!"

The guy's friend finally stood up and grabbed his shoulder. "Come on, Ron. You need to step back."

Ron shook the man's hand off. "You shouldn't be walking the halls of a posh hotel alone in that dress." He looked me up and down. "It was an easy mistake, sweetie."

Wyatt growled beside me. "You need to shut the fuck up right now. Come on Abby, let's go find Titus."

I stood there panting with my hands fisted. "I bet even your mother is sad your father didn't use a condom the day you were conceived."

Wyatt chuckled as he stepped in front of me, and Ron's friend had to hold him back. Wyatt finally steered me back down the hallway.

My hands were shaking, and I was so mad I wanted to hit something. "I can't believe that asshole propositioned me. Who does that? Do I look like an escort to you?"

"Of course not."

"Good answer," I spat.

We walked into the ball room, and Titus spotted us right away. He took one look at me and started stalking over.

"Aw, shit," Wyatt muttered. "Here we go again."

When Titus got to us, I stepped in front of him. "He helped me this time."

Titus paused and settled his hands on my hips. "Why are you upset then?"

"Some asshole grabbed my wrist and propositioned me when I walked out of the women's restroom."

"Where is he?" Titus growled.

"Wyatt pulled him off. I'm fine." I didn't want Titus to get arrested for beating someone up.

Titus turned to Wyatt. "Show me where this fucker is."

Connor walked over. "You guys aren't going to fight here, are you?" he asked cautiously.

Titus shook his head. "Not with each other. But Wyatt is going to show me the bastard who touched Abby and propositioned her outside the bathroom."

Connor rocked on his heels and rubbed his hands together. "Let's go."

I looked at the three of them and realized they were excited.

Titus looked around. "Jackson," he said in a raised voice. Jackson walked over when he heard his name.

"Stay here and watch Abby."

"Where are you going?" Jackson asked.

"To kick someone's ass."

They strode off and Jackson looked at them forlornly.

"I want to see this," Isa declared and ran after them.

Grabbing Jackson's hand, I dragged him behind me. "Come on."

By the time we made it back to the seating area outside the bathrooms, Titus had the pink-shirted golfer pinned up against the wall.

"I didn't know, okay?" the guy whined. "She's beautiful, and all dressed up in that short gold dress, walking around alone at night in an expensive hotel. If that doesn't scream escort, I don't know what does." He laughed nervously.

Titus shook the guy. "You don't approach or proposition a woman, especially one walking down a dark hallway by herself." He leaned in and lowered his voice. "And you sure as fuck don't touch her. She's with me and the hockey team."

The guy glanced over at Connor, Wyatt, and Jackson all scowling at him, and swallowed loudly.

"That's right, you bitch-ass mother fucker," Titus growled softly.

That's when we all saw it. The guy peed his pants, and he was wearing light khaki slacks, so there was no hiding it. Titus looked down, dropped the guy, and stepped back.

"I think you've learned your lesson." He turned around, saw me, walked over, and took my hand. "Is there anything else you need to say?"

I looked down at the guy's pants and shook my head. "No, I think you got the point across. Let's go hit the dessert bar, then go home."

"Well, shit," Wyatt muttered. "That was anti-climactic."

Connor patted his shoulder. "Titus is a 'less-is-more' guy." He looked at the man, whose eyes darted around wildly as he edged away. "And it's effective."

As we walked back to the ballroom, Titus leaned over and whispered in my ear. "When we get home later tonight, I want to peel that dress off and fuck you hard. Does that mean I'm an asshole too?"

"No, and I *want* you to peel off my dress. Let's skip dessert." We were out the door less than a minute later.

Chapter 21

S tella squatted down in front of the kennel and stared at the little guy curled up in the back corner. He watched us, but he didn't get up.

Titus had taken us to lunch that day, but instead of heading back home afterward, he'd parked outside the Palm Springs Animal Shelter.

He turned off his vehicle and looked at us. "I want to show you something."

My leg bounced nervously, and my hands clenched in my lap. "Are you looking for you?"

"I'm looking for us."

His words were like a shot of poison euphoria to my system. If he wanted to adopt an animal "for us" then he expected us to be together for a while. But it was reckless and irresponsible to expect our relationship to last after Titus got custody of Max.

"I don't know where we'll be in a year. Let alone five or ten years." I looked out the window. "And I don't want to break her heart when she has to leave a loved one behind." Stella would have her heart broken either way since she already loved Titus. A lump settled in my throat.

He studied me carefully. "I grew up with dogs, and want that for the kids. I also know where you'll be in a year. Come on."

Titus didn't wait for me. He was unbuckling Stella by the time I climbed out.

The little dog was a gray miniature schnauzer mix. He only weighed seven kilograms and stayed curled up in a little ball in the back of his pen.

Stella crouched down to study him. "What's his name?"

I looked up at the small whiteboard attached to his pen. "Russ, and he's three years old, just like you." I squatted down next to her. "He looks kind of scared, doesn't he?"

She splayed her little fingers on the glass. "Uh-huh. He looks sad."

Titus was still out in the foyer, signing in and talking with the woman at the front desk. But he'd told us which dog had caught his eye on the shelter's website.

An attendant walked up. "Do you guys want to see Russ? It takes a few minutes for him to warm up to people, but he's good on a leash."

The newer facility appeared to be well-run, and all the pens were clean and bright. But a couple of the dogs we'd walked by seemed so beaten down and sad. I could relate to their pain, and it depressed me.

The attendant opened Russ's kennel, and he finally raised his head. Shelly, based on her nametag, clipped a leash onto his collar.

He got up and slowly followed her out. Russ didn't seem to care he was getting out of the pen, but he came along.

Shelly handed me the leash. "You can take him out to the back patio area. There's a playground and some fake grass out there. And if you're interested after that, you could walk him over to the park across the street and get to know him a little better."

Russ turned and headed toward the back door with us in tow. I followed behind him. "He knows where he's going, doesn't he?"

Shelly smiled and walked with us. "Russ is one of my favorites, but I'm not going to lie. He's pretty depressed, and it's turned off a few potential new owners."

"This sounds like a stupid question, but do you know why he's depressed?"

"You're the first person to ask. Yeah, I think I do. His owner died unexpectedly, and the owner's girlfriend didn't want to keep him. So almost overnight, he lost his pack and his home. I'd be depressed too."

"Oh, poor little guy. Will you tell the tall man with the black shirt in the lobby where we are?"

Shelly's eyes lit up and she grinned wide. "You mean the Spartan? Are you two with him?"

My eyebrows went up and Shelly shrugged. "My wife and I are big Thunderbirds fans." She looked down at Stella and recognition hit. "Hey, I've seen you two on the jumbotron a few times. Well, hell. You're his girlfriend, aren't you?"

"I, hmm..."

She shrugged sheepishly. "We follow the *Hot Hockey Times* gossip rag online. There was a story not long ago about the Spartan's blond Barbie babe."

I choked. "Blond Barbie babe?"

"Yeah, that's your nickname. The article has a great photo of you watching him play with this scared, excited, almost constipated look on your face."

Stella tugged on my shirt. "Come on."

Shaking off the disturbing news that there was an article somewhere about Titus and me, not to mention a photo to go along with it that made me appear constipated, we headed out to the back patio area.

Russ stayed next to us as we wandered around the space. He stopped to sniff briefly at the bench leg and a shrub, but he seemed disinterested and disconnected.

Titus walked out a few minutes later. "What's his name?"

Stella stroked the dog's head. "Wuss. And he's sad." She was still working on consistently pronouncing her *r*'s.

I nodded. "She's right. He seems depressed. When we first saw him in his pen, he just laid there, curled up in the corner."

After studying Russ for a moment, Titus knelt and held out his hand. The dog flicked him a gaze, then looked away.

"My *grand-mère* had a little schnauzer, and he was great with kids." Titus considered Russ. "He's small, but not a miniature. And he looks like he's in good health. Let's take him over to the park."

While we walked, I told Titus what Shelly said about his last owner. We strolled along the boardwalk by the Tahquitz golf course, and finally stopped and sat on the grass.

That's when Russ walked over to Stella, nudged her hand, and laid down next to her, resting his chin on her leg. Titus and I watched them carefully, but Stella just patted his side and didn't fuss. Stella could be a little quiet and standoffish with new people too, so it seemed they had a few things in common. We took "Wuss" home with us a half hour later.

Over the next few days, we stocked up on dog supplies, and Titus had a dog door installed going into the backyard. I cringed as I watched the handyman cut a hole in the side of Titus's beautiful home.

"We can take him out when he needs to go," I reminded Titus for the hundredth time.

He grinned and shrugged. "It's too late, the hole's already there. It'll make it more comfortable for all of us."

"But, your beautiful home."

He wrapped his arms around me and kissed my forehead. "It's just a house. The people inside it are what make it a home."

His words hit me softly in the solar plexus. When I was a kid, my father often punished me for leaving toys on the floor or crumbs on the kitchen counter. He would've had a coronary before he put a hole in the wall for a dog to be more comfortable. I'd lived in his house for years, but it was never my home.

The first night, Russ slept under the kitchen table. The next couple of nights, he slept on the dog bed we put in Stella's room. On the fourth night, we found him curled up next to her.

Standing in her doorway, we watched them sleep. Russ raised his head, then laid back down when he saw us.

We backed out, and I turned to Titus. "I'm not sure if I should stop this now or let them figure it out."

Titus shrugged philosophically. "If she doesn't mind, let's leave it. He's not hurting anything."

I picked up my wine glass and sat at the bar. "I'm okay with that. What are we going to do with Russ when we go to Vancouver though?"

"Take him with us."

"But we're flying. And we're going out of the country." I cocked my head. "Is that even possible?"

Titus stood behind me and wrapped his arm around my shoulder. "Yeah, that was part of the reason for the vet visit. I needed to get some paperwork and verify his vaccinations are up to date."

This was a good reminder of how different our worlds were. He didn't think twice about taking a dog out of the country, and I didn't even have a clue a person could.

"What about flying with him?"

He shrugged. "I always charter a jet. And I pay them enough to fly whatever the hell I want as long as it's legal and meets their weight requirements."

"Russ is pretty small, so I think we're good there. Okay. It'll be fun to see Max's reaction to him. And Trixie's."

The next day, I received a phone call from another number I didn't recognize, but with the same area code where my parents lived. This time, whoever it was left a voicemail.

I stared at my phone as the call finally ended, and when the voicemail notification beeped, I jumped a little. Whenever a call came in from an unknown number, my heart always clenched.

Even if the calls were spam, a wrong number, or someone I might know but hadn't programmed their number into my contacts yet. It was another reason I hated my father.

Clicking the message open, I listened to it. "Hello, this is Betty from the U. S. Post Office on Greenwood Avenue in Seattle. I'm calling for Abigail Carver. We have mail for you here, but I don't have a forwarding address. We know it's in Palm Springs somewhere, but we need the exact address. Please call and leave it at this number, and I'll get your mail forwarded to you. Have a nice day."

Before I left Seattle, I set up a forwarding address to Claudette's parents. I trusted them not to give my address out, and so far I'd received junk mail and one tax form they forwarded to me. This was probably a phishing scam, but it was more likely my father trying to get my exact location.

Just in case, I looked online and found the post office located on Greenwood Avenue. I called the number and asked to speak to Betty, but no one worked there with that name. My hands shook as I ended the call. I was now certain my father knew what city I lived in.

Chapter 22

Titus's attorney sat across the desk from us, impatiently tapping his gold pen. Gary Whitmer wore his hair slicked back, had a receding chin, and wore an expensive suit.

When we'd walked into his office, he scanned me dismissively and didn't glance at Stella. While we were in Vancouver to see Max, Titus scheduled an appointment with him to find out what was happening with his custody case.

"I picked the best family law firm I could find, but I ended up with a lazy fuckwad as my attorney," he'd told me on the plane ride over.

Gary shifted in his oversized leather chair. "We'll be ready," he insisted. "The continued hearing is on the calendar."

Titus leaned forward. "That's bullshit. You're not ready, and you haven't done fuck-all to get ready."

The attorney waved his hand. "We still have time–"

"I've had some experience with legal matters, Gary. You need to get your documentation turned over to the opposing counsel and the court well before the hearing, and you haven't done anything. You haven't asked me for shit either. If your incompetence fucks up my case, I'll ruin you." Titus's deep voice was perfectly calm.

Gary quit tapping his pen and straightened. "I'll be ready."

"No, you won't. Because you aren't on my case anymore." As if on cue, a tall middle-aged woman in full makeup and a navy-blue power suit stepped in.

"Hello, Mr. Tremblay. I'm Fran Drummond, a partner here. I hope you're coming back to Vancouver next season because our hockey team needs you. My assistant told me you asked one of the partners to step in on this meeting."

Titus turned to Fran. "I was just telling Gary that he hasn't done shit on my case, and I'm firing him. Do I need to fire your firm as well or is there a competent attorney who can take over?"

The woman's eyes narrowed as she took us in. "Let's take this meeting to the conference room if that's alright. I'd like to have another partner sit in."

We walked into the glass-walled conference room. There were some nice toys and a play rug situated in one corner, and for the first time since we arrived, my shoulders loosened a little.

I turned to Stella. "We need to talk with these people. Do you want to see what toys they have?" I pointed to the corner.

She turned, the toys catching her eyes. "Okay."

Titus touched her shoulder. "We won't be long, *ma puce*. And when we get done, we'll go get Russ, then meet Max and find some lunch." She nodded and went to explore the toys.

Less than twenty minutes later, Gary had been fired—from Titus's case and the firm. It sounded like Titus wasn't the only one who'd complained about him.

Fran's partner walked out with a red-faced Gary, and Fran turned to us and sighed. "Is there any way I can talk you into continuing the hearing?"

Titus shook his head. "Fuck, no. It's been continued twice already, and Gary shouldn't have let the second continuance happen. What do you need from me?"

Fran rubbed her temples and stared at Titus's file on her computer. "I need... everything. Documentation about your preparations for custody of Max, photos of your home, proof you have a pediatrician lined up, a plan outlining your son's daily care, that kind of thing. There's nothing here."

Scooting forward, I put my backpack on the table and pulled out my laptop. "I've been collecting that information, and I have a file ready." Titus turned to me and tilted his head in question. "I told you I spoke with Laurel about this." I looked back to Fran. "By the way, his son's name is Max. He's almost two, and he's sweet and a little possessive of Stella. He also looks and acts a lot like Titus."

Nodding, Fran smiled and picked up a business card, sliding it over to us. "Can you send me the file? Here's my email address."

"I'll do it right now. We'd like you to review it before we leave today so you can give us a list of additional items or information you want before we walk out. I assume the judge will also have questions for us. Can we get a list of those potential questions?"

Titus's lips quirked, and he squeezed my thigh under the table. I patted his hand, pulled up the file, and emailed Fran a copy. She opened it and skimmed over what I'd gathered.

As she studied her computer, she slowly relaxed and her brow unfurled. "This is great. Very thorough." She glanced up at us. "We'll be ready."

Titus breathed out slowly. We owed Laurel, who'd talked to Ramone and emailed me with a few additional ideas.

When we walked back into Titus's condo, Russ trotted excitedly out of Stella's room to greet us. He'd warmed up a little over the past week, and he had no problem with flying.

"Hi, little guy. Did you miss us?" I squatted down and Russ came over for a head scratch.

After taking Russ out for a pee break, we met Trixie and Max at a big outdoor shopping mall. Russ pranced along next to us as we walked. Trixie was late again, and we waited for fifteen minutes before she walked up wearing a sleek black jumpsuit and red stilettos.

The outfit would have looked great if we were meeting at an expensive restaurant or a nightclub. But it was a weekday afternoon at an outdoor suburban mall. I looked down at my black leggings and patched jacket. I was probably under-dressed, but Titus hadn't complained.

Max's stroller was again loaded down with shopping bags. When his eyes lit on Titus, he immediately started slipping out of the stroller.

"Da Da," he chanted. Then he noticed Stella and his body seemed to vibrate. "Mine!"

Trixie lurched forward. "Fucking hell, Maxie. You're going to land on your head." He balanced precariously on the front of his stroller. Trixie plucked him up by his arm and deposited him on the ground, her red, manicured fingernails vivid against his little black jacket.

Titus knelt and Max ran into his arms. Stella stood next to me, bracing herself against my leg. After a moment, Max wriggled out of Titus's arms and threw himself against Stella. Russ backed up a little, and his leash wrapped around my leg.

Their combined body weight threw me back a few inches, but I chuckled. "Hi, Max. It's good to see you too." He didn't glance at me, but squeezed Stella and chattered happily at her.

I put my hands on top of their heads and looked at Trixie. "Hello. You look nice."

Her red lips curled down as she took me in with the two little kids braced against my legs and Russ standing next to us. "You're so sugary sweet, you make my teeth ache."

I raised my eyebrow. "That's better than making you nauseous, I guess."

Max noticed Russ just then and started pointing and jabbering.

Trixie turned to Titus and rolled her eyes. "I doubt she's going to keep you satisfied long. Not with your tastes, baby. Where'd you find her anyway? A Sears catalog? And they threw in the mutt for free, I bet." She laid her red-tipped hand on Titus's arm. "When do you plan to drop him off?"

I turned away to watch Max hug Stella again, then he squatted to check Russ out. I knelt to supervise the introduction.

Titus pulled her hand off his arm and raised his eyebrow. "Quit being a bitch, Trixie. We're flying out late Friday morning, so we'll bring him by around eight."

"Whatever, asshole," she snapped. "Do you want the stroller or not?"

Titus turned to me. "Do you want the stroller, *mon coeur*?"

Trixie froze, and her face paled. Titus had called me his heart in French.

"No, we have one in the car. But we need his backpack."

Trixie prowled behind the stroller, then turned and bent over so we had a direct view down the front of her jumpsuit. Her breasts were on full display in a black pushup bra. Titus didn't even glance her way.

She grabbed Max's backpack and walked back over, slamming it into Titus's chest. "Make sure he gets lunch."

When she took off, I looked up at Titus. "Well, that was... something. She likes you."

Shaking his head, he put Max's backpack on his shoulder. "We tolerate each other."

"You didn't see her face when you called me *mon coeur*." I wanted to ask him if he said it just to irritate her, but I didn't have the courage.

He shrugged. "I got Max out of the deal, so I try to be civil. We've got a couple of full days here. What would you like to do?"

"Connor said there's a neat aquarium and a zoo. He also talked about a science museum. Would you and Max like to see any of those?"

Scooping Max up, he put his other arm around my shoulder. "If you and Stella are there, Max and I don't give a shit. What do you think about the aquarium today since it looks like it might rain?"

"Sounds perfect."

The kids loved the aquarium, and so did I. We had to keep Max from slamming his hands against the huge tank with all the bright, tropical fish, and he squealed when a big octopus swam by. I made Titus take a few selfies of all of us together to send to Nana as we wandered through.

When we walked into Titus's condo building late that after-noon, Carla was checking her mailbox in the foyer. I knew we'd inevitably run into her, but I'd hoped it wouldn't be so soon. Her face lit up when she saw Titus, but she barely glanced at the rest of us.

"Hey! You're back. Oh, and you have a dog now." She knelt and made kissy faces at Russ. "What's his name?"

I held Russ's leash, and he stared up at Carla, then sat against my leg. "His name is Russ," I said quietly.

She straightened and gazed at Titus. "How long are you going to be in town? My offer of a good Canadian whiskey, a soak in the hot tub, and a full body massage is still open."

Titus wrapped his arm around my shoulders and kissed the side of my head. "I think you've met Abby. We also just got back from the aquarium and the kids are tired. Have a good night."

Carla gawked at us, with his arm wrapped around my shoul-der, and the kids flanking us. Then she turned to me and her face went pale. I felt a little sorry for her, even though she'd written me off as unimportant.

I held up my hand as we started walking to the elevators. "Nice to see you again." Titus pulled me closer when we got inside, and I watched the doors close on Carla's angry, hurt face, fervently hop-ing it was the last time I had to stand there while she propositioned him in the foyer.

On the last night in Vancouver, I made my homemade mac and cheese after we got home from the park down the street.

"Moe," Max said when he'd devoured the mac and cheese on his plate.

I gave him another scoop and smirked as I took him in. "You're a mess, little man. You even have noodles in your hair."

Russ had taken a liking to Max, mostly because Max dropped food on the floor and Russ got to clean it up.

I turned to Stella. "Do you want any more?"

She shook her head. "No, thank you."

Max lifted a sticky hand to check his head, getting even more ketchup and cheese sauce in his hair.

Titus pushed his chair back, grabbed a wet washcloth, and wiped Stella and Max down. "Let's get ready for bed so we can read a few books together," he said.

Stella and I cleaned up, then snuggled on the living room couch as we waited for Titus to give Max a quick bath.

When Max walked in, freshly bathed with his little hockey pajamas on, he came over and climbed up on my lap like he'd done it a hundred times. Then he grabbed Stella's hand and tried to pull her onto my lap too. When she understood what he wanted, she climbed up next to him and I wrapped my arms around both of them, sniffing their hair while they giggled. Titus walked in and leaned against the doorframe, smiling.

I squeezed the kids and then held up a couple of books. "Alright. Are we reading about stinky garbage trucks or how two of the three little pigs get eaten?" Stella laughed, so Max started laughing too. Then we took turns reading.

When we returned from Vancouver on Friday evening, a big package sat on Titus's doorstep, and my stomach lurched.

Titus glanced at it. "Are you expecting anything?"

"Yes. It's from Edna, the Cherry Box's assistant. Or, I guess my assistant."

Edna texted me a couple of days ago to let me know our manufacturer was sending a few proposed monthly subscription boxes for me to review and approve. Claudette and Gabriel would also be coming in a couple of days. Time had run out for me to tell Titus about my new online business, and the fact he hadn't heard about it from someone else was a minor miracle.

"I still haven't seen your website," he said absently, as we unpacked from our trip.

My eyes skidded around the kitchen, not making eye contact. "Yeah, about that. When Stella goes to bed, we need to talk." I cringed as soon as the words were out of my mouth. "It's nothing bad!" I paused. "At least, I don't think it's bad. But maybe you'll think..." My shoulders slumped.

He straightened and studied me. "Stella's dead on her feet. I'll tuck her and Russ in if you want to get ready for bed. And then we'll talk." Titus helped Stella brush her teeth and wash her face and hands. It had been a busy few days in Vancouver, and she crashed as soon as she crawled into bed.

I also cleaned up and changed into one of my kimonos. Then after kissing Stella goodnight and giving Russ a pet, I lugged the box into Titus's room. He walked out of the bathroom in his sleep shorts as I set the box on the end of the bed and sat next to it with my laptop.

Then I mentally straightened my spine and looked up at him. "I'm sorry. I haven't been totally honestbut in my defense…" I paused. "I don't actually have a good defense."

His brow furrowed, and he pushed off the wall. "Tell me."

Blowing a chunk of hair out of my face, I opened my laptop and typed in the Cherry Box website. "Let me show you. I'm a big coward and I worried about what you'd think."

Turning my laptop around, I showed him the website. "Claudette offered to sell it to me without any money upfront. I think it's as much a gift as a business transaction. The site makes good money, and it's something I can do while still being at home with Stella and Max."

He scanned the website, and his eyebrows shot up. He gently took the laptop out of my hands and sat down. "This is the online 'toy store' you're taking over?" he asked.

"Yes." I jumped up and started pacing as he scrolled through the site. "I can work from home and work smarter and not harder. Claudette has it running smoothly. The only thing is…" I ran out of steam and stopped rambling.

Peeling his eyes off the site, he fixed on me. "What?"

My body broke out into a sweat. "I don't… That is, I'm not…"

He set the computer down and studied my face. "Use your words, *cocotte*. Talk to me."

The dam broke, and all my insecurities spilled out. "I don't know what I'm doing! My background is in building and maintaining websites, and I know about drop shipping and that kind of thing. But I've had sex with exactly two guys." I held up two fingers. "And the first guy doesn't count because he was *horrible.*

And you? You're so far from horrible it isn't funny. I mean, I had an orgasm with you inside me, and that's not normal."

I continued pacing and rambling. "And the Cherry Box website? There are things on there that I've never even *heard* of. I've owned exactly one vibrator."

Stopping in front of the large package, I pointed at it. "And Edna sent me three Cherry Boxes to critique. How am I going to critique *anything*?"

I glanced back at Titus and lost steam. During my nervous rant, he'd leaned back against the headboard and laced his hands behind his head, my computer resting on his lap.

"What?" I asked.

His lips twitched. "I'm just listening."

"Maybe I didn't tell you exactly what I'd be selling, but I *did* tell you." I chewed on my bottom lip.

"Mm, that's a big stretch. You told me the online shop sold toys."

"That's actually accurate. A little misleading, but true."

He shook his head. "A *little* misleading? That's like saying the Mojave Desert gets a little warm in the summertime."

"I'm sorry." My shoulders slumped. "I should have told you."

"It makes me think you don't trust me."

Sitting next to him, I put my hand on his thigh. "I do trust you, as much as I trust Isa, or Claude and Gabriel." He grunted when I brought Gabriel's name up, but I pushed on. "I was embarrassed, and afraid you'd think it was wrong or inappropriate. Or some crap my parents would have spewed at me."

I realized that their constant disapproval and judgment still colored my life. My father's reaction would've been explosive and volatile, but Titus seemed amused and a little disappointed I hadn't just told him. If I wasn't careful, I could fall in love with this man.

He looked back at the website. "Why would I think that? It seems like a good opportunity for you, and it gives me so many ideas. Now, let's do some product research." Titus put my computer on the nightstand and swung his legs over the side of the bed. "We can unpack the boxes together. And I'll make sure you know how everything works."

I sputtered. "Wait, what? No!"

Chapter 23

He started toward the end of the bed where the large box sat, but I stood up and positioned myself in front of him with my hands up. "I'll open them tomorrow. I don't need your help, I'm a big girl."

"I know you are, and it's cute you think you can block me." He reached in and grabbed my waist, spun around, and deposited me behind him. Then he started pulling the tape off the large box before I fully realized what he'd done.

"How about I go through the subscription boxes tomorrow, and if there's anything I can't figure out, I'll ask you?"

"Or how about we go through one together tonight?" Pulling out a dark red box, he studied it. "Nice packaging." The red box had a black buckle holding it closed, with the Cherry Box logo stamped on top showing red lips licking two plump cherries.

"Give me that." I lunged for the box.

"No."

I jumped on his back and wrapped my arm around his neck, trying to reach it. "How about you give me the box, and no one gets hurt?"

He laughed and held it in front of him, out of my reach. With his other hand, he reached around and grabbed my ass. "Or how about we open a box and play together?"

Sliding off his back, I stepped around to his front and wrapped my arms around his waist. "You aren't going to let this go, are you?"

He grinned, holding the box up over his head out of my reach. "Fuck, no. And I want to see your reactions to every single item in those boxes. I'll get to watch you squirm, blush, and get all hot and bothered."

Backing up a little, I hopped a few times and tried to grab it out of his hand. "I'm already squirming and blushing." I couldn't help it, I started snickering when he brought the box down a little, teasing me with it.

He wrapped his arm around my waist, pulled me into him, and held me still. Then Titus leaned in and bit and kissed my neck. "Don't you want to know what's in it? I bet I can make you beg from just using one toy in here." His voice went even lower, and my insides clenched.

I stopped trying to grab it. "Oh, yeah? What if I can make *you* beg?"

He grinned and nipped my lips. "Even better. Let's do a little product testing tonight since you say you trust me."

Damn it, I couldn't say no now, and if I could get over my embarrassment and awkwardness, I did want to know what was in the box. And I wanted to do it with him. Lust and indecision swirled through me, my toes curling into the rug.

"Okay. I do need to open them, and I hear you're an expert."

His wicked smile gave me pause, but before I could change my mind, he pulled me over to the bed, turned us around, and sat me between his legs.

Then he quickly opened the box, pushing aside the wrapping, and pulling out a pair of large black dice in a red silk bag.

"Those aren't too bad," I said. Then I got a closer look. There were different sexual positions carved into one die, and explicit words like "suck" and "lick" on the other. Pointing to one of the positions, I turned to Titus. "I take that back. Is that even anatomically possible?"

He laid his chin on my shoulder. "Yeah, but it's a tricky one. We'll work up to it." I could hear laughter in his voice.

"Okay, then." I set the dice aside and pulled out a small bottle, reading the label. "Watermelon flavored edible clit sensitizing gel." My face flamed.

He took it and set it on the nightstand. "Well definitely be using that tonight." My insides throbbed in response, and I shifted my hips against him.

Pushing aside more wrapping, he pulled out a black lace thong with adjustable ties on the sides. There was something inside the small front panel, and when he flipped it around, I noticed a vibrator tucked inside.

"Is that a remote-controlled vibrator?" I asked.

"Yep. And the vibrator goes into this little pouch right over your pussy." He kissed my shoulder. "We'll try it tomorrow to see if the thong is a good fit, and what the distance is on the remote control."

"Oh, Lord." I held my thighs together.

He nodded to the box. "Why don't you pull out the next toy?"

"Because I'm scared."

Titus cradled my backside between his thighs. "But are you wet?"

"Yes," I admitted.

"Go on, they aren't going to bite."

Reaching in, I pulled out a small black box. When I opened it, a pair of silver nipple clamps with little flowers on them winked up at me.

I held the box up to Titus's face. "What were you just saying about not biting?"

Chuckling, he wrapped his arm around my chest. "I take that back. Those will bite."

He reached in and pulled out a black paddle shaped like a heart, with red ribbons tied around its base. "This one might bite too, depending on how hard I use it."

Watching Titus handle the paddle like he knew how to use it made my insides clench. Next, I lifted out a long, red satin sash. It looked like it could be used as a blindfold or a restraint. He made a low sound and twirled the paddle around, studying it and the blindfold together, like he was imagining using them on me. Then he set them down and pulled out the last item. It was a teal blue, bulbous toy with a base. It looked vaguely familiar, but I couldn't place it.

"Is that also a vibrator?" I asked.

He spoke softly in my ear. "It's a vibrating anal plug. It's not too big, but you'll know it's there." His thick, rigid cock seemed to pulse beneath my bottom.

I curled into him a little. I'd never had anal sex, and the mechanics of it were a little fuzzy to me. My breathing sped up, and my skin tingled where he lightly caressed me. Vivid images of Titus using some of the toys we'd pulled out of the box played in my mind.

Setting the plug down next to the paddle, he put the box to the side. Then he slid his hand down my stomach and guided his fingers across my slit. "You're so warm and wet, *ma bonne fille*. Are you ready to play?"

My hips shifted restlessly, and he curled his palms under my knees, lifted my legs apart, and draped them over his thighs. Cool air touched my damp pussy as he reached around me and ran his fingers over my clit again. I moaned and moved against him.

"I'll take that as a yes. Do you want to use the vibrating plug first?"

My eyes snapped open, and my legs tried to close but his knees held them in place. "After you."

He chuckled, gave my clit one more stroke, then rolled me onto my back and laid me on the bed. "I'm teasing. We'll work up to the anal plug, but I want to try the clit sensitizer and see how watermelon tastes with your pussy. And then I'd like to bite, suck, and then clamp your beautiful pink nipples."

While he positioned us so we faced each other on the bed, he slid his hand up my torso and cupped my breast. Then he ran his thumb across my nipple and rubbed it until it peaked. He sat up and pulled my kimono over my head, straddling my thighs. "Let's do some research. Starting with this."

Reaching over me, Titus grabbed the long, thick strip of red satin. "Have you ever had your hands tied during sex?"

"No." The cool, silky tie slithered over my skin, and my nipples went even harder. The only sex I'd had was usually in the missionary position, and it had been uninspired and one-sided. Until I met Titus, I didn't think about sex much. Now, it seemed like I craved it all the time.

"My guess is there's going to be wrist cuffs, ties, or some other type of restraint in the Cherry Box almost every month. For a reason." He leaned over and slowly gathered my wrists together and tied them up, watching my face as he worked.

"Why?" I whispered.

He shrugged. "A lot of people like giving up control, or feeling overpowered." Pulling me up a little, he wound the remaining length around his headboard. "Others like the element of danger and excitement. Some find it relaxing."

My legs shifted restlessly, and I tugged on the tie. Lust flared in my stomach when it held tight. "What do you like about it?"

He knelt back on his heels and studied me for a few seconds, his breath heavy. "The way you look, tied up and stretched out under me. Panting in need, with your cheeks flushed and your nipples stiff." His head tilted. "Speaking of nipples." He reached over and pulled the clamps out of the little black box.

My heart rate skyrocketed. "Oh, God," I whimpered.

He smirked and kissed my mouth hard and fast. "If you own an online adult toy store, you better get used to testing nipple clamps. And you might learn to crave the bite. These tits are a gorgeous

handful, and I want to feast. But for now, let's decorate them."
He leaned down and took each nipple into his mouth, working
them over until they were tight and hard.

I watched in fascinated horror when he grabbed a clamp and
attached it. Pain and something else shot through me, and my
back arched as I cried out.

He watched my face as I adjusted to the feel. "Is it getting
better?"

I panted and nodded. "It still stings a little."

His eyes sparked, and he reached down to cup my center. "And
you just went from wet to soaking. You ready for the second one?"

I nodded. As it bit into my stiff nipple, my head flew back. "Oh
Lord! Please," I panted.

He lightly flicked each one with his index finger. "See? I told
you I could make you beg using a toy in this box tonight. Now
let's see if I can make it two."

My hips shifted restlessly, and I tried to hook him with my feet.
"We can quit here. I think two toys are enough."

He crawled over me and grabbed the clit sensitizer from the
nightstand. "Or we can keep going, and I can eat out your water-
melon-flavored pussy. I vote for option two."

My thighs rubbed together. "What does it do?"

He opened the bottle and squirted a generous amount on his
fingertips. "It increases blood flow to your clitoris, and makes it
more sensitive." He slowly worked the gel into me, then leaned
over and tugged a little on the nipple clamps.

My torso jerked to the side, trying to get away from him. "I'm
going to ask Edna to include a torture device for men in the next
Cherry Box."

He grinned then leaned back and studied me. "You feel any-thing yet?"

"Yes. It tingles, and I want..." My hips shifted restlessly.

"Use your words, *ma cocotte.*"

Need turned to frustration, and my head whipped back and forth. "Tremblay, I swear to God if you tell me to use my words one more time, I'm going to rip out your tongue."

"If you did that, then I couldn't do this." He leaned in and ran his tongue over my clit.

Fireworks exploded in my center, and frustration turned to red-hot desire. He licked and sucked on me, then slid a finger inside.

"Okay," I panted. "You can keep your tongue." I felt him smile against my pussy.

I hadn't understood that sex could be like this. Titus knew what my body needed and craved better than I did. He monitored my responses and checked in with me frequently to see if I was still wet and panting for him.

Titus lapped and flicked my clit until I vibrated underneath him. He knew where to touch, and how much pressure or friction to use. I'd ponder about how he'd gotten so good at this later.

He slid another finger inside me, and I lifted my hips off the bed, trying to get closer to his mouth. My hands tugged against the tie again, and if they'd been free, I would have grabbed his hair while he worked me. When he fluttered his tongue relentlessly against me, my orgasm broke, and I moaned out his name.

Working his fingers in and out while I spasmed around him, he wiped his mouth against my thigh. When my contractions eventually stopped, he crawled up my body and kissed me. I could taste the watermelon gel mixed with my juices, and when he pulled back, I licked my lips and gazed at him with heavy eyes.

"Please, I need you inside me."

"Fuuck me," he moaned. Titus lifted my hips up, notched his cock against my soaking wet entrance, and slammed into me. My body slid up the bed, and I braced my still-tied hands against the headboard as he hammered into me.

Reaching down, he grabbed my ankles and hooked them over his shoulders, then he lifted my hips up to meet his brutal thrusts. My eyes rolled back, but he reached down and wrapped his hand around my neck.

"No. You're going to watch me fuck you." Then he growled in French while he drilled into me, and even though I didn't know what dirty things he was saying, my pussy contracted around him in response.

He slowed down several times so he wouldn't come, and my insides hummed in pleasure. Suddenly, he stopped and pulled out.

"What are you doing?" I cried out.

Rummaging around, he pulled out the small vibrator that came with the thong. "Let's test one more thing from your box tonight." With a flick, he turned it on and adjusted the setting. Then he pressed it against me.

My clit still throbbed and pulsed from my orgasm, and when the vibrator hit me, my head flew back as my thighs tried to crush his hand.

He chuckled and wedged his body between them. "Too much?"

"Yes!" I howled.

He pulled the vibrator off and slammed back into me.

My muscles unclenched. Until he placed the vibrator back. "No...yes! Please! It's too... I can't..." But my hips arched up to meet him.

He continued thrusting. "Yes, you can. I want another orgasm out of you tonight." The vibrator buzzed against me as Titus flicked the nipple clamps with his other hand, and then he shoved deep inside me. And I felt his tip hit my swollen cervix.

The sensations were too much. I arched my head back and came on a long wail as he shoved inside one last time and flooded me with his hot come. He held my hips up, suspended against his cock, while he locked over me with the vibrator still pressed to my clit.

My mind couldn't hold a thought as it sizzled and crackled like a neon sign. My body hummed with an overload of endorphins and dopamine as Titus finally turned off the vibrator and gently laid me back down. I felt his fingers on my breasts, and when he unclipped the nipple clamps, blood flowed into my nipples.

"Ouch," I whispered.

He chuckled and bent down to suck each nipple, then kissed the tips. Even after everything we'd just done and two hard orgasms, a zing went through me. This man was methodically ruining me for anyone else.

Reaching up, he worked on the ties holding my wrists together, then massaged my arms. Finally, he sat against the headboard and pulled me into his lap, uncaring about the moisture trickling out of me and the sweat coating our bodies.

"Are you doing alright?"

My mind still drifted in chemicals, and it took me a moment to find my voice. "I think I'm high on something."

He smiled into my hair and squeezed me to him. "Product testing is my new favorite thing. But we didn't get to the vibrating butt plug."

"You say that like it's a bad thing."

Chapter 24

When Claudette and Gabriel arrived a few days later, I opened the door and threw my arms wide. "I'm so happy to see you guys!" I hugged Gabe long and hard, kissed his cheeks, then smacked his butt. "And you. Why haven't you kept in touch?" He looked me up and down and hugged me again, and I felt his comforting, sinewy frame.

Then I turned to Claude and loudly kissed both her cheeks. She wore a mustard yellow silk top and purple fitted pants, her innate Parisian style on full display.

Even though Claudette and Gabriel were a couple of years apart, they looked like fraternal twins. They were both tall, with curly, brown hair and lush black eyebrows. But while Claudette enjoyed nice clothes and fashionable shoes, Gabe usually wore jeans and pullovers. He still had a lean swimmer's build, but his eyes were more serious now.

"We missed you too." Claudette hugged me again. "Oh my God, I love this weather and sunshine, and this town has so much *style*. I can't believe I've never been here before."

"We'll show you around over the next few days. Come in." Stella stood in the entryway with Russ, watching us curiously.

Gabe stopped short and studied her for a few seconds. "Hi, Stella. Wow, you've grown so much. Do you remember me?" Stella searched his face, then looked up at me.

I got a little teary. "This is Gabe. He's the one who gave you your yellow blanket. We used to live with him before Grandma and Grandpa."

She hugged her blanket and smiled. "My blankie."

"I'm glad you still have it. You're so grown up." Gabe let out a breath, straightened, and glanced around.

We walked into the kitchen area, and Claude put her Hermès purse on the counter. "Nice digs. Where's Titus?"

"He's at the arena. They're finishing up some post-season stuff." I clapped my hands. "I'm so happy you're here. I can't tell you how much I missed you."

Pulling out a few appetizers and drinks, we sat around the kitchen bar and caught up.

"Gabe, how's work? Do you still see Elias?"

"Work is fine, but I'm thinking about taking over Mom and Dad's export business."

I nodded, not surprised.

He glanced at the windowsill above the kitchen sink where a basil plant grew. "I remember you growing herbs around the house when we lived together. I miss your cooking." He gazed around the kitchen. "Elias is engaged."

My eyes went wide. "What? No way."

We were sitting around the bar laughing and talking when Titus walked in. Stella ran over and wrapped her arm around his leg.

He squeezed her shoulder as he studied us. "How was your day, *ma puce?*"

She smiled at him. "Good. Can we play?"

"Absolutely." He looked back down at her. "We'll play hockey after dinner, alright? I need to meet your mom's friends."

He came over and wrapped his hand around the back of my neck, then tilted my head back for a kiss, and murmured in my ear. "Introduce me."

"Of course. And my day was nice too."

He smirked and kissed me again. "Good."

I introduced everyone, and Claude gave Titus a little wave. "It's nice to meet you, even though you've beaten me out of being Stella's second favorite person."

"She loves hockey like she loves her yellow blanket, so that gives me an edge. I hear you're moving to Berlin soon, and Abby's buying the Cherry Box. We've enjoyed testing the products."

Claudette started laughing.

"Fucking hell," Gabe muttered.

My eyes went wide. "I can't believe you just said that."

Titus shrugged. "It's true. Last night when I used the water-proof handcuffs–"

My hand slapped across his mouth. "They get the idea, and Stella is *right here*. Nobody wants to hear the details." He grinned under my hand.

"I do," Claudette volunteered.

The doorbell rang, and I carefully pulled my hand away, ready to cover his mouth again if he continued talking.

Claudette put her drink down. "I'll get it. I'm sure it's Isa and Connor."

We heard them greeting each other. Titus and Gabe stared at each other, and Gabe's eyes narrowed.

"You've been invited to Martini Monday," I heard Isa say as they all walked into the kitchen. "I want you to meet the rest of our friends here."

Connor shook Gabe's hand, and Isa gave him a big hug. "Hey, I missed you." She turned to Connor. "He's one of our other best friends, and Abby lived with him for a couple of years."

Connor's eyebrows shot up. "Two years, huh? Were you two an item? Did you share a bed?"

Isa turned to Connor. "I know you like to needle Titus, but don't embarrass Abby."

"No." Gabriel turned to me. "We never did, unfortunately."

My body locked and my mouth fell open. What did he just say? Connor started laughing.

Titus leaned against the counter and crossed his arms. "*C'est ma femme.*"

Gabe smirked. "*Pour l'instant.*"

I translated their French the best I could. *She's my woman. For the moment.* Then they started speaking rapidly in French, and I lost the conversation.

"Well, fuck." Claudette put her hands on her hips and started talking to Gabriel in French. She sounded exasperated.

"I wish we knew what they were saying," Isa muttered.

"Me too." I watched them and wiped my sweaty palms on my shorts. Gabriel had always treated me like a little sister, and then a best friend. I didn't understand what was happening. Had I missed any signs? My mind raced as I tried to make sense of the situation.

Isa pointed to Connor. "You look way too pleased with yourself." Connor's lips twitched, but he gave her an innocent shrug. She stepped forward and clapped her hands at them. "Okay, you three. It's pretty damn rude to speak French in front of us, and I'm starving. Let's order pizza and then play street hockey with Stella."

Pointing between Gabriel and Titus, I scowled. "Are you two going to tell me what that was about?"

Titus pulled me in for a kiss. I struggled for about two seconds, but when he nipped my bottom lip, I went still and kissed him back.

He raised his head, studied my flushed face and hooded eyes, and smiled. "No."

I could hear Isa and Claude laughing and Gabriel swearing. Then Titus walked out to the garage with Stella to set up the hockey nets. We ended up pulling out a couple of brooms, and even a mop, since we only had four little hockey sticks.

I turned to Claudette. "We play out here a couple of times a week. It's been one of her favorite gifts. Thank you again."

Claude smiled as she took in the cul-de-sac with all of us standing around, holding comically small hockey sticks or brooms. "This is exactly what I hoped for when I gave it to her."

I fought the lump in my throat. "I want to come visit you in Berlin."

"I'm holding you to that."

Connor and Titus became the captains by default, and Stella went over and stood next to Titus.

"Smart girl," Isa muttered. Connor swatted her butt, and she yelped. "What? You've been retired for almost six years. You're probably rusty."

"We'll see how rusty I am tonight, little girl." He grabbed her around the waist, and she laughed.

We split up into teams and laid out some ground rules, then played a few surprisingly competitive games.

"Fuck!" Gabriel hissed when Titus hit him hard with the puck for the second time. Titus grinned.

We played until we broke a hockey stick and a broom, and it was too dark to see the puck. After putting the set away, we sat around on the back patio enjoying the perfect desert evening and sipping drinks. Soft lighting illuminated the palm trees, and the smell of rosemary scented the air while a lone cricket chirped in the bushes. I loved these desert nights.

When Stella started falling asleep, Titus carried her inside, and I got her ready for bed. We kissed her, tucked her in, and walked back outside together.

When we sat again, Isa asked Claudette about the Cherry Box. "Are you ready to hand over the reins?"

Claudette smiled. "Yes. It's been a lot of fun getting it set up and established. But I'm ready to move on to a couple of other projects."

Connor leaned forward and grinned. "So, you're the friend who gave Isa a monthly subscription to the Cherry Box. I've enjoyed the fuck out of those. Best present ever."

Claude snickered and inclined her head. "Thank you, I'm glad you both liked it. And now I'm selling the business to Abby since I'm moving out of the country soon." She turned to me. "And Titus says he also enjoys the boxes."

I groaned and took a big sip of wine. "Oh, Lord. No one wants to hear this."

Connor threw a chip at Titus. "Lucky bastard."

Isa leaned forward. "Claudette, we told our friends about the website, and they love your product reviews."

She smirked. "Here's a tip. I only write those when I'm a little drunk. Either on wine or post-coital chemicals."

Titus grinned. "I'll help her with the post-coital chemicals."

"I can't hear this," Gabriel muttered and stood up.

I went stiff and my heart rate spiked. "Gabriel, stop. Why are you doing this?"

"Abby, you're ten years younger than this cradle-robbing bastard. And he's already gotten another woman pregnant and didn't stick around. Do you really want to go through that again?"

My breath froze in my lungs. I couldn't believe he'd throw that at me. "You don't know–"

Titus squeezed my hand and straightened. "It's alright. If I were him, I'd feel gutted too." Then he turned to Gabriel. "She lived with you for two years and you didn't make a move. She lived with me for two months, and I knew I'd do whatever I needed to lock her down." He leaned in and growled, "And I'm fucking *keeping* her."

Gabriel considered Titus. "She was young and scared, and she'd just been royally fucked over by that stupid sperm donor. And for the first two years of Stella's life? *I* was there." Gabe hit his chest with his palm. "I gave Stella that little yellow blanket, helped change her diapers, fed and played with her." Gabriel ran his hand through his hair. "So yeah, it does fucking gut me to see you with them."

Isa stood. "Connor and I are leaving. You guys need to talk without an audience." She looked at Titus and Gabriel. "Damn it, I love you both. But, Gabriel, your timing sucks and you're an ass for putting her in this position."

We all stood, and Gabriel turned to me. "I'm sorry I didn't make you and Stella come with me when I left Seattle. You don't know how sorry I am, and I understand you're with him now. But I want to talk to him alone. Will you give me that?"

My heart squeezed painfully, and I slowly turned to Titus.

He cupped my cheek. "We'll be fine."

"Please don't hurt him."

"I won't physically hurt him, but there's not much I can do about the rest."

I nodded and rested my forehead against his sternum, breathing him in. I reached out and squeezed Gabe's hand as I walked out with Claude.

The full moon illuminated the street as we walked around the block to give them privacy. I'd never strolled in the neighborhood at night before. It was so peaceful and quiet in the moonlight.

"How did I miss it?" I asked softly.

She glanced at me. "When you first moved in, it was just friendship. I don't think he meant to fall in love with you, but by the time he graduated, and you insisted on moving out and letting him get on with his life, he didn't know how to tell you."

I stopped and faced her. "He never said or did anything that made me think he felt that way."

"Gabe probably thought you needed time to grow up a little, and he could come back for you. I'm guessing this, but I know him better than anyone."

"He's one of my best friends. I don't want to lose him."

"He'll have to decide that. We didn't know how bad things were with your parents last year." She turned to me, her eyes shimmering with tears. "I'm so sorry."

Guilt and shame rose in my chest. I thought I'd finally moved past having my father taint all my relationships. "It's not your responsibility to take care of me, and Gabriel shouldn't have felt obligated to protect me and make sure we had a roof over our heads. And now I've hurt him." My voice broke.

"Don't take on that guilt. It's not your fault you moved in with a hot-as-hell, ripped, French Canadian hockey player who looks at you like he adores you but also wants to tie you up and breed you."

"You've been reading too many dark romances again, haven't you?"

She snorted and looked up at the starry sky. "There's no such thing."

"I don't know what to do to make this right. He and Elias gave up so much for Stella and me."

"Abby, you aren't a burden, and it wasn't a hardship. They love you and adored all your fussing and cooking. And the fact that you're sweet, beautiful, and a little snarky didn't hurt either. Damn, I remember being jealous of the treats and lunches you made for them. No wonder Gabe loves you."

Memories of our little house with the crooked porch and overgrown hedges flitted through my mind. It always smelled vaguely of mold and cedarwood. Elias's guitar hung on the wall, and we'd used a blue flowered sheet as the front window curtain. It hurt me to think that time could be tainted for Gabriel now.

When we walked into the house, they were standing in the kitchen waiting for us. Neither one of them looked happy, but at least they hadn't killed each other.

Before Claudette and Gabe left a few minutes later, Gabriel studied me carefully, pulled me in for a long hug, and then walked out.

After they left, I turned to Titus. "What happened? My mind feels like marbles on a trampoline. What did he say?"

"That he loves you and not in a platonic way, and I better treat you well. He's also worried about your parents. You had no idea?"

Rubbing my forehead, I stared down at the floor. "No. He always introduced me as his roommate or 'good friend.' They used to talk about some of the girls on their swim team in front of me." Spinning away, I started to pace. "I don't understand. Why would he do this?"

Titus rubbed the back of his neck. "I'm not young enough anymore to think I know everything. But my guess is he developed feelings for you while you lived together, but thought it was better not to tell you."

Tears welled up in my eyes. "I didn't want him to give up his life for us, and I didn't know how he felt."

Exhaling, he opened his arms. "Come here, *cocotte.*"

I walked into his embrace and wrapped my arms around his waist.

"Fucking hell. I can't believe I'm defending that bastard, but don't be too hard on him. It would be brutal to be him right now."

Chapter 25

"**D**amn it," I muttered to myself as I hunched over my computer, racking my brain. My critique email to Edna about the Cherry Boxes was overdue. But between the situation with Gabriel and my raging hormones whenever I thought about what to write, I wasn't getting much done.

I finally called Edna. "You know that input you and the manufacturer wanted about the sample Cherry Boxes?" I asked.

"Yes," Edna drawled out.

"I'm struggling. We, uh, tested some of the products–well, most of them. But a couple of things I just haven't worked up to yet. Can I give them partial feedback?"

Edna sighed, then started chuckling. "Damn it. Claudette won our bet."

"What bet?"

"Whether you'd have the nerve to test the products with Titus, or if you'd pawn it off on your Martini Monday friends."

"And what did Claudette bet?" I asked, wondering if I really wanted to know.

"That once you came clean and told him what kind of business you were buying, he'd be all over trying out the boxes with you, but the anal and spanking stuff you'd probably struggle with."

"I hate you guys."

"No, you love us. I bet that you wouldn't work up the nerve. Of course, I'm at a disadvantage because I've never seen or met Titus before."

"You're definitely at a disadvantage," I muttered.

She laughed. "I need to come to Palm Springs and meet you both face-to-face. I'll make it easy for you. Every box needs some type of restraint and spanking item. Every few months, you want to spice it up with something out of the ordinary, like a plug or electric play. Or a novelty toy. Send me your critiques on what you did use, and I'll fill in the rest."

"Okay. I'm going to hang up now. My face is on fire from mortification and embarrassment, and I need to go put it out."

She chuckled again. "I'll look for your email. Have a good day, sweetie." We hung up, and I groaned.

"What's got you so worked up?" Titus asked from the door-way.

I jumped. "I didn't hear you come in. I'm trying to critique the Cherry Boxes Edna sent and give her my feedback. That was her on the phone."

He grinned and walked over. "What's your feedback?"

"Not much."

"Can I read it?"

"No." I closed my computer.

His eyebrow went up. "No?"

I raised my own eyebrow, but I was still blushing. "No is a complete sentence."

He grinned. "True. At least tell me your favorite toy so far, and I'll tell you mine."

I sat back and thought about it. And blushed even more. "Maybe the peppermint massage oil." Remembering all the places and ways we'd used it made my body heat all over again.

He grinned. "I smelled like a candy cane afterward, and every time I get a whiff of peppermint from now on, my dick is probably going to get hard. But it was worth it."

"The holiday season might be a little tricky for you. What was your favorite toy?"

"It's difficult to choose just one. Maybe the nipple clamps." He wrapped his hand around my neck. "Or the paddle."

My heart sped up. The heart-shaped paddle had been the biggest surprise for me. I didn't think I'd like it when he pulled it out on the second night. But Titus made it into a game, and he'd been careful to monitor my reactions. Now, I squirmed just thinking about it.

He let go and leaned against the counter. "What'd you tell her about the vibrating anal plug?"

That thing seemed to mock me. Staring up at the ceiling, I groaned again. "Nothing because I still haven't tried that blue menace yet. As you're well aware."

Laughing, he leaned down and kissed me. "I know. Are you afraid?"

I knew what he was trying to do, but it didn't work. "Hell yes. I'm an anal virgin, but somehow I own an online sex toy shop. Nothing like a little pressure."

He twirled my barstool around and pulled my thighs apart. "I can help you with that." He leaned in and growled against my neck. "And make you like it."

I shivered and grabbed his waist to steady myself.

On Monday evening, after getting ready for the Martini Monday party, I gazed at myself in the bathroom mirror and didn't recognize the girl standing there. No ghost white complexion or anxiety in my eyes, and I wasn't wearing my usual shorts and t-shirt.

When Titus took us shopping, he'd asked the flirty saleswoman to pick out a few things for me. She'd found a cute black dress with crisscross straps in the back, and several other pieces of clothing. So far I'd loved everything. I tried the dress on tonight and was surprised and irritated at how well I liked it. The clerk did have good taste.

When I walked out into the kitchen, Titus scanned me carefully. "Now I have another reason why black is my favorite color."

"Besides the fact that it hides stains and bodily fluid?" I asked, remembering why he said he'd liked it.

He slid his fingers under the straps on my shoulders and pulled me in to meet his lips. "Besides that. Are you sure we can't stay here tonight?"

Just then, the doorbell rang. "That's the babysitter."

He sighed philosophically.

We picked Claudette up from their short-term rental that evening, and I turned when she slid into the back seat alone. "Gabe isn't coming?"

Her mouth tightened. "No." I stared dejectedly out the window as we drove to Laurel's house.

Then I looked back at Claudette in the rearview mirror and smiled, even though my heart felt heavy. She wore a bell sleeve V-neck coral print dress. It was perfect for a cocktail party in Palm Springs.

"You look very vintage and high fashion. You'll fit right into Laurel's neighborhood, and I think your outfit even matches her neighbor's front door."

The women were excited to meet Claudette, and Laurel had chosen cherry-themed cocktails in honor of the Cherry Box and our ownership transition.

Laurel grinned when we walked in. "I'm sure Ramone here, who is my unwanted fashion consultant and harshest critic, will approve of your outfits."

Ramone turned around, scanned us both, then raised his martini glass. "Ladies, you look fabulous, and even Fern would have wholeheartedly approved."

Claudette smiled and stopped in front of Ramone. They gave air kisses like pros, and she stepped back. "It's nice to meet you. Now, which one is Fern?"

Ramone's smile dimmed a little. "She's Laurel's late aunt. Fern started the Martini Monday tradition almost fifty years ago." He scanned Claudette, in her gold Channel sandals and chic silk dress. "I think she would have enjoyed meeting you."

Laurel smiled a little sadly. "I think so too." She wore a skirt with vibrant red cherry clusters on it. Pointing to the bar, she led the way. "We're celebrating the Cherry Box tonight. We have a sour cherry gin martini, a sour cherry negroni, and a cherry lime cosmopolitan."

"And whiskey," Titus added, as he held up a bottle of expensive, single-malt Canadian whiskey. "I figured I could provide it this time."

Jonathan sighed contentedly. "Good to see you. And your delightful Canadian whiskey."

"So tonight's theme is based on an online sex toy store? I love it!" Martina snorted.

Sebastian took orders and expertly mixed the drinks while Laurel assisted him. Most of the men opted for a two-finger pour of the Canadian whiskey.

Zeke raised a cut crystal glass to Titus. "I know we've had our differences in the past about whether the word 'shit' or 'fuck' is more versatile and universal, but I think we can both agree that this is some good fucking shit."

Slowly, the women migrated outside to the same spot where we'd talked about the Cherry Box a few weeks ago.

Isa turned to Claudette. "Is the transfer complete?"

"As of tonight at midnight it will be." Claudette raised her glass in a toast, and everyone followed.

Martina pointed her glass at Claude. "Your product reviews are the shit, and I think your buyers feed off each other. I laughed so hard, my stomach started cramping."

"Titus said he loves product testing with Abby," Claudette volunteered.

Isa leaned forward. "You should have seen how big Abby's eyes got when she showed me a sleek red leather flogger that came in one of the test boxes."

Laurel raised her hand. "Do you have a box specifically for water play?"

I turned to Laurel. "I can answer this one. There's a box called 'Soaking Wet' and everything in it is waterproof."

"Titus said you enjoyed the waterproof restraints the other night," Claude added helpfully.

Laurel gazed out over at her pool and grinned. "I'll be ordering that one."

Gabriel and Claudette planned to fly out on Tuesday afternoon. That morning, Andrea was cleaning the house, and she'd brought her young daughter Carmen with her. I asked if she'd watch Stella for a few minutes.

Titus had gone to work out, so I drove to their short-term rental to see if I could talk with Gabriel before they left. I couldn't leave things the way they were.

When I knocked on the door, Claudette answered. "Did I miss a breakfast date?" she asked.

"No. I want to talk to Gabriel before you fly out this afternoon. And we're still on for lunch."

Claudette studied me, then swung the door wide. "Come in. He's probably just getting out of the shower, I'll tell him you're here."

I looked around the rental as I waited, shifting from one foot to the other. The townhome was in a newer development close to Titus's home. It had been decorated with mid-century modern furniture, bright pops of color here and there, and black-and-white 1950s prints of some of the Rat Pack.

A few minutes later, Gabriel came out alone. He stopped in the doorway when he saw me standing there, wiping my hand against my pant leg.

"You do that when you're nervous or anxious." He pointed to my thigh.

"Do what?"

"Rub your palms on your legs."

I quickly pulled my hand away. "Well, I am nervous. And anxious. Can we talk?"

"Yeah." He walked into the living room and sat on the velvet blue couch.

My mind wandered through all the things I wanted to say, or thought I should say. But I kept circling back to one thing.

"You never told me. I... I didn't know."

He turned toward me and put his arm on the back of the couch. "No, I didn't."

"Why?"

"Because I was afraid you'd reciprocate out of guilt or obligation, and I was a coward."

I tried to think back to that time. Maybe he was right, or maybe I would have been attracted to him. There were so many things about Gabriel worth loving. But I'd never know because in that instant I realized I didn't want anyone but Titus

Studying Gabriel's face, I saw the pain behind his even stare, and there wasn't a way for me to answer without causing him more pain. So I gave him the truth.

"I don't know how I would've responded."

He pulled back and broke eye contact. "Okay."

My mind scrambled to find the right words, the best words. Reaching out, I grabbed his thigh. "But I do know that you'll always have a part of my heart, and those days with us in that rundown, little house are seared in my memories. Up until that time, it was the happiest I've ever been. Please, Gabriel. You're one of the best people I know, and I don't want to lose you."

He sat still for a moment, then sighed and leaned forward. "Me neither, sweetheart. Are you happy? Does he treat you and Stella well?"

"Yes. He's gruff and protective. And sweet."

He studied me. "Do you love him?"

I punched his shoulder. "Probably. But I'm not ready to admit it yet because it scares the hell out of me."

He nodded tightly. "Alright, I'll try to get along–for you." He sat up and carefully cupped my jaw, giving me a chance to pull away as he swept his thumb across my cheek. "Your fucking father needs to go to jail for what he did to you and Stella."

I clasped his wrist and squeezed. "We're good now. Better than good. Go live your life, be happy, and stay my friend."

He leaned in, gave me a soft kiss, and smiled even though pain shadowed his eyes. And both our hearts broke a little, for different reasons.

My eyes were red from crying when I walked into the house a little later. Titus sat at the bar working on his computer.

When he saw my face, he straightened. "What's wrong?"

"Where's Stella?"

He surveyed me. "Playing with Carmen in her room. Andrea's just finishing up."

I walked over and laid my head on his chest, and he sighed, stroking my hair. "You talked to Gabriel." It wasn't a question.

"Yeah. He promised to try to get along with you."

"I'd like it better if he keeps being an ass." He pushed my hair to the side and kissed my jaw.

"I hurt him," I whispered.

"Fuck," he muttered without heat. Standing up, he pulled me out to the back patio, then sat down on the cushioned loveseat and settled me in his lap. "Tell me."

Laying my head on his chest, I breathed him in. It was strange coming to Titus for comfort about hurting another man. But somehow it also felt right.

"He never told me how he felt because he didn't want me to feel guilty or obligated. I didn't have a clue." It felt so good having him stroke my hair.

"Huh. I hate to admit it, but the fucker has a valid point. It didn't stop me, though." There was no remorse or guilt in his voice. "If he had told you how he felt, you might be with him right now."

That alternate reality seemed strange to think about. "It was different from the start with you. By the end of the first week, I liked you even though I was still afraid." I wrapped my arms around him. "And you purposely tried to drive me crazy wandering around the house without your shirt on half the time."

He chuckled. "Nice to know. I walked in one day when you were bent over in one of those tiny pairs of shorts you wear, looking for something in the fridge. The bottom of your ass cheeks were hanging out a little. I had to go beat off in the shower to get rid of my hard-on."

I shifted on his lap, my insides warming. "I'll have to bend over in front of you more often."

"Please do. How were things with him when you left?"

"A little better. But it's never going to be the same, is it?"

He didn't hesitate. "No."

The truth stung, but I knew he was right. "You're doing a bad job of comforting me."

His lip twitched. "Let me work on that."

He bent and kissed my mouth, then licked my lower lip. I opened for him, and his tongue slipped inside. Straddling his lap, I lowered onto his hard length encased in his jeans. As I rubbed against him, I moaned softly while we kissed.

Just then I heard the patio door open and quickly jumped off his lap as Stella walked out to find us.

Titus laughed and patted my butt cheek. "Don't worry, we'll finish this tonight."

Chapter 26

Nerves crawled through my stomach, and all Isabella's jokes about being thrown into a Canadian jail raced through my mind as we walked into the courthouse in Vancouver that morning for Max's custody hearing.

Trixie's outfit reminded me of a sexy secretary Halloween costume. She sat next to her attorney at one table in the courtroom, and Titus and his attorney sat at the other.

She wore a black pencil skirt with a long slit up the side and a suit jacket that looked two sizes too small. Her button-down shirt was open to mid-chest, and she had on her fire-engine red stilettos, with matching red lipstick and nails.

My simple, cream-colored shirtwaist dress couldn't have been more different. Max and Stella sat with me a few rows behind Titus.

"Ms. Drummond." The judge looked down from his elevated podium to Titus's attorney. "As the moving party, we'll begin with you."

"Your Honor, Mr. Tremblay has been trying to establish joint custody since his son was born. But the mother keeps demanding a higher child support amount than the law dictates." Fran paused for effect. "We're here because she wants more money, and she's using the child to try to get it."

Trixie's attorney stood up. "We object. At the last hearing, the court also ordered Mr. Tremblay to show he has an appropriate family environment and is fully prepared to take on the care of his three-year-old child, and all that entails."

Fran stood again. "The child's name is Max, and he's actually two years old." She turned around and smiled at me. "As the court can see, Max is content in Mr. Tremblay and Ms. Carver's care, and he's become attached to Stella, Ms. Carver's three-year-old daughter."

When Stella heard her name, she looked up for a second, then went back to playing with Max.

Fran went on. "We've also provided documentation regarding Mr. Tremblay's home showing the safeguards he put in place, who Max's pediatrician will be, and an approximate schedule of care. Frankly, Your Honor, joint custody should have happened when Max was born. Children need both parents in their lives, and having an active, caring, appropriate father who wants joint custody should be celebrated."

Trixie's attorney, Mr. Cutter, tried to sputter through reasons why Trixie had withheld joint physical custody for so long. Then Judge Farrell asked Titus several standard questions before turning to me.

"Ms. Carver, are you prepared to assist Mr. Tremblay with child supervision and the care of Max?"

I stood up. "Yes, Your Honor."

"Do you live together?"

"We do."

"Are you romantically involved?"

My cheeks heated, but I smiled. "Yes."

"You turned in a criminal background check with..." He looked down at his computer screen. "Two speeding tickets. I wish most of the people who come before me had that kind of record. Tell me about yourself."

I hoped I didn't have to discuss the Cherry Box with him. While he seemed nice, he also looked a little rigid. "Stella is my three-year-old daughter. I'm twenty-three years old, and I design and help clients maintain websites and online businesses. I have a small one myself, and I work from home."

I silently begged him not to ask me about what kind of business it was.

"How long have you and Mr. Tremblay been together? And how did you meet?"

My hands were damp, but I resisted rubbing them on my dress. I'd thought about how to answer this question.

"One of my best friends did an internship last year with the Thunderbirds' medical staff. Titus has a back injury and often visited the medical office there. She's the one who set us up."

Judge Farrell winced. "I'm aware of his back injury. I was at that game when it happened."

He seemed sympathetic to Titus, so I pushed forward. "Titus is a kind, affectionate, patient man off the ice."

The judge chuckled. "Yes, those are traits you'd want to leave on the bench if you're a professional hockey player."

I smiled back at him. "True. Stella loves him, and she doesn't like that many people. He plays street hockey in our cul-de-sac with her most evenings, and reads books to her, helps with meals, and does all those things a loving parent would."

"So you believe Mr. Tremblay is an appropriate, nurturing father?"

I tried to remember everything I'd rehearsed, but in the end, I just went with my heart. "Yes, absolutely. I know not everyone is fit to be a parent. Believe me, I know. But Titus is, and Max deserves that. He deserves to learn how to skate and play hockey from his dad. And wrestle on the living room floor, or go to the library together. Maybe go rescue a sweet little mutt from the animal shelter because Titus wants him to grow up with a dog." I glanced down at Stella's little runners. "Titus will teach him what being a kind, decent person means."

Judge Farrell studied me. "Thank you, Ms. Carver." He turned to Titus. "How's your back?"

Titus stood again. "It's getting better, Your Honor. I'm playing with the Thunderbirds in Palm Springs and doing a lot of physical therapy."

The judge leaned forward and looked at Trixie's attorney. "Speaking of that. Mr. Tremblay makes a fraction of what he used to make, and the child support hasn't been adjusted. Yet your client wants a higher amount? Can you explain her legal reasoning?"

Her attorney couldn't. The judge then asked if they wanted to take a recess to try to reach a stipulation. Over an hour later, the parties reached an agreement. Titus would have joint custody and continue to pay the same child support amount he'd been paying, but custody would shift, and Titus's home would be considered Max's primary residence. But the biggest win by far was that when Max reached school age, he would reside primarily with Titus. I sat there, stunned and ecstatic.

When we walked out of the courtroom, Titus shook Fran's hand. "Thank you for stepping in."

"Abby is the one you should thank, and I apologize again about your first attorney. I'll file the stipulation and send you a copy of the signed Order when I get it." She shook her head. "Trixie is very fortunate you didn't push for attorney fees and the lower child support amount, but it was a great leveraging tool." She looked down at Max. "She essentially sold primary physical custody for a higher child support amount, and not having to eat your attorney fees."

The judge had read the terms of their agreement out loud, including the amount of child support Titus would continue to pay Trixie. The amount seemed so large me, but Titus didn't seem to care.

"I want custody of Max, so it's money well spent. She can be a bitch, but she's his mom, and she loves Max in her own way. We just needed to get through this bullshit."

Trixie walked out without her attorney. Fran said goodbye and took off as Trixie walked over to us.

"Are you flying out today or tomorrow?" she asked Titus.

"Tomorrow. If you want him tonight, I understand. And I'll bring him back in a couple of weeks as per the agreement."

She shook her head. "You keep him tonight. He'll just spend the day whining for Stella. And her." She waved her hand vaguely in my direction.

Just then, Stella tugged on my skirt. "I need to go potty."

I looked down and took her hand. "There's one right here. Let's go." We went in together, and as we finished up and were washing our hands, Trixie walked in.

She didn't waste any time. "Are you proud of yourself?"

I straightened and looked at her in the mirror. "Pardon?"

She walked over and stood in front of me, pointing her sharp red fingernail at my face. "You're a prop, and we both know it. Titus found himself a little vanilla girl, who also happens to be a single mother, to drag in front of the judge. And two speeding tickets? Jesus, what a dull, boring person you must be."

"That's an opinion." I turned to Stella so we could walk out, but Trixie kept talking.

"No one buys that you're together, and you'll probably be gone by the end of the month."

Her accusations stung because she was partially right—at least in the beginning. When Titus and I first met, I *was* a prop.

"Our relationship isn't your business, and you need to step back."

"Or what? Remember, I know how Titus really likes to fuck."

"Today isn't about us. It's about Max, and his right to have both his parents around, as long as they're decent and appropriate."

"Are you saying I'm not *appropriate*?"

"Not always."

"Listen, you stupid little bitch. I don't have to take your shit." She flung her hands out and shoved me. Stella stood behind me, and Trixie pushed us both against the counter. I heard Stella hit her head and start crying.

I whirled around to kneel in front of her, checking her head. She cried as I looked her over, but she seemed okay, and slowly quieted down. The incident probably scared her more than anything, but it reminded me of all the other times she watched my father shove me around.

Slowly, I stood and turned to face Trixie. I wanted to slap her smug face. "If you ever hurt my little girl again, you'll regret it," I snarled.

She put her hands on her hips and scoffed. "Oh? What are you going to do? Browbeat me to death? Or do you think you can take me in a fight?"

I quirked my head and stared at her. "Yes, I think I could. But that wouldn't be satisfying enough, and it sets a bad example for the kids." I walked right up to her, and she quickly backed up. I'd surprised her, and she teetered a little on her stilettos. "What I *will* do is spread rumors that you have several serious sexually transmitted diseases, you're mentally unstable, and have stalkerish tendencies. I'm sure the good folks at *Hot Hockey Times* would love to print the story. No one would touch you after that."

"You little cunt, you wouldn't dare. Titus doesn't need you anymore. And if he does let you stay around, it'll be out of pity."

Her words dug in and hit at my insecurities, but I turned and took Stella's hand. "Come on, little bug. We're done here. Let's go get lunch with Max and Titus." We turned and walked out.

As we stepped into the elevator, Titus studied me and then took my chin. "What did she say to you in the bathroom?"

"It doesn't matter. Let's go get lunch."

A few bailiffs recognized Titus and approached him to take selfies and talk hockey with him in the courthouse foyer for a few minutes. By the time we walked outside, Trixie caught up with us.

She stood on the courtroom steps, tapping her foot. "Your little bitch girlfriend threatened me in the bathroom."

Titus sighed. "Her name is Abby, and Max and I are pretty damn lucky to have her in our lives."

She narrowed her eyes. "I don't want Max around her."

"You need to close your mouth and walk away," Titus murmured.

"I bet she lays there like a stiff board when you fuck her, and she has no idea what you like or how hard and dirty you need it. You can cut her loose now, you got what you wanted."

My heart lurched, and I felt like throwing up. Her words were aimed to hurt, but what if she was right? What if I wasn't experienced enough for him? I loved our sex life, but maybe Trixie knew something I didn't. And what if I really was just a "prop" to him?

But Titus wasn't like that, and he would never treat me that way. I turned away and started down the steps with the kids. They didn't need to hear this.

Titus stared flatly at her. "She's so far out of your league it's laughable, and she deserves better than me. But she's *mine.*"

Max looked up from where he and Stella were hopping down the courthouse steps, oblivious to all the drama. "Mine! Mine, mine," he yelled back at Titus.

Titus smirked and turned away from Trixie. "That's right, little man. Come on, let's go eat lunch with our girls."

That evening, Trixie's accusations circled in my head as we wrangled Max and Stella into getting ready for bed. We'd spent the afternoon at Charleson Park on the waterfront with Russ, and walked along the path there, enjoying the sunny spring day. There was a wooden pirate ship at the park, and Max and Stella ran around it, exploring the enchanting space. If Trixie's words hadn't been nagging at me, it would have been the perfect afternoon.

Titus turned to me while we walked with the kids and Russ. "I'm so damn relieved to have the case behind us."

Taking his hand, I squeezed it and kissed his scarred knuckles. "Me too. I didn't want to find out what Canadian jails are like."

He grinned and leaned down to murmur in my ear. "That wasn't going to happen, but I'll put handcuffs on you later if you want to pretend with me."

I melted against him. "Yes, please."

Max seemed content and didn't let Stella out of his sight, and Titus kept grinning at him all afternoon. We tucked Max into his bed that night, knowing he'd be hopping out of it minutes later to go sleep next to Stella and Russ.

We left them to it. Titus pulled me into the bedroom and turned to me. "Tell me."

"Tell you what?"

"What happened between you and Trixie in the bathroom."

I slumped in his arms. "It's over, and I don't want it to affect your time with Max. Just let it go."

He gazed at me. "No."

"No?"

"You heard me. And I've been told 'no' is a complete sentence. I can always call Trixie and ask her."

"You're not going to call her." I poked his side for even suggesting it. "She said some stuff about us not really being together, about me being a prop for you and shitty in bed, and then she pushed me and Stella into the sink. Stella hit her head."

Titus went still. "She did *what*? Is Stella alright?"

"Yes. She has a small bump on her head, but I think it scared her more than anything."

"Trixie is going to be sorry she ever opened her fucking mouth," he growled.

I had to tell him the rest of it. "She's right, I did threaten her. Then I got Stella out of there."

His nostrils flared, and he nodded and turned away. Titus didn't try to reassure me that what Trixie said wasn't true; he didn't say anything to me at all the rest of the night.

When I got ready for bed, Titus was still in his office talking on the phone with the door closed. I fell asleep before he came to bed.

Max seemed wound up and full of energy the next morning, while Titus and I were both tired and quiet. We didn't talk much on the way home, each of us lost in our own thoughts.

When we got back from Vancouver, I picked up the mail. Along with all the junk mail and advertisements, I noticed a forwarded letter from Claudette's parents with the State of Washington, Division of Child Support on the return address. When I opened it, I found a check for over twenty-one thousand dollars addressed to me.

My mind couldn't compute what I was seeing for a few seconds. I shakily looked through the attached documents and read the letter stating the biological father's checking account had been garnished in the included amount. I briefly wondered if they'd collected money meant for a tuition payment or another large purchase. But then I decided I didn't care. Kyle had left me pregnant, broke, and alone. He could go screw himself.

For the rest of the evening, my brain ricocheted from one thing to the next as I thought of that check for over twenty thousand dollars sitting in my top drawer. I could feed and clothe Stella for quite a while, and even afford preschool for her. I could also get new tires for my car now. And if I needed to, I now had enough money to get an apartment.

The next morning while Titus was still at the house, I went running by myself for the first time in over a year. It felt strange not running behind Stella's old, squeaky stroller.

George stopped me first, and we discussed how his mom was doing. Next, I ran into Vern and Bowen in their driveway as they were coming back from pickleball. "Where's little Ms. Stella this morning?" Vern asked in his lilting southern accent.

They had on matching purple velour shorts today. "Hello, gentlemen. You both look very coordinated. Stella's home with Titus and Max. How were the gingersnaps?"

Bowen smiled. "They were delicious, thank you. How did you know they're my favorites?"

I didn't have the heart to tell him Vern had requested them last week. "Lucky guess."

When I got back from my run, I noticed Titus's lovely mint green door. I smelled rosemary in the air, and a wave of both contentment and melancholy hit me. This house, and even the neighborhood, had become my refuge. If Stella and I needed to leave, I would miss it so much.

The next day I took the kids and Russ to the fire engine park near Isa's house and met her and Elodie there. Max jabbered nonstop, and Stella seemed to understand a good portion of what he said.

Isa shook her head as she watched the kids play. "It's almost surreal to see Max here. Titus worked on getting joint custody for so long."

I reached over and pulled a leaf out of Max's hand before he could shove it in his mouth. "My stomach felt queasy for most of the hearing, but honestly? The worst part was Trixie cornering me and Stella in the bathroom afterward and knocking us into the sink."

Isa's head jerked to me. "What the hell?"

I told her about the altercation. Sighing, I leaned over and scratched Russ behind his ears. "The worst part is Titus didn't deny anything when I told him what she said."

Isa was quiet for a few minutes, and I walked over and helped Max go down the slide a few times. When I sat next to her again, I knocked her leg with mine.

I knew she had something she needed to say. "It's okay, Isa. You can tell me what you're thinking."

"It might be nothing. He said once that he wasn't marriage material and never planned to get married." She sighed. "But he seems to adore you and Stella. Please talk to him about whatever you're thinking."

"Yesterday, I received a check in the mail for back child support. It's enough for me to move out, get my own apartment, and afford groceries."

She threw her arm around me. "Thank God! I'm so glad they caught up with that loser asshole. But will you promise me something?"

"Of course. I owe you."

"Will you talk to Titus before you make any big decisions? I know it's only been a few months, but you two belong together. It would be a tragedy if you gave that up without even fighting for it first."

"I will. But during one of our question-and-answer sessions a while back, Titus told me he's been a single athlete with a 'skewed moral compass.' Maybe marriage and monogamy don't interest him."

"Please talk to him."

I nodded. "We'll talk. But I never want him to feel stuck or obligated. That wouldn't be fair to him after all he's done."

He'd told Isa he didn't plan to marry. I sat back, feeling dejected and heartsick. It was time to evaluate my life objectively and impartially. I didn't know if I could continue living with Titus, knowing he might never feel more than affection for me, and eventually, maybe even regret that.

Chapter 27

Atear ran down my cheek as I sat at the kitchen bar, watching Titus and the kids play in the pool through the kitchen window. I hastily wiped it away and looked back at my computer.

My newest client's website was a mess. The site advertised Pete's Pool Service in Scottsdale, Arizona, but none of the links worked, and someone had listed the wrong phone number on the contact page. I muttered to myself as I quickly went through and fixed it.

After finishing, I returned to watching Titus and Max in the pool. Max floated on his back with his eyes closed while Titus held him up, both of them looking peaceful and content. Titus started giving the kids swim lessons the day after we got back from Vancouver. Stella sat on the steps, watching them, and both kids had on bright yellow swim floaties.

Not everything was going well, though. Since we came back and I'd had my conversation with Isa, Titus and the kids had been almost inseparable, but he seemed to be pulling away from me.

He was quieter, and something bothered him. Maybe he need-ed space and freedom, but didn't know how to ask.

I'd also slept in my old room the last two nights, and Titus hadn't protested or commented. Max decided he wanted to sleep with Titus instead of Stella the first night, so I'd quietly gone and slept in the other room. And stayed there last night.

Trixie's words had also burrowed into my brain and seemed to play on repeat. Titus never denied her claims when I told him about the altercation, and that probably hurt the most.

It was past time for us to talk. When I heard the patio door open, I looked up to find the three of them standing just outside. They were all dripping wet. I quickly wiped my face and stood up.

Titus regarded me, then pointed to the towels they'd left on the kitchen table. "Will you hand me those? I forgot to bring them out."

"Of course." I grabbed the towels and walked outside, em-barrassed he'd caught me crying. I avoided his eyes and helped dry Max and Stella off.

"Are you guys hungry?" I asked the kids. "I made home-made chicken pot pie."

"Uh-huh." Stella nodded.

Max jabbered and held onto my legs while I dried him off. I smiled down at him and patted his back. "I'll take that as a yes, little man."

Looking up at Titus, my smile dimmed. "Do you want to bathe them before or after dinner?"

"Now. So when they start fading, they'll be ready for bed. Then we can talk."

I *really* hated it when people said that. Swallowing back dread, I nodded. "Okay. It's probably time."

His eyes darkened, and he scanned my face again. We got the kids bathed and into their pajamas, then sat down and ate homemade chicken pot pie. I barely tasted the meal as my mind churned. When the kids finally started winding down, I took them into Stella's room to cuddle and read a couple of books while Titus took a phone call.

They both started drifting off, and I slowly extricated myself. As I tucked them in, I looked up to see Titus in the doorway watching me. He tilted his head toward the hallway, and I nodded and walked out after him.

Taking a few quiet, deep breaths, I tried to bolster myself for our conversation. I paused in the kitchen, thinking we could talk there. But Titus took my hand and pulled me into his bedroom. Then he shut the door and turned to me.

"Tell me."

I didn't know what he wanted me to tell him. "I don't under-stand."

"You've been retreating since Vancouver. So just fucking tell me what's going on in that brain of yours," he growled.

My eyes narrowed and some of my sadness drained away. "*I've* been retreating?"

"Yeah. You went back to the other bedroom, for fuck's sake. Don't mess with me right now."

Somewhere in the back of my mind, it registered that I'd never seen him angry before.

Well, I was mad too. "You're the one who stopped talking to me. And when I told you what Trixie said? You didn't deny it, you just clammed up." My anger turned to pain. "And you haven't touched me since. She said you needed someone more experienced. More adventurous, more... whatever." I wanted to say trashy.

He stared at me for a moment, then closed his eyes and put his hands on his head. "Son of a bitch."

He wanted me to talk? Fine. I'd talk. "We accomplished what you needed me for. It worked, and now you have joint custody of Max. I'm so happy for you two. And Trixie was right, I did make a good prop. But now? If you want us to move out, we will. I have a little money." If he said yes, it would gut me.

Titus put his hands on his hips, a grin spreading across his face. "No fucking way." Then he started chuckling.

"I swear to God, if you laugh at me right now, not even your mother can save you."

He covered the space between us and wrapped his arms around me, but I stiffened under his touch.

"We're fucking idiots," he growled.

"Speak for yourself, jackass." My voice sounded muffled against his chest, and he laughed again. Then he walked us backward toward the bed and tipped us over on it.

"There's no way you're moving out, and don't bring it up again unless you want me to really use that fucking ridiculous heart-shaped paddle on your ass. I've been agonizing that you'd want to leave after Trixie got in your face and hurt Stella."

I stilled. "Why? You didn't hurt Stella, Trixie did."

"Yeah, but she's *my* fucking mess. I've turned a blind eye to her temper tantrums and cruelty, but I'm done with her bullshit."

The stiffness slowly seeped out of me, and I leaned back to look at him. "She's not just your problem, she's our problem." My eyes shifted away. "As long as I'm living here."

He rolled me onto my back and propped himself over me. "Why wouldn't you be living here? It would break Max's heart if you and Stella left." I turned my head away, but Titus took hold of my chin, turning me back to face him. "It would break *my* heart. Don't let Trixie get to you. I've learned to ignore her bullshit, which irritates the hell out of her."

"I'll try, but it was difficult when she had me cornered against the bathroom sink. With those red lips and nails, I was getting serious Ursula vibes."

Titus's mouth twitched, but then he grew serious. "Do you remember what I told you the first time we fucked, and you came on my cock?"

The abrupt change in topics made my mind skip like a scratched record and sent heat sliding through me. "Hmm. What you said probably paled next to the mind-blowing orgasms you gave me."

I laid my hand on his cheek and soaked him in. Being close to him, feeling his hard warmth, and smelling his comforting scent, made me tear up a little. I'd missed it over the past two days. But it was time to find out what he wanted. I took my hand away, and he sat up, pulling me onto his lap.

"I told you that you're mine."

"Isa said you told her you never planned on getting married." I held up my hand. "I'm not angling or asking for a proposal, but I can't keep sleeping with you and... having feelings for you if you don't want a serious relationship. It wouldn't be fair to any of us."

He sighed. "Fucking hell."

His words sent a shaft of pain through me, but I held onto my composure. Quickly sliding off his lap, I started backing away. "It's alright, and I understand. But we can't stay because my decisions don't affect just me anymore–"

He reached out and pulled me back to him, then settled me between his thighs. "You're staying, and for the love of God, quit second-guessing and twisting the fuck out of what I say. I told you that night that you're *mine*. And I didn't mean until the hearing, or when Max got here. Or for a few months."

"But what about–"

"I don't even remember that conversation with Isa, but I'm sure I did tell her that. Because until you, I never wanted a woman to be here when I got home, or hang out with me and Max, or sit in the stands cheering for me. Even though you chew your fingernails and wince through most of the game."

"No, I don't," I denied.

"You do, and it's amusing as hell. I'm also not the only player who's noticed either. We're so good together when we're not letting other people fuck with our heads. I like your sassy mouth, and I'm addicted to your pussy. It's also sweet as hell to see you in your little kimonos in the kitchen, looking sleepy and thoroughly fucked while you make coffee or breakfast."

I sat still and thought about what he'd said. He made some good points. "Trixie said–"

"I don't give a single fuck what that woman said. Trixie can't stand that even without all the shit like hair extensions, heels, makeup, and expensive clothes, you're gorgeous and hot as fuck. And Abigail?"

"Yes?" Leaning in, I laid my head on his shoulder and wrapped my arms around him.

"You get back in my bed, and don't move out again unless you want me to use that wicked red strap that came in the last Cherry Box on your ass."

I snorted. "You could try."

"Are you daring me? Because I'm always up for a good challenge. But tonight I think we'll use the blue plug."

I squeaked as he grabbed me around the waist and rolled me onto the bed. Straddling me, he leaned down and kissed me, long and deep.

"I love sliding my hands across your soft skin." He ran one hand up my shirt and squeezed and pinched my nipple.

My hips shifted restlessly between his legs, and he leaned over me. "Do you want me to bury my cock in your wet little cunt?" My heart fluttered in my chest, and I nodded.

But he smirked. "Use your words, Abigail."

"Yes, damn it."

"Good enough. Now raise your hips." He pulled down my shorts and panties, then cupped me between my legs. "This is mine." Then he yanked my shirt and bra off, held my breasts, and worked my nipples. "And these lush little tits are mine."

I gulped in air and shifted underneath him. Then he put his thumb on my bottom lip and pushed my mouth open. "And this goddamned mouth is mine." He slid his thumb inside. "Now suck."

My body heated at his words, and I wanted to strip him bare, crawl on top of him, and impale myself on his cock. But I opened my mouth and took his thumb inside, sucking and licking on it.

"Good. You've gotten talented with that agile tongue of yours." He pulled his hand away and peeled off his own clothes, then leaned over and rummaged in his nightstand, pulling out four red leather cuffs and nipple clamps.

My eyes went wide. "Those weren't there before."

"I wanted quick access." He held up the cuffs and grinned. "And I want to tie you spreadeagled across my bed tonight. I've missed your pussy and we're going to make up for lost time. Do you trust me?"

I stared at the cuffs and clamps, and my nipples pebbled. "Yes."

"Good." Grabbing my hands, he put the cuffs on. Then he slid down my body and cuffed my ankles. Leaning back on his heels, he palmed his thick, hard cock absently and stroked himself.

"Lay back and spread your arms." He studied me intently, and I stared back at him. "Now, *bonne fille*," he murmured.

Slowly, I lay back and raised my arms. He leaned over me and secured my arms. I hadn't noticed the straps before now.

"Where did those come from?" I whispered.

"I installed them before we left for Vancouver. You look a little spooked, so I'll hold off on tying down your ankles. For now." He ran his hand up my thigh and bent over me to work my clit with his tongue. Then he crawled up my body and teased and sucked on my nipples. Finally, he knelt above my head and held up his cock to my lips.

"Open." I parted my mouth, and he pushed inside. Swirling my tongue around his shaft, I slowly started sucking. He watched me as he worked himself to the back of my throat. "Relax and open. That's it. Aw, fuck!"

His head went back, and he pumped himself inside my throat a few times, but he pulled out before climaxing. Tears leaked from the corners of my eyes, and saliva covered my chin.

He leaned down, pressed my lips open, and spit inside my mouth. "Swallow it—now. I want something of mine inside your stomach if it's not going to be my come tonight."

I swallowed down his spit and then licked my lips. His eyes flared, and he laid his hand on my throat and squeezed lightly. "There's my *bonne gentile fille.*"

My body craved his dominance and his commands, and I moaned his name with lust and need as my vision blurred from tears and extreme emotions. Titus brought me to my knees, and then he gave me what I hungered for when he consumed and overwhelmed me like this.

Positioning his shaft at my opening, he palmed my cheek and brushed my hair out of my eyes. "I'm going to pound inside you until my cock can slide in and out of your well-fucked, little pussy with ease. And you're going to take every inch of me."

Then Titus drove inside me. It took several hard strokes to work himself to the hilt, and I arched up and threw my head back. He felt like heaven, like he belonged inside me, filling and stretching me.

"That's it. Take it all. Let me see your beautiful tits bounce while I fuck you." He started rhythmically thrusting into me, then he lifted my hips and reached around and fingered my back hole. "I'm going to take your tight little virgin ass soon, but we'll stretch it for you first." He coated his fingers with my juices and slid one inside me there.

I pulled at my restraints and panted beneath him. "Titus, what are you–Oh, my God!" I wailed. He'd just shoved another finger inside me. My head thrashed as I begged him to stop, then fuck me harder. The stretch and burn of his fingers triggered my orgasm, and I locked up and came all over his cock. White hot lust slammed through me while a red haze coated my vision.

My climax triggered his own. Groaning, he slammed into me, held my hips tight against him, and spilled his hot come deep inside my channel. Even after he stopped spasming, he held me to him. My heart still pounded, and chemicals flooded my system as a fine sweat coated my body. I still couldn't seem to grasp a thought.

He leaned over, laying his sweaty forehead on mine. "You're a beautiful fucking mess. And now that we know you like anal play, let's try the vibrating plug."

Chapter 28

I jerked and twitched in his grasp. "It was a fluke, a one-off!"

He grinned wickedly. "Let's find out, shall we?" He let go of my hips and slid out of me. "Stay right there." He smirked and patted my hip, then walked into his bathroom.

I looked up at my cuffed wrists and realized he'd made a joke. After cleaning up, Titus took a wet washcloth and wiped me down, taking extra care between my cheeks.

"Okay, I'm clean back there," I wheezed.

"I'd still like to paddle your ass for sleeping in the other room. But the plug works too." He reached over and pulled it out of his nightstand.

My eyes went wide, and I tugged at the cuffs. "Holy hell, what else do you have in that nightstand?"

Pulling out a small container of lube, he held it up and grinned. "Funny you should ask."

"If you even try it, you better sleep with one eye open."

He leaned over and kissed my nipple, then licked and blew across it. It instantly puckered. Titus licked and worked the other nipple, then took the small, silver clamps and attached them to my nipples as I softly whined through the sting.

Sitting up, Titus turned on the vibrating plug and slowly brought it down my body until he laid it against my clit. "Don't worry, by the time I work this inside your little hole, you'll be begging me for it."

My back bowed, and I started panting. "I hope you step on a Lego in your bare feet."

Wincing, he chuckled. "That sounds painful. Let's see if I can change your mind. And I promise I won't put this inside your ass unless you ask me to."

Titus edged and played with me until I called him a few choice names, demanded he fuck me again, then eventually begged for the damn plug.

He picked up the lube and squirted some on. Holding it up, he stared down at me. My stomach slowly flipped over, and I gazed up at him with half-lidded, dazed eyes.

"Get on your knees and bend over, *bonne fille*."

I panted, then rolled over on my stomach and worked myself onto my knees. With my hands still cuffed, I struggled to get into position while he watched me.

He ran his hand down my back and cupped my globe. "Now rest on your elbows."

I hesitated, and he laid the vibrating plug on my pussy again, but pulled it off before I could come. I bent over on my elbows.

"Spread your legs wider." Sliding my knees farther apart, I opened for him. He stroked the backs of my thighs. "That's it.

You look so fucking beautiful with your wrists and ankles wearing those red cuffs and your ass up in the air, ready to take whatever I give you."

Using his thumb to pull one of my cheeks wide, he then worked the tip of the vibrating plug into my hole. I panted as he slowly pushed it inside me. The pressure built, and I shifted and whimpered at the sting. Titus worked slowly but relentlessly, and the strange sensations made my insides clench around the plug.

He lightly swatted my ass. "Relax and loosen up. That's it. Now push back." Titus held it still for a moment and bent over me. "Do you know why I made you beg?" he murmured.

"No." I breathed through the tightness and the sting.

"Because I want you to understand inside that sweet, tortured mind of yours that you trust me completely to take care of you and give you pleasure, even if it's with a little pain and discomfort." Then he worked the whole plug inside me, the flat end laying snug against my crease.

Reaching around, he slowly rubbed my pussy. "And that's what I'm going to do."

Then he pulled the plug out and worked it back in several times while he massaged my clit. Minutes later, I threw my head back and wailed my release.

We were eating lunch a few days later when Titus casually mentioned his parents would be arriving in Palm Springs in a couple of hours. I stared at him blankly.

"I'm sorry, I think I misunderstood. Did you just say your parents are going to be here in–" I glanced at the microwave clock. "Two hours?"

He continued eating lunch. "Yeah."

I dropped my fork, stood up, and started talking fast. "Are they planning to sleep over? How long are they going to be here? Do they know about me?" I spun and started toward my old bedroom. "I'm not ready!"

He glanced up. "Where are you going?"

"To change the sheets in the spare bedroom."

"They're not sleeping here. *Maman* likes to stay at a spa hotel and get 'the works' when she visits. Whatever the fuck that means."

Max threw a piece of chicken, and Russ caught it in midair. They'd made a game out of Max throwing his food.

Titus grabbed his hand before he launched the next piece. "You need to eat a bite now. Russ gets one, then you eat one." Max fisted a little handful of chicken and peas, shoved it in his mouth, then threw another piece to the dog.

I turned and came back to the table. "So they know about me."

"Of course."

"How long have you known they were coming?" I asked suspiciously.

"A week."

"Why didn't you tell me before now?" I cried, wiping my palms on my shorts.

"I didn't want you to worry for a week." He eyed me. "Now I'm thinking two hours might have been too much warning."

I sighed and looked up at the ceiling. "This morning when I woke up, I marveled at how well everything seemed to be going. I should have known better."

Without taking his eyes off me, Titus reached out and grabbed Max's sippy cup before he could throw it. "If you hit Russ, you could hurt him."

Stella got up and bent down to pet him. "Don't hurt Wuss, 'kay?" She picked Max's plastic spoon off the floor and put it back on his tray.

"Thanks, Stel." Titus studied my face. "They want to meet you two and see Max since they missed out on most of his first year."

"I'd like to meet them, too. I'm just nervous, and I want them to like me."

He pulled me to him and cupped the side of my neck. "They'll love you. And if it makes you feel better, they hate Trixie." In some ways, that did make me feel better.

After we cleaned up the lunch mess, I scrubbed the kitchen and vacuumed the family room while Titus helped the kids straighten their rooms. Then I stood in my bra and panties in the closet, agonizing over what to wear. Titus walked in while I stood in front of my small collection of clothes.

He wrapped his arms around me and ran his hands up to cup my breasts. "This is nice, although you naked is my favorite. But you probably need to wear pants at least."

The heat of his hands seeped into my skin, and I leaned back against him. "I was thinking of wearing a little summer dress. Is that too casual?"

"No. Especially since I'll have easier access to your pussy after they leave." Titus and his dirty mouth. I shivered, and he reluctantly let go. My green sundress would do, I decided. It was only a little faded and made my eyes look almost normal.

Suddenly, my head went up. "It's quiet."

"Yeah, it's nice."

"Silence is nice unless children are involved. Then we'd better go see what's broken."

He smirked. "Good point."

I pulled on the sundress, and we walked into the kitchen where we heard soft giggles. Following the noise, we found Stella and Max sitting on the floor eating graham crackers and drinking orange juice. Russ snuck a piece of mushy cracker off Max's fist, and both kids had orange juice stains down the front of their shirts.

I sat next to them on the floor. "What are you guys doing down here?"

"Having snacks," Stella answered.

The doorbell rang just then, and I glanced up at Titus. "It figures."

He smiled. "I'll get it."

At that point I didn't have enough time to clean them up and change their shirts, so I let it go. "Looks yummy. Next time, let me know so I can have a snack with you."

"'Kay." Stella handed me her cup, and Max held up his gooey hand.

"Thank you, that looks delicious." I took a small sip and pretended to eat Max's offering. "Titus's parents are here. Let's wash our hands and say hello."

I stood and jumped a little when a tall man with a head full of messy white hair came around the corner. He looked like Titus, except he wore dress slacks and leather shoes.

"Where's my little Max?" His deep voice sounded at odds with his words.

"He's down here, Mr. Tremblay. We're just having a little afternoon snack on the kitchen floor." Russ barked once. "With the dog."

Titus's father took us in and grinned. I blinked and realized where Titus got his looks.

Titus's mother walked into the kitchen and smiled at us. Her short, gray-blond hair framed her smooth, made-up face. She wore a chic linen tunic and beautiful jade jewelry.

"Abby, these are my parents, Arthur and Florence." Titus gestured to them.

Stella peeked around the corner of the bar and stepped next to me. I waved awkwardly. "Hello. I'm Abigail, and this is my daughter, Stella."

"Hello, Abigail and Stella." Florence looked up at Titus. "He's never lived with a woman before, so you must be something special."

My smile slipped. "I'm not special, believe me."

Max stood up, and I remembered the mushy crackers. Picking him up, I took him over to the sink. "Let's wash your hands, little man."

When he was clean, I set him down and faced our visitors again. Arthur and Florence studied us for a few seconds until I shifted nervously and put my hands on the kids' shoulders to draw them into me.

"Can I get you anything to eat or drink?" I asked into the awkward silence.

Florence cleared her throat and stepped forward. "Yes. Something to drink sounds lovely, and I'm so happy to meet you."

Over the next hour, we opened a bottle of wine and a few beers, then sat in the family room and talked while the kids played with an indoor hockey set.

Florence smiled when I pulled it out. "Oh, I'm so glad they like it."

"Did you give this to Max? They play with it all the time."

"We did," she confirmed.

Arthur walked over and watched me set it up. I gazed up at him. "Did you play hockey too?"

He nodded. "I was never as good as Titus though. I didn't live and breathe it like he does. Do you like hockey?"

"Yes, but not as much as Stella. It gets a little intense for me sometimes, and it seems like there's a lot of blood."

Arthur nodded and rubbed his hands gleefully. "I know. Titus, you remember the player who caught his teammate's blade and got his throat sliced?"

"Yeah, it was Zednik. He was a little before my time." Titus glanced over at me. "He made it. They took him into surgery right away. It took the Zamboni a while to clean up all the blood though." My stomach roiled a little.

Arthur nodded enthusiastically. "And the player who caught that slapshot and lost the tip of his finger?" He looked at me and grinned. "It was still in his glove." I set my red wine down.

Titus threw the soft puck over to Stella. "There was also Verbeek, who lost his thumb in a farming accident. His game actually improved after that." By the time they wound down, I felt woozy.

Florence leaned forward. "It reminds me of the time you split your knuckles and broke your thumb beating up that player from Toronto." She turned to me. "The man tried to force himself on an inebriated fan. That's where Titus got the scars on his knuckles."

I studied Titus. "I didn't know that. How long ago?"

Titus gazed down at his hands and closed them into fists. "Five, maybe six years ago. It's a memory I'd rather forget."

Florence winced. "I'm sorry for bringing it up."

Arthur pointed to Titus. "That player and a couple of his teammates are the ones who triple-checked Titus against the boards and injured his back."

My stomach twisted when I thought of the scar along his spine. We watched the kids play for a few moments.

"Titus has a lot of scars," I murmured without thinking.

Florence raised her eyebrows. "Really? And have you seen them all?"

There was no good answer. "I'm going to take that as a rhetorical question."

Titus laughed and wrapped his arm around my neck, pulling me into him. Then he kissed me thoroughly. "Sometimes if my back is acting up, she'll give me a massage. And hers are much more enjoyable than Phyllis's, our physical therapist. But the last part of Abby's massages are my favorite."

My face flushed so hot, I imagined it glowing. "Oh, God. They don't need to know that!" They laughed, and the conversation drifted to what Titus might do next season.

Before his parents left a couple of days later, Florence took me to get a pedicure and a massage. She was appalled when I told her I'd never had a professional pedicure before.

"You need them to help get rid of dead skin and keep not just your nails, but your feet healthy," she told me as we sat in the salon while the nail technicians massaged our feet.

"Good to know." I didn't have the heart to tell her I couldn't afford professional pedicures.

She glanced at me. "When Titus turned thirty, we started to worry we'd never have grandchildren. And then he got hurt. I guess you could say we got a grandchild out of that."

"Trixie."

She rolled her eyes. "We love Max. Trixie, not so much."

Thinking about that woman gave me heartburn, so I changed the subject. "Tell me about his back. How long was he in the hospital?"

"Not too long. But the recovery took a while." She gazed out the spa window, lost in her thoughts. "The doctors said if he wasn't so muscular and tall, he might have been paralyzed."

"What happened to the player who assaulted the fan?"

Florence sighed. "He got dropped by his team because of the allegation. But another team picked him up a year later since the woman didn't want to testify, so no charges were filed."

"Is the guy still playing?"

Florence got a gleam in her eye that scared me a little. "No. After Titus's back injury, there was a serious brawl with some of Titus's former teammates, and the player is done. Permanently."

I didn't like violence, but in that instance, I thought the man deserved what he got. "His back bothers him sometimes, but he's never irritable or mean about it, and he doesn't take it out on us."

Florence searched my eyes and laid her hand on mine. "That's not his way. Titus and his dad are two of the most even-tempered men I know. Well, with their loved ones anyway. They find more interesting or enjoyable ways to get what they want." She raised her eyebrow. "That's not to say Titus doesn't get grumpy sometimes."

"That's true." We gave each other a knowing grin. Even when Titus got annoyed or grumpy, he still usually made me smile.

By the end of their stay, I felt more at ease with Titus's parents than I ever had with my own parents. Even Stella warmed up to them.

At the end of the week, Titus flew Max back to Vancouver. He also planned to spend a few days taking care of some business there. Max didn't seem to understand he was going back, but Stella did.

She hugged and kissed him, then patted his head. "Bye, Max. Love you." He hugged her back and kissed the front of her shirt.

"Say hello to Carla and Trixie for me," I said, then bit my tongue. "I'm sorry, that was snarky."

Titus grinned and pulled me to him, then kissed me with a little tongue. "I like that you're jealous. It shows you give a fuck. According to Keith, Carla moved out of the building last month, and the less I have to talk to Trixie, the better. She's livid." He smirked.

"Why?"

He cupped my jaw. "Because after she went after you and Stella, I took back the Mercedes she's been driving and stopped paying her weekly spa treatments and monthly condo dues. Even her fucking phone bill."

"What? I didn't know. Why would you pay for all that?"

He shrugged. "Bribery. So I could see Max without her jerking me around. But now I have a court order, and she fucked up when she hurt Stella. I'm done with her shit."

I kissed him again and hugged him tight. "Hurry back, the house will be too quiet without you guys."

"I ordered something from the Cherry Box. Don't open it until I get home."

"You know I can get anything for free, right?"

He shrugged. "I liked going through the website and picking out a few toys myself. And reading your reviews."

"Oh, Lord," I moaned.

He grinned at my discomfort. "I can almost picture what we were doing with each toy. Your customers seem to love it."

I covered my face. "Why is it okay to have perfect strangers read my write-ups, but I get mortified–and turned on–when you read them?"

He chuckled. "I get a fucking kick out of watching your reactions whenever we try out a new toy. You go from sputtering and blushing to begging and–"

I put my fingers over his mouth. "You like making me squirm, don't you?"

He bit the pad of my index finger, and his beautiful lips tipped up. "You have no idea."

Chapter 29

When Titus and Max left, the house was so quiet, we decided to make brownies and take them to the neighbors. We'd stayed home so Stella wouldn't miss her first day of preschool. It had been a small miracle she'd gotten accepted so quickly.

I called Isa with the good news. "The lady who first took my application told me the wait was at least four months long."

"Did you tell Titus you were on their waitlist?" she asked.

"Yes. He and Max came with us when I checked out the school and dropped off her information."

Isa laughed. "That explains it."

"What do you mean?"

"Abby, you've been living with the man for months. What does he do if he wants something?"

I thought back to him methodically getting joint custody of Max, and his patient way with me and Stella. And the sex. So much delicious, dirty sex. He'd even gotten me to try anal, and made me like it–damn him–just like he promised.

I cleared my throat. "He finds a way to get it."

"That's right. If he wants something, he gets it. And he doesn't lose his temper, or get upset. He works for it and finds a way to make it happen."

"You're right. He's like a velvet bulldozer, and he usually makes me happy he got his way."

She snickered. "Somehow, I don't think you're talking about preschool anymore."

Smiling, I looked down at my curled toes. "No, I'm not. You're saying he bribed them."

"Probably. We tend to forget he and Connor are loaded, and they can buy pretty much whatever they want."

The next afternoon, Harley Emerson called me out of the blue as Stella and I were finishing up another letter to Nana. This time, we'd taken a colorful child's placemat from our favorite Mexican restaurant and drawn all over it.

Harley was one of the Martini Monday crowd, an attorney like Laurel, and she'd recently gotten engaged to Damien. "I know this is unexpected, but Zeke needs to talk to you and Titus as soon as possible. He thought it might be better if I called you first."

My stomach dipped. "Titus is in Vancouver for the next couple of days. Is everything alright?"

"Damien's tied up, but Zeke and I can meet you at your house in half an hour. We need to talk."

Twenty minutes later, the doorbell rang. Harley and Zeke stood on the doorstep with matching serious expressions.

"Come in." I introduced them to Stella, then knelt in front of her. "I need to talk to my friends for a few minutes. Can you play with your toys?"

She nodded but didn't take her eyes off Zeke. "Can I have another brownie?"

I had to grin. She wasn't above exploiting the situation.

"Sure. But just one more, okay?" She took her brownie and skipped off to her room.

Turning to Harley and Zeke, I eyed them. "Would you like a brownie? Or a drink?"

Harley shook her head. "Let's go out to the back patio. I don't want Stella to overhear anything that might upset her."

I led them out to the outdoor dining table, and we sat down. Zeke didn't waste any time. "Is your father Calvin Carver?"

The sound of his name coming from Zeke felt like two different worlds crashing together. I could feel the blood drain from my head.

"Yes," I whispered. "Oh, God. He's looking for me, isn't he?"

Harley glanced at Zeke, then turned to me. "He's not just looking for you, Abby. He's telling people you're too mentally unfit to care for Stella, and you ran away with her a few months ago. It sounds like he found you through a few hockey articles and online photos of you with Titus. He called MAD Investigations this morning and talked to Zeke about paying them to track you down."

My lunch tried to crawl back up my throat as my mind slowly processed the news. I raised my shaking hand to my brow and tried to think. "He wants Stella? But why? He hurt her, and my parents barely tolerated her. I have to keep her safe." Panic and fear flared as I tried to catch my breath. "I need to protect Max too. What if he's here when my father comes? Oh God, I have to leave. Stella and I have to run."

Zeke grabbed my shaky hand. "Abby."

Getting to my feet, I tried to shake Zeke off. "I... I have a little money now."

He shook his head. "You're not running."

I almost doubled over with terror. "Please, please don't tell him where I am. Or at least give us some time."

Zeke held on to me. "Sweetheart, we'd never tell him where you're at. We're here to protect you."

Harley stood up and took my shoulders. "Abby, running is the most dangerous thing you could do. Take a few deep breaths, you're having a panic attack. Come on now, breathe with me." I tried to take in air, but my throat felt constricted. She turned to Zeke. "Will you grab some water?" He nodded and strode back into the house.

"Look at me," Harley ordered. When I gazed up at her, she took my hands. "I'm an attorney, and I know the law. Your father doesn't have a leg to stand on, especially since I heard you came here bruised and traumatized from him."

Some of my fears ebbed, but I still wanted to throw up. "You don't know him. He doesn't care about the law." I shuddered. "And he hates to lose."

Harley's eyes went hard. "He's going to lose this time, and you are not running."

When Zeke came back out with a glass of water, he had his phone to his ear. "Yeah, Harley's talking to her," he said. He paused and studied me. I was still terrified, but I wasn't trying to run. "She seems more in control, but I'm still worried. Okay." He stopped in front of me and held the phone out. "It's Titus. He wants to talk to you."

I took the phone in my trembling hand and put it to my ear. "Titus? I'm so sorry. I didn't want to bring this to you." I started crying softly. "We'll leave–"

"Abigail, you and Stella are not going *anywhere*. Do you understand? I'll be home in six hours, and I need you to be there when I get back. And quit fucking talking about leaving." I could hear him breathing heavily.

The fight-or-flight instinct still coursed through my body, but his voice soothed me, and his words helped cut through the haze.

"Okay. We'll be here." My voice dropped to a whisper. "But I can't go back. Zeke said he's telling people I'm mentally unfit, and I ran away with Stella." Tears spilled down my cheeks.

"Yeah, and he's full of shit. Zeke agreed to stay at the house until I get home, and then tomorrow we'll contact the police in Washington. You're going to make an official complaint, and push for charges."

I nodded. "Okay. I can do that."

He sighed. "I need to make some phone calls to get home. But remember, if it comes down to it, you already know how to prove you're a fit and stable parent. When we were in Fran's conference room, you pulled out documentation, photos, and a fuck-ton of shit to show I was fit. You can do the same for yourself."

My mind settled a little. Having a plan and something productive to focus on helped center me.

"You're right." I looked down at the ground and admitted the truth. "I hate that he... terrifies me."

"I know he does, but you aren't alone and isolated anymore. We're a team." Even though he was over a thousand miles away, he helped talk me back off the ledge. He was right, we were solid together and brought out the best in each other.

And then it hit me–I was deeply and irrevocably in love with this man. He was it for me, and I wanted to spend the rest of my life with him.

When he hung up, I handed Zeke his phone back. "Thank you. I lost it there for a few minutes, but I'm alright now. I'm not going to run."

Zeke patted my shoulder, knocking me to the side a little. "It's understandable. I'm just glad I didn't have to make Harley tackle you." Harley rolled her eyes, but smiled.

Isa and Connor arrived at the house less than an hour later. Isa hugged me, then pulled a bottle of whiskey down from the liquor cabinet. "Harley said that psychotic asshole father of yours is trying to hire a private investigator to find you."

I nodded, eyeing the whiskey. "Since when did you start drinking whiskey?"

"Since Calvin Carver crawled back out from under his rock. I usually drink a sip or two, shudder, and hand the rest to Connor."

Connor gave me a one-armed hug. "Titus told me he'd kick my ass if I let you leave. So don't leave."

How many babysitters did Titus think I needed? "Zeke's here watching me too. He's out on the back patio, and Harley just left to grab some food."

Isa raised her glass. "Good. After you tell us what's going on, we'll make a party out of it."

Zeke filled them in on his conversation with my father. I couldn't listen to it again, so I took Stella swimming while they talked in the kitchen.

Isa came outside a few minutes later with a red face and fire in her eyes. "If I knew we could get away with it, I'd murder that son of a bitch and dump his body out in the desert for the turkey vultures to find."

Even with my wet swimsuit, I hugged her tight. "I love you too, Isabella."

Several hours later, Titus made it home with a new stuffed animal for Stella. This time, it was a little skunk. I'd never been so happy to see anyone in my life.

Stella hugged his leg, and he picked her up. "Hey, *ma puce*. I missed you."

She patted his face. "Me too."

He set her down and walked over to me. Cupping my cheeks, he carefully studied my eyes. "Are you okay?"

Tears blurred my vision, but I willed them back. "Yes, and thank you for coming home early. I'm so sorry you got involved in my mess."

Shaking his head, he kissed me. "It's *our* mess, remember?"

Connor grabbed Titus's shoulder before he and Isa walked out. "Keep us posted, and let me know how I can help, eh?"

"Thank you for coming over. She's still here, so I'll have to kick your ass another day."

Connor smirked. "That's never going to happen."

Titus walked out with Zeke and Harley, and they stood talking in the driveway for several minutes before everyone left. Stella and

I put on pajamas and got cleaned up, and when he walked back in, he found us curled up together in her bed.

Grabbing a book off Stella's nightstand, he squeezed in next to us. "I've always liked *Goodnight Moon*." And then he quietly read to us, his deep voice soothing and calm.

Martina dumped the contents of her bag onto the counter several days later. Pepper spray, a whistle, and a gun clattered out. On second glance, the gun looked like some kind of stun gun.

She pointed to me. "You need to protect yourself. I know Titus is working on a few things, but you can also be smart."

I gingerly picked up the stun gun. "Why do you have this?"

Laurel patted my shoulder with a gleam in her eyes. "Trust me, that thing is worth its weight in the finest Belgian chocolate."

Martina smirked. "Don't you mean gold?"

"No. Gold doesn't make you want to orgasm."

"Good point." Martina turned to me. "Laurel zapped her father in the nuts with this last year."

I winced. "I bet that hurt."

"It did." Martina agreed. "I saw the whole thing, and the sound he made was almost inhuman."

Laurel studied me. "The whole incident was premeditated. He needed an incentive to leave me and my little brothers alone, and I gave him one."

It had been almost a week since Zeke and Harley came to the house with news about my father searching for me. I'd been anxious and jumpy since then.

"How? What did you do?"

"I decided to hit him where it hurts. We figured out what matters most to him and then threatened it. He loves money and power more than anything. And that's where we aimed."

Martina sat next to me. "So what does your father love the most?"

Thinking back to my childhood, my father seemed to be motivated by money too, but also control and dominance over the people around him. And he used religion to justify it.

A glimmer of a plan started percolating in my mind. My back straightened, and I looked up. "I think I have an idea, and it's unorthodox."

Laurel smiled. "Like Aunt Fern used to say, either do it in style or don't bother doing it. Tell us."

That night, after Stella fell asleep, Titus and I lay in bed as I told him my plan. "Laurel and Martina came over today."

"Yeah?"

I propped my head on my hand. "Did you know her father attacked her last year?"

"I heard something about it. What happened?"

I told him what I knew. "She provoked him and used herself as bait."

"No."

"No?" I echoed.

"It's a full sentence." He reached over and palmed a breast, and my slit grew wet. "You're not using yourself as bait."

He was right in this instance, even though I wanted to keep arguing with him just to see what he'd do. "Stella and Max are usually with me, so I agree it would be too dangerous. But she gave me an idea."

His fingers slid further down and he started stroking me. "Tell me."

Chapter 30

Later that week, Titus and I met with Zeke and Damien in their office. I'd taken some of my child support money and hired their firm to help me.

Titus and I had our first major fight over my paying their retainer. "Abigail, you can use your child support money for Stella's education. Or to buy a better car, or blow it for all I care. But I'm paying the fucking retainer."

What Titus didn't know was that I'd already paid it. "It's done. I hired them yesterday, so we can quit arguing about it. They're also giving me a steep 'friends and family' discount. Today is my first appointment, and you can come if you want, but *I* need to do this. For me. To prove to myself I can." My breath hitched.

He put his hands on his hips and scowled. "And I need to help protect you. You're not alone anymore."

"I know. But for so many years, I felt like I was. He tried to chip away at my independence and will." I thumped my chest. "Even my soul." How could I explain what it was like to have the people who should've protected and nurtured me be the people I feared the most?

I thought back to that little girl who could never understand why her father always criticized, nitpicked, and punished her. "I think some wounds have to be excised alone at some point. No friends, no partner, no family. Just me. To show myself I've moved past him, and he didn't win."

He studied me, his jaw still clenched. I stepped in front of him and wrapped my hands around his cheeks. "You make it possible for me to even think about facing him. And you've never made me feel afraid or worthless—just the opposite. You're my rock, my Spartan. And I love you."

He closed his eyes for a second and sucked in a deep breath, then he gathered me to him. "Fucking hell, you know how to gut a man, don't you? I love you too. Now, let's take care of that bastard so we can get on to better things."

Later that afternoon, we sat in Zeke and Damien's conference room, and I laid out my ideas.

By the time I finished, Damien looked intrigued. "This isn't typical, but it should be effective."

Zeke grinned and shook his head. "It's never a dull moment with you ladies, and you're all a little fucking crazy. Send us a copy when you get done."

Over the next few days, I also called the police station nearest my parents' home and spoke with an officer there. Laurel had prepared me regarding what to say, how to file a report, and the issues I'd face.

The officer on the line sighed. "Ma'am, you state he assaulted you several months ago. Why did you wait so long to make a report?"

"I didn't plan on making a report, but a few days ago he tried to hire an investigation firm where I live to track me down, and it's just a matter of time before he finds me. I live in another state over a thousand miles away. I have appropriate housing, employment, a pediatrician for my daughter, and she's just started preschool. But he's *still* harassing and threatening me. It's time to fight back."

"Alright, that's a reasonable explanation. Do you have any photos or evidence?"

"Yes. I do." Luckily, Isa had taken a few photos on our road trip, and my bruised face was visible. When she forwarded them to me last week, I wondered if she'd taken them so I'd have the proof if I ever needed it.

Next, we tracked down my old school counselor who'd tried to intervene. Sandra Denton had moved from Seattle to Miami several years ago, and Zeke helped me find her.

"Abby Carver. Of course I remember you. How are you?"

"I'm getting there, Ms. Denton. Thank you for talking to me."

"Call me Sandra, you're an adult now. How can I help you?"

I laid out my life with my father and didn't sugarcoat it. Then I asked her if she would provide a statement regarding her trying to help me all those years ago.

She sniffled. "Of course I will. I'm sorry I couldn't stop him."

"Thank you again for caring enough to try."

Next, I contacted the school where Sandra Denton made that report over ten years ago. They sent me to the district office, and when the administrator found out what I wanted, he sent me to the school district's legal office.

"Ms. Carver, it's been over ten years. I'm not sure the school even has those records anymore."

I rolled my eyes. He probably just didn't want to be bothered. "They do, Mr. Lenard. I already called them. I also sent a formal request for all my records. The law states schools who receive federal funds must provide a person their records upon request."

He sighed. "Alright, Ms. Carver."

My blood started to boil. I hung up and puffed out a long, frustrated breath. "Lazy asshole."

Isa sat on the floor, playing Uno with Stella and Elodie. She looked up and snickered. "This is a side of you I've never seen before. I like it. Dad always said when I get in trouble, I should pray for help, but also work like hell to get myself out."

I smiled because that did sound like Javier. Turning back to the kitchen table where all my notes were spread out, I squared my shoulders and called my old pediatrician's office to request my medical records. My pediatrician had also been my father's friend.

It was time to stir the hornet's nest.

Except for my father, we'd settled into a nice, peaceful routine at home. Titus spent most mornings training and working out, but he had a lighter schedule since the season ended. When Max wasn't with us, and Stella went to preschool half days on Thursdays, Titus stayed home and we messed around on every conceivable surface in the house.

Last Thursday morning, Titus had tied me down spread eagle on the kitchen table, then he'd teased and fucked me for an hour straight while he fed me strawberries and whipped cream, and ate them out of my pussy. He called those days our thirsty Thursdays. I was like one of Pavlov's dogs–when Titus murmured those two words in my ear and told me what he had planned, I got wet and broke out in goosebumps.

Max was with us this week, so we had to get a little creative. I grinned as I thought about our late-night swim last night. There'd been a full moon, and Titus decided we should go skinny dipping after the kids went to bed. It had turned into a long, salacious bout of pool sex with waterproof toys and a ball gag from one of the toy boxes. I tended to get a bit noisy.

Titus texted me later that morning.

Titus: How are things at the house, and what are your plans for the day?

Me: We're straightening up and I'm working on my to-do list.

Titus: Am I on it?

Me: Always. It says "Do Titus" right at the top.

The days were turning hot here, so we usually ate out on the back patio for breakfast or dinner but stayed inside during the afternoon. It was perfect for swimming though, and Stella and I were tan and sun-kissed for the first time in our lives.

Claudette Face Timed me from Berlin, and we talked while she sipped a big glass of wine. "You're my damn hero, Abby."

"I miss you. And I didn't know wine glasses came that big. How are you?"

"So good," she drawled, taking another sip. "A couple of work buddies and I rented a fancy apartment in Seville last week and explored southern Spain. And we drank sooo much good wine."

"Such a hard life," I mocked.

"Well, look at you. All tan and glowy. And I love that little jumper you have on."

"Titus loves them too."

"Uh-huh." She tipped her glass to me. "I bet he does."

Claudette put her wine down, her face getting serious. "Did you email a media presentation to your father's church congregation about him physically abusing you?"

"Yes, I did. How'd you hear about it?"

"That whole damn zip code heard about it. Child abuse being covered up by a church congregation and a pediatrician is a serious thing. Mom and Dad even knew about it, and Gabriel called me. He's worried about you."

I chewed on my lip. "A few of them helped my father gloss over what happened to me, and I thought if I put them all on notice, it might keep him away."

I set kids' lunches down in front of them and stroked their hair.

"Thanks, Mommy." Stella picked up the sandwich I'd cut into a heart shape and took a huge bite.

Claudette whistled. "Shit, that's ballsy. So, what happened? Have you heard from any of them?"

"Yes. And some responses have been... surprising." I gazed out at the red hibiscus flowers blooming in the backyard.

Max bit off a piece of sandwich and spit it onto the floor for Russ. "Doggie," he babbled and pointed, as if Russ didn't know exactly where the food landed.

"One is enough. Now you eat," I told him.

"How have they been surprising?" Claude asked, drawing me back to our conversation.

"Most of the emails were supportive, and several people seemed horrified and outraged. It's caused a major firestorm that I didn't expect."

"They're churchgoers. Most of them probably want to do what's right and have good hearts. Although your perception might be a bit different." Claudette cocked her head. "What, exactly, did the presentation have in it? Send me a copy."

I sighed. "Some incidents are distressing, and a few people tried to help me over the years that I didn't even know about." I rubbed my forehead. "I feel ashamed for some reason about what happened to me, but also relieved and unburdened to get it all out. That probably doesn't make sense."

"It does. What were some of the surprising things you found?"

"My kindergarten teacher got in a shoving match with my mother over finger-shaped bruises on my arms. She was suspended for a week." I had to stop talking for a minute and collect myself. "My father stopped physically hurting me for a long time after that. I didn't even remember her until I read that report."

Claude gazed at me, her eyes shiny. "Abby, I think you're a fucking warrior."

Her vehemence warmed me. "An internet warrior, maybe. Okay, I'll send it to you." I pulled up the file and emailed her a copy. Then I waited while she skimmed through it.

The presentation included snippets of reports from the kindergarten incident, me missing school for a week after my father whipped me, my school counselor's report, a broken arm he'd given me the summer I went to camp, and some photos over the years that I'd scrounged up. I also included Zeke's email verifying his conversation with my father.

Claudette's face went pale as she read, but her expression stayed stoic. "Abby, I want to read through it and call you back, okay?"

We hung up, and she called me back an hour later. Her eyes looked red, which made me tear up. "Damn it! I need you to be the strong and cynical one for me."

"Fuck being strong. I'm pissed." She had to stop and get herself under control.

"He fucking *broke your arm*, Abby. I didn't even know. It's why he let you go to camp that summer, isn't it? That cock sucking asshole tried to hide it."

I shrugged philosophically. "That was the best summer I ever had. It was probably worth the broken arm."

Claudette stood up and walked around with her hands on top of her head. "The school administrators knew, and your fucking pediatrician needs to have his license revoked. The hospital staff had suspicions, and at least they tried to follow through."

Stella brought her plate to the counter and held up her jelly-smeared hands. "My hands are icky."

"Hold on," I told Claudette. "I need to clean them up." I hoisted her to the sink, washed her hands and mouth, then pulled Max out of his highchair and cleaned him up too. He babbled and complained while I wiped his mouth off.

"We're gonna play, Mommy," Stella said when I set Max back down.

"Sounds good. Tell Claudette goodbye, and then keep your door open so I can yell at you guys if I need to, okay?"

"Kay. Bye!" Then they ran off.

Claudette smiled, even though her eyes were glassy. "She's talking so well, and they seem happy. You're all tan, outdoor water babies now."

"It's so nice, and we love it here with Titus and Max. I just wish my father would leave us alone."

"What do you think he's going to do about you exposing him?"

Sighing, I picked at my lunch. "I don't know. It'll be something, I'm just not sure what."

My life felt a little like one of those scary movies where the girl walks around doing normal things while *Psycho*, slasher-type music plays in the background, foreshadowing the coming of the bogeyman.

Chapter 31

Titus: Are you wearing one of your little cock-teasing dress-es?

I read Titus's text and looked down at my shorts and old tank top. I'd just cleaned the kids' bathroom since Titus and I were trying to potty train Max, and he hadn't quite learned how to aim yet. I finally talked Titus into having Andrea come clean only once a week.

Me: I will before you get home this afternoon. They're nice and cool.

Titus: How about no bra and panties?

Me: The voices in my head are telling me no.

Titus: Don't listen to them.

Me: That sounds... interesting, but I'm probably going to be busy not doing that.

Titus: Up to you, but I'll make it worth your while. See you in a few hours.

The rest of the afternoon went by in a haze as I debated whether to wear panties or not.

When Titus got home that evening, he sat in one of the big recliners in the family room with the kids on his lap, while they crawled all over him as they told him about their day.

After Max and Stella wound down and went off to play, he came over to where I sat at the bar and slid his hand up my thigh.

Then he slowly grinned. "No panties. You didn't listen to the voices in your head." Leaning in, he nuzzled my cheek and pulled my thighs apart. Then he slid a finger along my slit. "You listened to your pussy instead. Smart choice."

He worked my clit and ran his thumb across my nipple over the fabric of my dress.

I moaned softly. "That feels...so good. It's going to be a long evening. And I have to be careful not to bend over."

He grinned and stepped back when I started panting. "A little anticipation will be good for you."

I tried to pinch him. "I don't need a proctologist to tell me you're an ass for getting me all worked up and then leaving me hanging."

Shrugging, he evaded my fingers and gave me a hard kiss. "But I'm *your* ass."

Wrapping my arm around him, I stood up and kissed him, then slid my other hand down his stomach and squeezed and rubbed his length. When he started groaning into my mouth, I broke the kiss off and stepped back.

"Isn't karma a bitch?" I patted his cheek and turned to walk away. He pulled me back, bent down, and threw me over his shoulder.

"Hey! What are you doing?" I laughed and struggled.

"We have six to ten minutes before they come looking for us. I can work with that." Titus strode into his bedroom and shut and locked the door. He laid me down on the bed, and when I turned and started scrambling on my hands and knees to get away from him, he grabbed my ankle and pulled me back.

Then he unzipped his jeans and wrapped his arm under my hips to keep me in place.

"Mouthy, handsy girls get this." He lined up his cock to my wet opening and slammed inside.

"Oh, my fucking God!" My head flew back as he grabbed my hips with both hands and shoved inside me again.

He flipped my dress above my hips and smacked my bare ass cheek. "No, *bonne fille*, you're fucking me. Try not to scream or moan the house down this time." I could hear the grin in his voice. He smacked me again, and the pain and heat made my pussy clench around him.

"Go... fuck... yourself," I panted.

"I'm busy right now. Fucking you." Reaching around me, he found my clit then rubbed and flicked it relentlessly until I braced my hands on the bed and started pushing mindlessly back at him.

"Harder! Oh sweet Jesus, deeper!"

"That's it. Fuck yourself on me," he growled. His words made my brain sizzle, and I rammed myself even harder at him. His thrusts became uneven and just as he slammed into me one last time, my pussy clenched around him, and I came. He didn't give me a chance to scream out loud, but wrapped his huge palm around my mouth and the lower part of my face while I wailed out my orgasm, and he spilled his come inside me.

When we finally came down, he laid his forehead on my sweaty back. "I'm stealing all your panties if this is what it gets us."

The next morning, I went for another run before it got too hot outside. Titus and the kids were starting to make breakfast, and he planned to meet Connor at the arena around ten, so I had plenty of time.

I finished my two miles and headed back toward home. As I turned into the cul-de-sac, a car pulled up to the side of the road in front of me. I crossed the street to avoid it, but a man stepped out and faced me. I glanced at him, then my heart slammed in my chest and my ears started ringing.

He looked so ordinary in a blue button-down shirt, chinos, and wire-rimmed glasses. But I knew what lurked beneath his bland, modestly handsome exterior.

My father started toward me, raising his hands. "Abigail, I want to talk to you."

My mind went into a free fall, and the years of living on edge and in fear flitted through my hindbrain. I doubled over a little as fear and shock slithered through me. His hand snaked out and grabbed my wrist, like he'd done so many times before, then he started dragging me toward his car.

"Abby, thanks for the brownies. They were delicious," I heard someone say from behind me.

The comment was so incongruous that it jolted me out of my daze. I turned and saw Walter standing there in his usual blue scrubs.

Planting my feet hard, I violently yanked my arm out of my father's grasp and straightened. "Walter, I've never been so glad to see anyone in my life." I turned to my father and rasped, "Don't ever touch me again, or you'll regret it."

Walter caught the tension and glanced between us. "Abby, do you know this guy?"

I nodded slowly as I backed up. I didn't want to turn my back on the man in front of me. "He's my father. I filed a criminal report against him in Washington State, and now he's being charged with child abuse and assault against me."

Walter straightened and his eyes narrowed on Calvin Carver.

He ignored Walter. "I just want to talk, Abigail. You owe me." His voice went from cajoling to bitter. "I raised you, then forgave you and even gave you a place to live when you acted like a slut and a whore."

Walter raised his eyebrow and looked at me. "Is he for real?"

I nodded miserably and met my father's stare. "I paid rent to live in your cold, partially finished basement. And you beat me when I wanted to leave. Not sure how that means I owe you."

He pushed his glasses up his nose. "God has forgiven me. I lost my patience and acted rashly, but you bore false witness against me when you sent that email to my congregation." His voice rose.

I forgot how he liked to color his speech with religious jargon sometimes. "God may have forgiven you, but I haven't. I hate you so much. Just leave us alone." My voice shook, and fear and adrenaline raced through me.

"God will punish you for this unless you drop those charges, and I know where you're living now, in sin with a whoremonger."

Walter gently pulled me onto his driveway. "She asked you to leave, you fanatic weirdo. She's on my property, and I'm telling you to leave too."

My father's face went red, and I knew without a single doubt he would have gone after me if Walter wasn't standing next to me.

"You're a harlot and an abomination, having a child and then living with men out of wedlock." He pointed a finger at me. "And I *will* find a way to put the fear of God in you."

Walter pulled his phone out and took a few photos of Calvin. "I'm calling the cops and having you arrested for trespassing and disturbing the peace if you don't leave right now."

My father stared at me without blinking for several seconds, then turned and walked back to his car. We watched him pull away.

"Abby, that man is creepy as hell. You need to be careful."

I turned and hugged Walter. "Thank you. I'm so grateful you were here."

He patted my shoulder awkwardly. "Me too. I'm walking you home, then I want to talk to Titus, okay?"

Titus sat at the kitchen table with the kids and smiled when we walked in. But his smile faded when he saw my face. "What's going on?"

Walter raised his hand. "Hello, Titus. We just saw Abby's father in the cul-de-sac. He grabbed her and started dragging her to his car, and then spewed several threats and slurs at her."

Titus stood and strode to me, cupping my face and looking into my eyes. "Are you alright?"

My legs felt shaky, and not from my run. I held onto his arms, feeling their strength and thickness. "I'm not going to lie. It scared me, but I'm okay."

Titus tucked me into him and turned to Walter. "I've never met him before. Tell me your impressions."

"There's something way off about him. He kept saying weird religious shit, and his eyes were cold. He also seemed to think of Abby as... under his control, or maybe his property." Walter looked at me. "He also said he'd find a way to put the fear of God in you. Don't run alone anymore, okay?"

A couple of mornings later, Jackson and Rudy showed up at our house around eight. When Titus let them in, I looked at him questioningly.

Jackson smiled and raised his hand. "Hey, we're going to be your running partners this morning before we go train."

"Oh, I'm sorry you guys came over. I'm just going to skip it until things settle down." I glanced over at Titus, who raised his eyebrow.

"You're not fucking skipping it. Even though you bitch about it, I know you look forward to your morning runs. And so does half the damn neighborhood."

He turned to Jackson. "It turns into a social event every time we go out for a walk or play in the cul-de-sac. Since we don't have a double stroller yet, I need to stay and watch Stella and Max."

"Yeah, and one long-distance run won't kill us," Rudy said.

Jackson smacked the back of his head. "Don't make her feel guilty."

"What? It's true. Long-distance running isn't the best way for hockey players to condition."

I shook my head and smiled. "Well, you're in for a pleasant surprise. My runs are short and quick, and the best thing I can say about running is how good it feels right after you stop."

We stretched a little, then I took off at my usual pace. Jackson and Rudy flanked me, and about half a mile into the run I glanced over and noticed Jackson scanning the streets as we ran.

He turned to me. "What was your dad driving the other day?" he asked.

"A bronze-colored Hyundai. I'm sure it was a rental. Why?"

Jackson pointed down one of the side streets to a man sitting in his car. "Is that him?"

My gait stuttered a little, and adrenaline raced through me. "Yes."

He stopped abruptly and pulled out his phone. Then Jackson walked toward the bronze car with his phone up. I slowed down and stopped as anger coursed through me. That fucker came back and was waiting for on a side street. Rudy stayed with me and moved to my other side, so I stood closest to the curb.

Jackson got within about ten feet of the car, when my father turned on the engine, pulled out, and sped away. He stared flatly at me when he drove by.

I stopped and bent over, putting my hands on my knees when he was out of sight. Rudy leaned over and studied my face. "You okay? You're not going to faint or anything, are you?"

Straightening, I put my hands on my head. "No. But I do want to kick something."

As we stood there, Vern walked out in a velour leisure suit, this one red with black striping. "Honey, Walter let the neighborhood know your daddy is stalking you. He's been parked there for almost an hour. That's not good."

I sighed. "Hi Vern. No, it's not. This is Jackson and Rudy, Titus's teammates."

"Is that velvet?" Rudy asked, studying Vern's jumpsuit.

Vern shook his head and ran his hand down his front. "It's velour, so it washes up like a dream and is fabulously comfortable."

Rudy nodded. "Nice, and those are Thunderbird colors. Where'd you order it?"

Somehow, Rudy's distraction with Vern's jumpsuit settled my nerves.

"We're finishing this run," I declared. I was done letting my father dictate my life.

Rudy sighed. "Okay."

When we walked into the house a half hour later, Max and Russ were wrestling over a rope toy in the living room. Titus stood watching them with a cup of coffee in his hand. He glanced at us when we filed in and knew right away something was off.

He turned to Jackson. "Was he out there?"

"Yeah. He sat parked on a side street about a half mile from here. Vern, your neighbor, came out and said he'd been waiting there for her. Something's not right with that guy."

Titus nodded and turned to me, wrapping his hand around my neck. "Zeke said your father's first hearing for the criminal assault charges is next week in Seattle. I'm sorry, but we need to be there."

"Damn it." I sighed and laid my forehead on his chest.

Chapter 32

Zeke called a few days before we planned to fly out to Seattle and wanted to talk to us before we left. Titus had just gotten home from taking Max back to Vancouver, and he came with me to their office.

Zeke cut to the chase. "When I did a background check on your parents, I thought it odd neither of them are listed as your grandmother's trustees. I don't think they're even in her will."

Nana was the only close living relative I had besides my parents, but she'd been in the memory care facility for almost eight years.

I cocked my head and studied him. "My maternal grandfather was a real estate investor and made some money that way, and my parents used to complain about him never giving them anything. He passed away when I was young."

"Your grandparents were well off. Did you know that?"

"Yes." I shrugged. "But Nana has lived there for years, and God knows how many times I've heard my father complain about how expensive it is."

"It shouldn't matter to him, since that's what her money should be used for. Do you know who your grandmother's estate attorney is?"

"Someone at Boeger and Boeger Law in Florida. I remember the name because it sounded almost like booger." I grinned sheepishly. "I was young the first time I heard it."

Zeke snickered. "I'd probably remember it too. It's a puzzle, isn't it? Your dad seems so fixated on controlling you, and it makes me wonder why."

"He always used religion and saving my soul as his reasons. And my mother went along with it."

Zeke leaned forward. "I think it might have as much to do with your grandmother's will as religion. I'd bet good money you're her heir."

A few days later, we flew to Seattle for the hearing. The courthouse was built in the Pacific Northwest architecture style, which meant a lot of wood, glass, and metal beams. The overcast sky drizzled rain and mist, but the grass and lush green trees smelled earthy and wet. I didn't miss the perpetually gray skies in Seattle, but I'd forgotten how much I loved all the deep, vibrant colors and life the rain brought.

After we passed through the metal detectors, Titus grabbed my hand as we walked inside. Connor had also come with us, but Isa had started working, so she and Javier watched Stella.

The prosecutor was expecting us. "I'm Deidra Cunningham." She gave me a firm handshake and spoke quickly. "It's problematic that you waited several months to make the report, but the fact he's stalked you since the charges were brought should sway the judge. And Zeke Deegan's report was very informative. I assume you want me to request a no-contact order?"

"Yes. He scares me, and last week while I was out running, he grabbed my arm and started pulling me toward his car." I told her what had happened. "I just want him to leave us alone."

Her eyes sharpened. "Was this in Palm Springs?"

"Yes, and Zeke should have sent you a few medical and public school records and some photographs."

A terrifying smile spread across Deidra's face. "He did. Let's see what Mr. Warner has to say. He's your father's attorney. I'll ask for a no-contact order for both you and your daughter."

"Thank you."

She held up a hand. "I have to warn you, whoever said the wheels of justice grind slowly didn't lie. It could be months before a resolution is reached." I'd seen this first-hand from Titus'ss custody case.

As we walked toward the courtroom, my heart started racing with dread at the thought of seeing my father and mother again. Titus and Connor flanked me as we walked inside. My father and his attorney sat at the defendant's table, and Deidra walked to the prosecution's table. We slid in a few rows behind her.

My mother sat directly behind my father. I studied her out of the corner of my eye. She styled her gray-blond hair in a straight, severe bob even though it was naturally curly like mine. She'd worn the same hairstyle since I was a child, and her clothes were bland and conservative. She sat still with her hands folded in her lap, not glancing my way.

I studied her now and tried to reconcile my feelings for her. It didn't take long—I didn't have any besides maybe dislike and anger. My grandmother had been the one to cuddle and love me as a child. She'd lived close enough back then that I'd spent a lot of time in her care. Between her and my friends and their families, I'd been able to scrape up enough love and nurturing to survive.

But it was no thanks to my parents. I realized as I sat there staring at her profile, I was done. Not mad, or hurt, or even upset. Just done. I turned my head and stared at the front of the courtroom, not glancing at her again.

The bailiff called the case, and the judge turned to Deidra. "Ms. Cunningham, we're here for a preliminary hearing. Have you spoken to Mr. Carver's attorney?"

Deidra stood. "No, Your Honor. We'll need to continue, and we're requesting a no-contact order against Mr. Carter for both his daughter and granddaughter."

My father's attorney stood. "Your Honor, my client does not waive his right to a preliminary hearing since he feels there is no evidence whatsoever, and he also strongly objects to a no-contact order. The alleged victim waited months before contacting the police, and my client states she's unstable and lives out of state."

Deidra shook her head and glanced at the opposing counsel. "Your Honor, Abigail Carver is here today. She flew in from Palm Springs. I've spoken with her, and she's given me detailed medical and school records. I also find it offensive for Mr. Carver to state she is 'unstable' when there is no proof of that whatsoever."

My father whipped around in his seat to stare at me, sitting between Titus and Connor.

Deidra continued. "Mr. Carver went to Palm Springs and accosted her less than a week ago. Then two days later, he sat in his car not far from her house, waiting for her. He may be the unstable one, and this could be grounds for a felony charge of intimidating a witness. There is video of him in her neighborhood, and I received a copy of a car rental agreement and a round-trip flight for Calvin Carver last week to Palm Springs. The alleged victim states Mr. Carver has been violent and abusive to her for most of her life, and she has records that back this up."

Zeke and Damien had come through for me in a big way. The judge pinned Mr. Warner and his client with a dark, quiet glare. "Mr. Warner, would you like a few minutes to confer with your client and the prosecutor?" he asked quietly.

Mr. Warner clenched his jaw and glared down at his client. "Yes, Your Honor."

The court recessed, and they went into a conference room while we waited in the hall. My mother didn't go into the room with them. A few minutes later, we heard yelling and what sounded like a chair or a fist hitting the wall. Then a red-faced Mr. Warner came out and spoke with Deidra for a few minutes.

Not long afterward, the bailiff reconvened the hearing and Mr. Warner addressed the judge. "My client agrees to the no-contact order, and we'll waive the preliminary hearing."

The judge nodded curtly. "Very good, Mr. Warner. If there isn't anything else today, we'll schedule the next court date and adjourn."

I let out a long, soft breath and grabbed Titus's hand, giving it a firm squeeze. The temporary no-contact order wasn't a lot, but it felt like the first time anyone had publicly acknowledged my father's abuse toward me. It felt so good, I wanted to go somewhere and just weep with relief.

We all exited the courtroom, and I walked over to thank Deidra while Connor and Titus hung back.

"Thank you so much," I said, shaking her hand vigorously. "It feels like the first time anyone has believed me. My pediatrician and a few school administrators were church friends with him, so he was always able to hide it."

Deidra studied me. "I have a lot of cases, so I'll admit that I only glanced through the files your investigator sent over. But I'd be remiss in my duties if I didn't tell you that you probably have a strong civil claim against the pediatric office and the school district. You should think seriously about talking to a private attorney."

I stood still, a little shocked at what she'd said. And then her eyes widened as she looked behind me. I turned around in time to see my father shove Titus, then take a wild swing and hit Titus in the cheek. Titus barely moved.

"Well, fuck," Deidra muttered admiringly.

I screamed Titus's name and tried to run to him, but Deidra reached out and grabbed my shirt. I stopped short and noticed Titus just standing there with his arms at his sides. What the hell was going on? Connor stood several feet away with his arms folded, watching the altercation with an amused smirk.

My father's fists clenched as Titus leaned forward and said something low enough so no one else could catch it. Calvin's face turned a mottled shade of red, and bile rose up in my throat.

"Just watch." Deidra held onto me.

"You'll burn in hell, right along with her!" My father screeched at Titus. "She's been nothing but a willful little bitch since the day she was born."

"A bitch? Since the day she was born?" Titus chuckled and shook his head. "Do you really think that, or are you angry and bitter her grandmother passed you and your Stepford wife over so Abby would inherit?"

My father took another wild swing at Titus, hitting his cheekbone. Then Titus struck so fast that I almost missed it. He clocked my father in the middle of his chin with a quick, brutal jab, and Calvin Carver went down like a puppet getting its strings cut. He lay still on the floor for a few seconds, then moaned. I'd heard a distinct crack when Titus hit him.

The bailiff stepped forward as Titus moved back, holding both hands up.

Connor pointed down. "I've been standing right here and saw the whole thing. This asshole hit him twice before Titus defended himself."

Deidra let go of me with a gleam in her eyes. "It looks like we need to add another assault charge–in a courthouse, no less–to your charges, Mr. Carver."

Over the next hour, we filled out reports while a police officer detained my father, and the EMTs were called in. Because it turned out Titus had broken his mandible. After the police reviewed the courthouse video, we were free to go.

Titus ordered a ride as we walked out of the courthouse.

Connor grinned gleefully. "You broke his jaw. Did you mean to do it?"

Titus put his arm around me. "Fuck, yes. I hear a broken jaw hurts like hell and is a bitch to recover from. He should be too worried about how to talk and eat for the next few months to focus on Abby." I turned and stared at him with my mouth open.

On the ride to the airport, I gazed out at the traffic, not seeing anything. My mind went back over the day's events, and I felt hollow and fuzzy, like I'd burned through too many emotions and my heart needed a chance to regenerate.

Connor sat in the front passenger seat, and Titus pulled me into his side as far as our seatbelts would allow. His craggy, handsome, but slightly bruised face carefully searched mine.

Over the past months, since Stella and I showed up at Titus's door, battered, wounded, and clinging to the hope that we could be safe in this scarred hockey player's home, he'd slowly and carefully nurtured us, giving us unconditional love and protection.

And then there were the uninhibited nights and stolen moments during the days when I learned to love and play and revel in intimacy, not feeling like a "whore" or a "harlot."

I didn't realize tears were falling down my cheeks until he reached over and gently wiped a few away with his thumb. I gulped and tried to hold back a sob.

"It's okay. Cry, scream, do whatever you need to."

Tears dripped down my nose, and mascara probably streaked my face. But I didn't care. Without turning around, Connor reached back and handed me a wad of tissue.

"Thank you." I wiped my face and blew my nose, then turned to Titus. "You let him hit you. Twice." I pushed his shoulder, but my heart wasn't in it. "Why would you do that?"

"Because I wanted to."

"But why?"

"Because I *really* wanted to lay that motherfucker out, but it needed to be self-defense, or you'd probably be waiting for me right now at the police station. I thought two half-assed punches from him first should clear me."

My lips twitched. "You're a very detail-oriented person, aren't you?"

He grinned and wrapped his arm around my shoulders. "When it matters? Yeah, I am. Now let me tell you—in detail—what I want to do with you when we get home." As he whispered in my ear, my breath sped up and I grabbed hold of his knee and squeezed.

Chapter 33

Over the next month, things settled down at our house. Max came for two weeks, and then left again, and Stella settled into preschool and played with Carmen when Andrea brought her along.

Stella followed Titus around, especially after Max left, and Titus started showing her how to do things. I watched from the kitchen window one morning as Titus talked her through checking my car's oil and tire pressure. I shook my head and smiled as I watched them.

Summer came to Palm Springs with a vengeance, and we put up a few shade sails in the backyard so we could go swimming to break up the heat. I'd gotten into the habit of wearing mostly sundresses or skirts, and Titus went out and bought me a dozen more. They were cooler, and he said he liked the easy access. I liked it too. Most of the time I wore panties, but sometimes I didn't, and he always liked to check.

He'd come up behind me and slide his hands up my skirt to palm my ass cheeks when the kids were in the other room. After they went to bed one night, he pulled me out to the back patio, sat in one of the patio chairs, and freed himself. The warm dry air swirled around us, caressing my skin, as he pulled me on top of him and fucked me in the hot desert evening, covering my mouth as I came around his massive cock.

The next day, I sat with Isa in Connor's kitchen. "What the hell are those?" Isa asked me as she looked over my shoulder at my computer screen.

In the other room, we could hear the girls playing together. Titus and Connor had gone to the arena to meet a few other teammates to condition together.

I grinned and held up my computer so she could see better. "These are a selection of specialty dildos I'm looking through for my online store. They're letting me test a few out for free. See anything that interests you?"

She set her coffee mug down and took my computer. "They all interest me, but maybe not to try on myself." She pointed at the screen. "What's that one?"

"It's an octopus tentacle dildo, but I'm not sure what I think of the florescent yellow color. Tentacle fetishes and tentacle porn is a thriving subculture."

She stared at it. "Huh. My fun fact for the day. What about this one?" She pointed to a sparkly pink, girthy dildo covered with rubber spikes.

I squinted at the screen. "Those spikes could go either way, but it's from the Princess Pleasure line and they have a good reputation. Let's test that one." I picked up my coffee and took a sip.

"If you were buying a dildo and wanted something unique and fun–besides the trusty six or seven-inch vibrating Rabbit–what would you choose?"

She stared at the screen, scrolling through the selections. "Damn, I didn't know there were so many choices. I mean, there's rubber, glass, metal, ceramic. And that's not including the size, color, or features." She squinted at my screen. "What's elastomer, anyway?"

"Silicone. Those are more flexible. So what interests you here?"

She handed my computer back to me, still staring at the screen. "Do I have to tell you?"

"No, but it would be nice to know. Tell you what, I'll order it and you and Connor can product test for me."

"Do you and Titus test all your products?"

"Not all of them." I shifted in my seat. "I'm working up to the extreme fetish stuff. I might have to get a few other product testers for it."

She turned to me, and her mouth curved up. "I know who would test your extreme fetish products for you."

"Who?"

"Martina and Iz."

I leaned in. "Are they finally together?"

Her eyebrow went up, and she smirked. "Yeah, and it was like a bomb went off. Iz finally put his size fourteen foot down. Right on Martina's ass."

"Karaoke night this Friday. You in?" I asked.

"Abso-fucking-lutely." We both laughed. Martina was the karaoke DJ at Iz's bar, and it would be fun to see the fireworks.

They'd been dancing around each other for almost a year and had some interesting history.

Isabella looked back at my screen and pointed to a dildo that looked like a hammer and had an action-hero theme to it. "That one."

I squinted at the screen, then leaned back. "Huh. Connor's nickname is The Hammer. Could that have anything to do with it?"

She blushed but smirked a little. "The nickname fits him well. How's the business going, anyway?"

"Good. Actually, more than that. It's fun, and the money has been a godsend. Edna, my assistant, is also like the crazy aunt I never knew I always wanted."

She smiled. "I'm glad. You deserve decent people in your life. Have you heard anything from your parents?"

I logged out and shut down my computer. "Just a few things second-hand. A few church members have kept in touch since I sent that email out. It sounds like my father was ostracized when it came out how he'd treated me. They've stopped going to their church. He's also struggling with his broken jaw."

"Karma can be such a sweet little bitch. It serves them both right."

"Maybe I should feel bad about what happened, but I'm just relieved."

She leaned back. "And I feel bone-deep elation and satisfaction. What's going on with his criminal charges?"

I shrugged. "The prosecutor said he's going to plead no contest. And the no-contact order will stay in place permanently, thanks in part to Titus and their run-in after the hearing."

"When are you going to see your grandmother?"

"In a few days. Titus is coming with me. I haven't been able to afford it until now, and it's been so long since I saw her."

Isa reached over and held my hand. "You said she's in the late stages of dementia. She probably won't recognize you, but I like to think people can sense on some level when someone they love is present."

Titus and I flew out to Florida. Weston seemed like a nice city, and I'd visited a couple of times when Nana first moved here.

The center where she lived seemed more like a luxury hotel than a memory care facility. The round, circular driveway had an enormous fountain in the middle, and flowers and tropical plants bloomed everywhere. When we walked into the reception area, a tall decorative wrought-iron gate ran across the entrance.

I pressed the intercom. "Good morning. How may I assist you?" a friendly voice asked.

"I'm here to see Edith Stuart. I'm her granddaughter, Abigail Carver, and my significant other is also with me."

"Just one moment."

Titus raised his eyebrow. "Significant other?"

"Boyfriend didn't seem quite right. You're way more than that." He leaned in and kissed my hair.

"Yes, here it is. Ms. Abigail Carver. You've been approved by her attorneys to visit anytime. I'll buzz you in, but please wait for someone to meet you. A note in her file states her caregiver wishes to speak with you."

We heard the gate unlock and pushed through. The covered courtyard inside held several comfortable sitting areas and dining tables interspersed with large urns of flowers. We waited on the other side until a middle-aged man wearing a nametag approached.

"Good morning, I'm Jeff." He shook our hands, then motioned for us to follow him. "Let me show you to Edith's apartment. She doesn't get many visitors since her daughter and son-in-law were removed from the list a few years ago."

I paused and glanced over at Jeff. "Why were they removed?"

Jeff gave me a side look. "You'll need to speak with them about that."

I stopped and held up my palm. "There's a criminal no-contact order against Calvin Carver. Please, did he do something to hurt her?"

Jeff sighed and stopped walking. "They tried to pressure her into signing an addendum to her will and trust, and it got ugly. She's not competent to do so and hasn't been for years. We've been waiting for you to come see her, Ms. Carver. She's dying."

The news wasn't unexpected, but it still hit me. "Until recently, I didn't have two dimes to rub together. I couldn't afford to come see her, but I sent her letters and cards. And voice recordings. Did she get those?"

Jeff smiled for the first time. "Yes. Come look." We followed him to the left wing of the facility and took the elevator to the third floor. The caregiver answered the door with a smile. Her shirt had little flamingos on it, and her hair was braided with colorful beads at the ends.

"Hey, Jeff. She's in a good mood today."

"This is Destiny, Edith's assigned caregiver. She's been with her almost since the beginning. Destiny, this is Edith's granddaughter, Abigail Carver."

"I know who she is."

We stepped into the sunny apartment. There was a small sitting area and kitchenette, and a door leading into what I assumed was Nana's bedroom.

And there was Nana, sitting in a recliner by the balcony windows, looking at the palm trees outside. I slowly walked over and knelt next to her chair. She didn't respond, and her shoulders were hunched. Her hair was thinner and completely white now, and she'd lost so much weight. Jeff was right, she'd faded away to almost nothing.

"Hi, Nana. It's me, Abby." She didn't look at me. "I came to see how you're doing, and to bring the last picture Stella and I drew for you. It's of us playing hockey outside in our cul-de-sac."

She still didn't move, and I pulled the picture out of my bag. "Stella loves hockey now, and she keeps asking when the season is going to start again."

I'd drawn the houses and palm trees, and Stella drew in the goals and our stick figures. It was hard to tell, but I think she even included Russ.

I stepped in front of her and held it up. Nana finally focused on me, and then looked at the picture.

"My Abby likes hockey too," she said softly. A ghost of a smile flitted across her lips, and then it was gone. Her gaze lost its focus, and she looked out the window again.

Tears gathered. "Yes, she does. And she also loves a big, huge, scarred hockey player." Titus folded his arms and shifted beside me.

Sitting next to her, I told her about Stella, Titus and Max, and our life in Palm Springs. I also told her I thought she would love it there, and I wished I could have visited her more.

She didn't talk or glance at me again, and Destiny finally stepped forward. "She's getting tired. This is usually her naptime, and there's something I want to show you in her bedroom."

Destiny, with a little help from Titus, transferred Nana to her bed. When I walked into her bedroom and looked up, I stopped short. Her wall was plastered with bright, childish drawings, photos, clippings, little receipts, and brochures I'd sent to her over the years.

I wandered over to the right side of the wall and saw the brochure from Zoo Lights and a photo of Stella and me on the jumbotron at one of Titus's games. Isa had taken it for me.

Destiny tucked Nana in and stood beside me. "She wanted to keep everything, so we started tacking them up on her wall. Then we put the bed here, even though it's a little wonky, so she could see the things you sent her over the years while she laid here."

I put my fingers over my lips. "They're all here."

"When these started coming..." She pointed to a photo of Gabe and me. "We thought at first he was Stella's father."

I turned to her. "He's one of my best friends, but he's not her father."

Destiny glanced at Titus, then studied me. "I wondered if you'd end up together, the way he looked at you." She pointed to a photo of Gabe gazing at me on Stella's second birthday. It was right before I moved out. "Anyway, I read all your letters to her, several times."

I grabbed her hand and squeezed. "Thank you for doing this." I motioned to the wall. "And for reading my letters to her." My voice was husky with emotion.

"It's nothing, and we all looked forward to it. Your letters about the Cherry Box have been a staff favorite."

I blushed and my eyes went wide. "Oh, God. I forgot I told her about it."

She leaned in and murmured, "We looked up your website during our lunch break the other day. Best lunch break we've had in years."

Titus smirked. "I can imagine."

She grinned. "Most of the staff drops by to see Ms. Edith and talk with her about your latest letter and pictures or photos. Everyone here knows her, thanks to you." She glanced at Titus. "We also looked you up. I read the story about you beating up that hockey player who assaulted the fan, so we figured she'd be okay with you."

Titus shook his head. "A story about me beating the shit out of someone made you feel better about me?"

Destiny grinned, then her smile faded. "Yeah, it did. I'm sorry about your back."

"Thanks." He gazed down at me. "It worked out for the best."

I took his hand and turned back at the wall, entranced. It laid out the story of my life over the past few years—in letters, pictures, and little memorabilia I could send to my grandmother in an envelope. Titus and I looked over the contents. There were letters when Stella was an infant. Photos of us celebrating Stella's birthdays. A picture of her in Gabe's arms after a swim meet, and some of us at Pike's Place in Seattle.

Later, there were selfies of Stella and me looking a little thinner with fewer smiles and less information that reflected the year at my parents' house. And then there were the twenty or so letters, clippings, brochures, and photos of us with Titus and sometimes Max. Those were the most colorful. We appeared happy, healthy, and tan. And we looked like a family.

Nana's wall showed the life Titus breathed into ours. Before we left, I pulled my phone out and took a video of everything to show Stella when she got older. Then I kissed Nana's sleeping head, and we walked out.

"Her mind is pretty much gone," Destiny murmured. "But what you gave her over the last several years was pure love in a weekly envelope. It's become an installation of someone she adored and cared about. And we all feel like we know you." She turned to gaze up at Titus. "Take care of them for us."

Chapter 34

Before flying back to Palm Springs in the morning, our last visit was to see Darren Boeger, my grandmother's attorney. Their law offices were on the second level in downtown Weston on a charming street lined with palm trees and bright pastel shops. Based on their décor, it looked like they'd been there since the 1970s.

Darren shook our hands. "Ms. Carver, it's nice to meet you face to face. Before Edith's dementia took her memory, she assured me you were nothing like her daughter and son-in-law."

"Please, call me Abby. I just wanted to give you my current information and see if there's anything I need to do for her. I would have come sooner, but I just couldn't afford it."

Darren leaned back and sighed. "Edith put money aside for you to visit her. I take it your mom didn't tell you."

"No." It felt like someone just punched me in the gut. I put my fingers to my temples. "Why wouldn't she tell me?" My father's abuse had been direct and intentional, but my mother's cruelty and apathy sometimes hurt more.

"Are you aware that you're Edith's sole beneficiary? I'm sorry to tell you her care has taken a good chunk of her net worth."

I shook my head. "Don't be sorry, that's what it's there for. And I'm so glad she has Destiny."

He smiled and patted my hand. "Edith was right, you're nothing like your parents."

That night, we stayed at a luxury hotel in Fort Lauderdale and planned to fly out the next morning. While Titus checked us in, I stood in the lobby feeling emotionally drained and weary.

"How're you doing?" Titus asked, taking my hand and leading me to the elevators.

"I'm alright. It was hard to see her like that. She used to be so sharp and witty, and when we got together, we'd play games or just chat and laugh about so many things."

"It's a good reminder to go visit my *grand-mère* soon."

I nodded. "You should."

The suite he'd booked was on the top floor. It had a private spa on the balcony and was almost as big as the main level of my parents' house. We walked in, and I slowly set my bag down on the couch, then turned in a circle to take it all in.

"Wow. This is so nice. You didn't need to do this."

"I wanted to. They guarantee the rooms are soundproof, and after we order room service, no one is going to interrupt us while I'm fucking you in at least twenty different positions, on ten different surfaces, over the next five hours."

My insides clenched, and need rolled through me. "Oh, God."

Titus walked over and wrapped his hand around my neck, pulling me in for a long, wet kiss. "Starting now, we're going to take adult vacations together every few months so we can get some time together alone besides just our stolen thirsty Thursdays. Then I can fuck you anywhere, and you can moan and scream all you want."

"Yes, please," I whispered and went in for another kiss.

Groaning into my mouth, he walked me backward until I hit the wall. "We'll do room service later. Take your panties off."

I gazed up at him, my mind awash in need.

"Or I can rip them off for you." His lip twitched as he watched me try to process his demand.

Sliding my hands up under my dress, I hooked my panties and slid them down my legs. I stepped out, then leaned over to undo the buckles on my sandals. The shoes had a heel and straps that wound around my ankles a few times.

He shook his head. "No. I'm going to fuck you in those." His eyes grew heavy. "Now unbutton your dress and slide it off. Unwrap your perfect, beautiful tits for me."

The man might be a professional hockey player, but he was also a professional dirty talker. My center slicked as I reached up and undid the buttons on my bodice, then let the straps slide off my shoulders. The dress hit the floor, and I stepped out of it. My silky cream bralette was see-through, and Titus's eyes gleamed as he traced my cleavage.

"You're a fucking vision. Now take your bra off. Slowly." He followed my movements. "That's it. Cup your tits, then work your nipples for me. I'd love to have nipple clamps to put on you right now."

The phantom bite made me shudder as I pinched them, my hips involuntarily moving against him.

He lifted me by my waist. "Wrap your legs around me."

Lust and adrenaline slid through my center, and my toes curled in anticipation. I never knew exactly what Titus was going to do or say when we fucked, and the uncertainty always made my clit pulse with need. I curled my thighs around his hips and rubbed myself against his hard length.

"Tonight, we're going to fuck here against the wall, then on the couch, the table, maybe the bed, and then out in the spa. And that's where you're going to take me up your ass while I spank your little pussy just the way you like it."

My insides clenched hard, and my neck arched back.

He pulled my arms above my head and held them there with one hand. "I've never fucked you against the wall before, and I have a few ideas." Titus always had ideas, and I usually blushed, then shivered, then climaxed my way through them.

The next morning when we left the hotel to fly back to Palm Springs, I felt sore and thoroughly used, and I couldn't stop blushing every time I thought about how well we'd utilized that hotel room.

A few days after we got home from Florida, Titus pulled me over to the couch after Stella went to bed. "The Vancouver coach called. They want me to come back, and training starts in a few weeks."

My stomach flipped over and my mind raced with a million thoughts. "Oh, my God! That's great!" He wasn't smiling. "Isn't that great?"

He nodded thoughtfully. "Yeah. When I came here last year that's all I wanted from this season." He turned and gazed at me. "I need to move back to Vancouver."

He hadn't said *we* needed to move, just that he would. Getting back into the pros was all he wanted out of his season, not a girlfriend with a three-year-old child. My heart stuttered and seemed to crack inside my chest.

"*You* need to move back?" I asked as I stood, wiping my hands down my thighs. "This is what you wanted–to get back into the pro league."

"It is. At least for the next few years. If I do go back, I'll probably play for a couple of years, then retire and coach for a few more years because to my fucking surprise, I like coaching." He shook his head.

I smiled despite the growing pain in my heart. "You're a great coach. The players love your grumpy ass."

Until that moment, I didn't realize my heart could ache like this. That heartbreak could be a physical thing, and I could be so happy for someone, even as they were quietly decimating me.

I turned around to look out the window. "Am I in your plans somewhere?"

His head snapped up, and he stalked to me and spun me around–only to see tears gathering in my eyes. "Why the fuck are you crying?"

"Because you didn't ask me to go with you!" I struggled against his hands. "I'm so happy for you. This is what you've been hoping for–what you wanted."

"Of course you're coming with me. And if you don't want to move to Vancouver, I'll stay in the minor league–although I'd rather not." He pulled me into him. "We belong together. When are you going to get it through your thick, hard head?"

I reached around and pinched his ass. He didn't flinch. "Why are you pinching me?"

"Because you could have been clearer, and said '*we* need to move to Vancouver, Abigail.' Or, oh, I don't know, '*we* need to be there by August.' So it didn't feel like you were ripping my fucking heart out!" I yelled as I finished.

He stilled for a couple of seconds, then sighed. "I see your point, *cocotte*. But you need to let it sink in that you and Stella aren't going anywhere unless it's with me. In a few months, I'm going to ask you to marry me. And a couple of years after that, I plan to start discussing having another kid with you."

With each sentence, he knocked the breath out of me. "Oh, my God!"

"*Now* what?"

"I just need a minute, or ten, to absorb those verbal bombs you dropped."

I felt him grin against my hair as he gathered me close. "I adore you, *mon coeur*. Since you came to my door with your gaunt, battered face and your scared little girl, I've been enamored with your sweetness and wicked mouth. That first day, when you told me your bedroom was 'very nice, and very white,' I wanted to laugh–and punch whoever gave you that black eye. I'm addicted to your warmth and sunshine, and I never want to live without it. Now, are *we* going to Vancouver or not?"

My Palm Springs friends hadn't been lying when they said summer could be brutal here. But the next few weeks flew by as we prepared to move to Vancouver.

Stella didn't seem to care since we flew there frequently, and she loved having Max around. So Titus rented a home near Connor's house in West Vancouver to see if we liked the area.

Two days before we left, the doorbell rang. Stella and I had just finished making shepherd's pie while Titus cut up fruit for a salad.

"You expecting anyone?" he asked absently.

"No."

He washed his hands. "I'll get it."

"Okay." I slid the dish into the preheated oven and started setting the table when I heard Titus's voice at the door.

"Stella deserves better than some spoiled little sodding fucktwit who runs at the first sign of trouble. They're both mine now."

My head came up, and I gazed at the hallway. I set the forks down and walked quietly to the front door. Then I heard another male voice talking.

"I just want to talk to Abby and see my daughter."

I froze as my heart seemed to constrict. *Kyle* was here? Why in the world would he be *here*? And how did he even know where we lived? Then it hit me, and a wave of anger and disgust swept through me.

Stalking over to the front door, I stepped into view and stood next to Titus. Turning to him, I took his hand. "I see you've met the fucktwit." Then I looked at Kyle. He was still handsome, in a boy-next-door kind of way. But the differences between him and Titus were glaring. And even more so on the inside.

"Who told you where I live?" I asked.

His eyes swept over me, and he swallowed. "Abby, I'd like to talk to you." He glanced at Titus. "Alone, so I could maybe explain a few things. And see where we go from here. Can I come in? It's hot out here."

I stared at him. When I didn't respond, he rubbed the back of his neck. "Look, I'm sorry for leaving you the way I did. For not reaching out..." He trailed off.

"You mean you're sorry for abandoning your broke, nineteen-year-old pregnant girlfriend who has abusive parents?" I asked in a conversational tone. "And not seeing your daughter one time, or paying one penny of child support until it was garnished from your bank account three years later?"

"Abby–"

"I'll ask you again. How did you know where to find me?"

"Your father, okay? He called and told me you were living here with this–" he looked Titus up and down–"hockey player and my daughter. He told me to come talk to you and see if I could make you see reason."

I let go of Titus's hand and stepped forward. "You stupid, weak asshole. You don't deserve to breathe the same air as this man, and Stella adores him. He plays with her, reads to her, gives her little Canadian stuffed animals to help her with bad dreams that your selfishness and weakness helped cause."

Kyles' face went red and botchy. "He's beaten people up, and he broke your father's jaw, for Christ's sake. And there are articles about him fucking his way across Canada."

"I don't *care*." I leaned forward. "Those articles are years old, and he treats us like gold. I love him so much I can't even contain it most days. I'd die for him, and he'd never hurt us the way you did."

Kyle's eyes got wide, and he looked at Titus again, then back at me. "I want to see her."

"You don't deserve her," I growled. "And you are not going to fuck with her head. You're barely her sperm donor, and after being with Titus? I know how truly shitty you were even at that."

Titus chuckled next to me. "You were too fucking stupid to realize what you had." His low, mean voice gave me happy shivers.

Kyle's eyes narrowed as he took us in. "I'll take you to court."

I snorted so loud, George and his mother two doors down probably heard me. "You can certainly try. But three years of complete silence, no child support, or even a phone call or birthday card definitely meets the abandonment statute."

His eyes flickered, and he swallowed.

"Go away, Kyle. Stella is so much better off without a weak coward like you, and I thank God you left. Because if you hadn't, I might not be where I am today."

"Abby, I have a right to see her."

I stared at him. "No, you don't. You abandoned us, and if you try to take me to court, I will hire the biggest shark of an attorney I can find, and I will bury you alive in legal fees. And the first thing I'll do is sue your ass for the rest of your back child support. Plus interest and attorney fees."

"I forgot what a sarcastic little bitch you could be. No wonder I ran." Kyle glared at me.

Titus unfolded his arms. "If you ever talk to her like that again, you'll be one sorry little boy. Now get the fuck off our porch," he said in a low, deep, conversational voice. It made Titus's words even scarier.

Kyle gulped, stepped back, then turned and stomped back to his car.

I rolled my eyes and turned to Titus. We walked back inside and closed the door against the evening heat.

"Zeke put in a top-of-the-line camera above the front door. Do you know what we just got?" he asked.

"Annoyed?"

"That too. But we also got Kyle's statement about your dad telling him to come see you on video. Calvin broke the no-contact order."

I smiled back. "So he did. The judge warned him about having even second-hand contact with me. We'll send Deidra that little present tomorrow."

He wrapped his arms around me and backed me up against the door. "You love me so much you can't contain it?" he asked. "I treat you like gold, and you'd die for me? That last one is a bit extreme."

Instead of joking around or pinching his butt, I laid my head on his shoulder and breathed in his familiar scent. "Everything I told him is true. My heart aches with how much I love you sometimes." I pulled back and gazed up at him. "So thank you—for loving and supporting me. For protecting us and being there through all of it."

He tucked a strand of hair behind my ear. "I love you too, *ma p'tite cocotte.* And I got you and Stella out of the deal, and a lifetime supply of Cherry Boxes. So I'm the lucky one here."

I rolled up on my toes and kissed him softly. "Let's go eat, and then later we can do a little product testing."

Epligoue

our Years Later

The arena in Vancouver where Max and Stella practiced and played wasn't too far from our home. I zipped up my jacket and watched Max and his team take the ice, the frigid air clinging to my skin. I missed Titus's body heat.

One of the kids tripped, and a couple of the players fell over when they skated into him. Max looked back at the small pile of bodies and shook his head, then skated smoothly onto the ice. He reminded me of Titus more every day.

We'd moved back to Vancouver, and Titus played three more seasons of professional hockey until his back, and a few minor injuries, reminded him his body wasn't getting any younger. I'd also been pregnant. When he told me he planned to retire, he shrugged philosophically and said it was time. Then he dragged me to the bedroom and gently tied me to the headboard.

"Max looks giant out there," Stella commented as she juggled little Felix in her lap next to me. Max would continue playing in the under-seven league until he aged out in a few months.

Felix looked up at Stella with his hazel–green eyes and messy blond hair and grinned happily. Then he shoved his little fist in his mouth and sucked. The little man was always hungry.

I braced my hands on my knees and looked down at my wedding ring for probably the millionth time. The beautiful thick gold band had a fissure with five small, brilliant rubies in it.

When Felix was born nine months ago, Titus slipped it off my finger, then leaned down and kissed me. "I need to borrow this for a few days to add a stone for Felix." I teared up, and he grinned.

During the last three months of pregnancy and a few weeks after Felix was born, I was an emotional mess, and I cried indiscriminately. Titus seemed amused by it, and he held, kissed–and did other things–to help me through the emotions and hormones. I grew a little hot, just thinking about it now.

"How do you feel about Max being in your league until you age up?" I asked Stella. She and Max would play together until Stella's next birthday.

She clapped Felix's little hands together and smiled down at him. "I like it, and he's better than most of the players on my team." Stella didn't know that a few of those players had a crush on her. She was still a little quiet and reserved around everyone but her family and close friends. It made those in her inner circle feel extra special.

Movement caught my eye, and I looked up to find Titus coming toward us. He leaned down and kissed me thoroughly until Stella started fake-gagging next to me.

"You made it." I smiled and stole another kiss.

Stella scooted around me and handed Felix off to Titus, then hugged them both and plopped down next to him on the other side. "Hi, Dad. Did you see Elodie in Palm Springs?"

Titus pulled out a small beaded friendship bracelet from his pocket. "I did, and she wanted me to give this to you."

Stella grinned and hugged him again.

The Thunderbirds had offered Titus the head coaching position when their last coach took a job in another league a few months ago. Titus was at loose ends after retiring, and the coaching position came at an opportune time.

The game began, and we watched the faceoff. "How were things at the house?" I asked.

We planned to move back to Palm Springs when the kids finished this school year. It wouldn't be a hardship since we visited often and had kept the house there.

"Good. I saw George, and he said they're excited to have us back in the neighborhood. He seems a little lost."

His mom and my grandma died within a month of each other just over three years ago. George and I got into the habit of taking walks together when I was in town, and we'd talked and processed our grief together.

My parents also divorced not long after Nana died, and my father spent a couple of years in jail for violating the no-contact order, violating his plea bargain agreement, and then for getting into fights in jail. Deidra had kept us informed.

Nana had been buried in Weston near Grandpa. Her service had been small, but Destiny and several staff members from her care facility attended. My mother didn't go.

The inheritance Nana left me still seemed like a lot of money, even after all her caretaking and funeral expenses were paid. I gifted a portion to Destiny, who probably meant more to Nana than her own daughter, and I put the rest into retirement and education funds. I liked to think Nana would have approved.

Titus wrapped his arm around me, giving me his body warmth. "How have things been here?" he asked.

"Hectic, but manageable. We miss you though, and the bed gets cold without you." I gripped his thigh and leaned over. "I've gotten used to you sleeping mostly on top of me."

A wicked grin curved his mouth. "You've also gotten used to sleeping with me still inside you," he murmured softly.

I blushed and my lips twitched. "That's only happened a few times. I can't help it if I'm nice and relaxed afterward."

Felix reached out and grabbed a thick hunk of my hair, pulling it toward his mouth. I bent closer to him so he wouldn't yank it out. The kid had a firm grip.

Titus gently unwrapped Felix's fat little fingers and kissed them. "*Non*, be nice to your *jolie maman*."

He tucked my hair behind my ear and studied me. "I missed you, and the little hellions too. I'll be glad to get us all back home in Palm Springs."

My eyes went soft, and I wrapped my arm around his neck. "You and our three little *angels* will always be home to me. Wherever that is."

He grinned, then leaned in and murmured what he wanted to do with me that night as Felix happily patted my blushing cheek.

Thank you for reading *Thirsty Thursdays: Book 4 in the Palm Springs Poolside Series!* Please leave a review–or even a simple rating!–on Amazon. Trust me, it's a good thing!

Leave a Review!

Have you read *Martini Mondays,* Book 1 in the Palm Springs Poolside Series? Read Laurel and Sebastian's story here! Get ready for another scorching hot Palm Springs Poolside read and find out the origins of the fabulous Martini Monday poolside cocktail party.

Read *Martini Mondays!*

Afterword

Do you want a chance to win free signed books, special sneak peek previews of new releases, and bonus features? Sign up for my newsletter at jlbrannick.com!

Thank you for reading *Thirsty Thursdays: Book 4 in the Palm Springs Poolside Series.* If you liked Titus and Abby's story, please leave a review on Amazon. Even a simple rating helps! Your reviews and feedback help authors share their novels and grow their reader bases. Trust me, it's a good thing!

Check out the other books in the Palm Springs Poolside Series at amazon.com/author/jlbrannick.

To my family and tribe—thank you for your support, humor, and patience. We make a great team and you're my favorite traveling buddies *ever.*

A special thank you to Marie-Pierre D'Auteuil, the amazing beta reader from Canada who reviewed and critiqued all things

Canadian, and the French Canadian pet names and terms. You make me want to write a series based in Quebec.

Thank you also to my beta readers and editors, Shelby Nesbitt, Gennifer Ulman, Susan Keillor, and Smart Mouth Editing, Inc. You help me in so many ways, and your funny, witty comments and sometimes brutal honesty help me create *much* better stories.

And thank you to my cover designer, Maggie Jackson, at Smart Mouth Publishing LLC.

Follow me on social media and subscribe to my newsletter for the latest news, free giveaways, exclusive bonuses, and new releases! linkfly.to.jlbrannick.

https://jlbrannick.com/
https://linkfly.to/JLBrannick

Afterword

Do you want a chance to win free signed books, special sneak peek previews of new releases, and bonus features? Sign up for my newsletter at jlbrannick.com.

Newsletter Signup!

Thank you for reading *Thirsty Thursdays: Book 4 in the Palm Springs Poolside Series.* If you liked Titus and Abby's story, please leave a review on Amazon. Even a simple rating helps! Your reviews and feedback help authors share their novels and grow their reader bases. Trust me, it's a good thing!

Leave a Review!

Check out the other books in the Palm Springs Poolside Series.

Other Books in the Series!

To my family and tribe—thank you for your support, humor, and patience. We make a great team, and you're my favorite traveling buddies *ever.*

A special thank you to Marie-Pierre D'Auteuil, the amazing beta reader from Canada who reviewed and critiqued all things

Canadian, and the French Canadian pet names and terms. You make me want to write a series based in Quebec.

Thank you also to my beta readers and editors, Shelby Nesbitt, Gennifer Ulman, Susan Keillor, and Smart Mouth Editing, Inc. You help me in so many ways, and your funny, witty comments and sometimes brutal honesty help me create *much* better stories.

And thank you to my cover designer, Maggie Jackson, at Smart Mouth Publishing LLC.

Follow me on social media and subscribe to my newsletter for the latest news, free giveaways, exclusive bonuses, and new releases!

Social Media Links!

www.ingramcontent.com/pod-product-compliance
Lightning Source LLC
Chambersburg PA
CBHW022009310726
48972CB00006B/1577